T LOST
DAUGHTER

An absolutely gripping mystery thriller that
will take your breath away

JANE ADAMS

A Ray Flowers Mystery Book 5

JOFFE
BOOKS

Joffe Books, London
www.joffebooks.com

First published in Great Britain in 2023

Cover art by Dee Dee Book Covers

ISBN: 978-1-83526-097-5

PROLOGUE

He remembers a time when everything was so simple. When the summer seemed to stretch endlessly and there were trees to climb and water, pumped from the well in the garden, so bright and crystalline and pure it sparkled in the sun. He remembered a time when they were all together and there were no tears, no doubts, no problems to overcome. When he was not alone.

The day they found the fox was what had marked the beginning of the adventure. It was hurt, attacked by a dog he had thought, it came limping into the field in bright daylight as though disorientated by its injuries, leaving a trail of vivid red spots on the pristine grass at the edge of the garden. That borderland where garden met farm, a strip of green, cropped and pristine where they had hunted for four-leaf clovers and where, when they were younger, Kit had made daisy chains. She had pretended to be too old for such activities now he recalled, they were all eleven and felt themselves on the brink of not quite childhood. Felt themselves struggling to be free of childish things, even while he knew they all craved them because to be a child was safer, simpler.

He recalls so vividly that sense that this summer was to be their last before the mysteries of adulthood impinged. A change of school, the prospect of exams, decisions to be made, new uniforms to be worn. But for now the summer stretched ahead and only the fox, bloodied and obviously in pain, intruded.

Paul remembered how she had taken a brick from the pile next to the house, and how she had been so matter of fact about it. The fox had flopped into the longer grass close beside the hedge and he had watched her as she approached slowly and so calmly the animal had barely raised its head. She had brought brick down so swiftly and so hard that it had no time to react. He remembered how he had wandered over, curious and disturbed. She had crossed back to the pump, washed the brick and replaced it on the stack while he and the brother had stared down at the now very dead fox.

He could not remember who had decided they should bury it, but he supposed it was the obvious thing to do, they could hardly leave it there to rot, it would stink the garden out. So they crossed from the neatly cultivated strip of land that separated garden from field, skirted the spinney, settling on an awkward corner of the field where the tractor turned and left the rough triangle of wildflowers, nettles, brambles and broken ground. With a spade taken from the garden shed and a bundle of old newspaper wrapped around the fox, they had dug a grave and dropped it inside, shovelling the earth back and pulling the brambles down to hide where it had been disturbed.

And then they had looked at one another and somehow he knew that a line had been crossed. "It was easy," she had said in answer to their unspoken question. Then added swiftly, "It was dying anyway, I didn't want to let it suffer."

It was, Paul remembered, the first time she had ever lied or dissembled or told them less than the truth about what she was feeling. She had walked away to avoid further question and they had looked at one another, he and the brother, and knew they both wished that they had been the one to fetch the brick and strike the fox dead.

Something shifted on that day, it was as though the ground beneath their feet became less solid, it was the day when the full potential of what they could achieve seemed to have been laid bare but was also the day that Paul had known that he must tighten his control, direct what came next so that this potential was not wasted. They had all grown up together, been closer than family, closer than anyone outside of their little trinity could ever imagine. He could not tolerate the thought of losing what they had; what he had. Most of all, he could not tolerate the idea of them becoming . . . ordinary.

Later, much later, when the girl had gone and had ripped their world apart, he had turned to the brother. Rob had kept journals, scribbled in his collection of notebooks since Paul could remember. That habit suddenly assumed far greater significance.

"Write this down," Paul had told him. "I will tell you what to say. You will be my amanuensis. You will be my gospel keeper. You will write our story down."

And so, he had, sometimes to Paul's dictation, sometimes from his own memory of what had taken place but always with Paul's sanction and approval. The story had to be right, the history written as Paul chose to remember it.

And sometimes, as the years passed and they both grew stronger, more determined, more skilled at standing outside of what others chose to call the normal world and what Paul considered ordinary and dull, sometimes what Paul wanted done was more than just the keeping of a record.

Rob did that too.

CHAPTER 1

"I've met someone."

Libby flinched. It hurt, even though she knew this had always been inevitable. She regained her composure, aware that Ashley was watching her nervously, then reached over and took her daughter-in-law's hand.

"What's he like? Can we meet him?" She felt Ashley relax and realized that the younger woman had been dreading this too. It had been three years since Aiden's sudden death. Of course Ashley would meet someone else. And of course that would hurt.

"He's . . . nice. I mean, more than that, but you know . . ."

He's not Aiden. That was what she meant. No one would ever be Aiden. She gave Ashley's hand a squeeze and then, keeping her voice carefully neutral asked, "Shall I get us both another coffee?" Give them both a chance to breathe.

Standing at the counter, waiting to be served. Libby glanced back at her daughter-in-law. The truth was she had always regarded Ashley as closer than that. The daughter she'd never had. She'd known Ashley for almost half the young woman's life. She'd been a long-term foster child of a couple in the same street, just a few doors down from Libby and her family, been to school with Aiden. Fallen for her son when the pair of them were still in their mid-teens and Aiden had fallen just as hard. Apart from a brief hiatus when they'd both gone to different universities and, in a half-hearted but determined sort of way had dated other people, they had been together.

Then they had married.

Then Aiden had dropped down dead in a supermarket carpark less than five years later.

And now Ashley had met someone.

"So," Libby said, setting their cups down on the table. "Tell me about him. Where did you meet?"

Ashley looked relieved and Libby could see just how much this confession had cost her.

"We met at the university. At a weekend conference on cross-curricular collaboration." She laughed. "Not actually as boring as it sounds. Anyway, he's an associate lecturer."

"So, hourly paid, no security and too much work." Libby said.

"Yep, all of that. But he's applying for a proper part-time post and I think he's got a good chance. He does some tutoring on the side. Oh, and his name is Tim Bennett. I suppose that's important too".

"It helps if I know what to call him, yes. So, can we meet?"

That anxious look returned to Ashley's eyes. "I don't know how serious it's going to get," she said softly.

"It's the first man you've shown even the slightest interest in," Libby said gently. "Of course you don't. But you like him enough to tell me about him, so—"

"So, yes, I'd like you and Dan to meet him. If you think that would be OK."

Dan would find it hard, Libby thought, but her husband loved Ashley as much as she did. There would be misgivings and doubts, but he wanted her to be happy.

"He's kind," Ashley said. "And he's not tried to push things, you know. I'd have run a mile if he had. You know I

5

saw a couple of people when I was away at uni, but there was never anyone else. Not really."

Not for Aiden, either, Libby thought. When people talked about soul mates, they might well having been talking about her son and this young woman.

And so, they made arrangements to meet, and it was only as Libby had driven home and spoken to Dan that she realized how little Ashley had really told her about this new man.

CHAPTER 2

"So that was the last time you spoke to her?" Ray Flowers asked. Libby Summers, late fifties, he guessed. Attractive and what his mother would have called 'well kept' and now clearly very worried. There was no mistaking the dark shadows beneath the carefully applied concealer. And besides, Ray had reason to know just how anxious this woman was. What havoc she was wreaking to try and get to the truth.

"Last time I spoke to her or heard from her. I tried to call that evening, but her mobile just rang out. I left a voicemail but she didn't return my call. Next time I tried, her phone was off."

"And you'd arranged to meet this new man. You went to that meeting." He knew this already but he wanted the story in her words.

She nodded. "I saw Ashley on the Tuesday, we'd arranged to go round to her flat for dinner on the Saturday. We arrived as agreed, at seven. There was no reply. We let ourselves in, Ashley had given me a key ages ago and she has a key to our place."

She paused, took a deep breath and he could see that she was reliving the shock. "She wasn't there. Nothing was there. All her possessions, just gone. Her books, her music, her clothes. Everything. Just gone."

"And you spoke to the police."

"Yes and to neighbours. They said there'd been a removal van arrive on the Friday morning, they saw it on their way to work that morning, but didn't see Ashley. Just the boyfriend. They'd seen him a couple of times, when he visited but they didn't speak to him."

"And the police?"

"A waste of space. They said Ashley was an adult and there was no evidence she'd come to any harm. That maybe she just went away."

"But you don't believe that? Maybe she needed a complete break from the past?"

"No!" She slapped her hand flat on the table. Then withdrew it hastily. "Look, we were always close and that didn't change when Aiden died. We'd speak most days. We saw one another three or four times a month. She'd been in and out of our house since she was just a little kid and that hadn't changed. It's nothing for her to just turn up, let herself in and spend the evening just . . . just watching TV, chatting. She's family."

Ray noticed the shifting tenses. Some present, some already past. "You're starting to think she may be dead," he observed quietly.

Libby Summers winced but nodded. "I can't think of any other reason why she'd not get in touch. It's been more than two weeks and not a word."

Ray was silent for a minute, just thinking. Finally he asked, "So what brought you to me?"

She looked a little embarrassed. "It sounds silly when I say it out loud. But I'd gone back to the coffee shop where we last met. I'd been back a couple of times. It was a regular meeting place for us and the staff knew her. I kept asking, had she been in, you know. But nothing."

Ray nodded. "Go on."

"Well, this was Monday, two days ago. I bought a coffee and I sat at our usual table. It was like . . ."

"Like you felt if you repeated the same actions it might bring her back. That's not silly." It was desperate.

"It feels like it. But I was sort of half listening, you know how you do in a busy place and I heard these two women talking. They mentioned your name. They said you'd found a missing person and I thought, well, maybe . . ."

"Who am I supposed to have found?"

"A daughter. She'd had a big row with her mum a few weeks ago and run away from home and you . . ." She was looking at Ray, waiting for some kind of confirmation. "You don't remember do you?"

"I don't remember because the last missing person's enquiry I was involved in was almost two years ago. And that was an elderly man. These days I mostly deal with corporate security, I don't do much of anything else."

"But—" She looked suddenly utterly downcast.

"I don't know if they were mistaken, or if you misheard what they said. But I've not been involved in finding a missing child." He paused, noting the devastation on her face. "That's not to say I can't or won't," he added. "But, Mrs Summers, I think there is something I should tell you first. This is not the first I've heard about your daughter-in-law's disappearance. Or the fallout from that. Tim Bennett, the man you accused of being her new partner. The man you believe to be responsible for all this. He's a friend of mine."

For a moment she stared at him and then gathered up her bag and jacket and stood up. "Well," she said. "Thank you for your time. But I wish you'd told me this over the phone, then I wouldn't have had a wasted journey."

"Please sit down, Mrs Summers, and hear me out. I didn't tell you because I thought it was important that we talk. I wondered what brought you to me. To me as opposed to any other private investigator, especially as one look at our website would have told you that Flowers-Mahoney isn't the kind of firm that deals with missing people."

"Well, now you know," she said coldly. "What does it matter? I've wasted your time and you've wasted mine." She turned to leave.

"Mrs Summers, I will look for your daughter-in-law."

"Don't trouble yourself. Wouldn't it be a . . . a conflict of interest."

Her tone was still cold but he could tell she was thawing. *She really does love this girl*, Ray thought. *She's really hurting.* "No, you and my friend Tim both have the same need, to find Ashley and to discover what really happened. My friend didn't know her. He'd heard her name because they're in the same faculty but not the same department and anyway he's an hourly paid lecturer, goes in two mornings a week and sometimes covers for other staff. He rarely even sees colleagues he does know, so—"

"That's what she said he was. Don't you see, he's just lying about not knowing her."

She turned and met Ray's gaze, then as though the fight had gone out of her, she slumped down in the chair once more and put her head in her hands.

Ray crossed to the coffee machine and produced a strong black brew for them both. He set one red mug down on the desk and sat back in his chair, sipping his own and waiting for her to regain her composure.

"She told me his name," Libby said at last.

"And I've no idea why she gave you that name. Maybe this new man in her life told her it was his. Maybe he knew enough to bluff his way through. He probably knew she'd do some checking, find the name on the departmental website. Why would she look for further confirmation?"

"But she might have gone to his office, checked him out. Why would this man have risked that?"

Ray shook his head. "Tim doesn't have an office. He shares space with other part-timers. There's a cubby hole on the ground floor where he has access to a computer and can sometimes hold tutorials, if there's no one else in there. The rest of the time he takes his students to one of the local coffee shops. The seminar rooms where he does his teaching are in a different building from where Ashley taught. Same faculty, different department. You know what the university's like, not everything's on the main campus and Tim does his teaching in one of the converted houses down on New Walk."

She picked up her coffee and winced, though he wasn't sure if it was because of the heat or the strength. She drank it anyway.

"The police have torn his life apart looking for a connection and found none. On the day the removal van was at Ashley's flat, and the neighbours testify to having seen the boyfriend, Tim and his family were two hundred miles away at a family wedding. He was not involved with your daughter-in-law. He was, up until very recently, a very happily married man with three young children."

"Was," she asked, her voice betraying unease.

"Daisy loves him, but you've made enough noise that there's a little worm of doubt in her mind."

"I'm sorry," she said softly. "I never meant to hurt anyone. I mean—"

"I know what you mean. You were scared and trying to make sense of what had happened and so you lashed out. Tim was an easy victim. First because you believed he might actually be guilty and then because you had no one else to blame."

She scowled at him. "You believe in straight talking, don't you."

"I do, yes. Especially if we're going to be working together on this."

"I still haven't said—"

He set his mug on the desk and spread his hands as though offering her a deal. "Your call," he said, "but the police won't help, you've already found that out. There's no evidence of foul play and the young woman is of an age to make her own decisions, so . . . But you want to find her and so does Tim because that's the only way he can truly get his life back on an even keel. Tim was never guilty, Mrs Summers, but the world now demands that he prove his innocence anyway."

"I never meant—"

"No, I know you didn't. But, Mrs Summers, even after the police had proved beyond doubt that Tim had no connection at all with Ashley, you still kept making waves." He crossed the room to a filing cabinet and produced a folder full of press cuttings and printouts. He laid them on the desk in front of her. A picture of Ashley stared back from the topmost one. A pretty girl with laughing eyes, dark skin and a mass of tight curls that looked almost blonde, in the black and white picture. A picture of Tim, shocked and white-faced stared out from another. "Going to the press was cruel. He can't go into work, he can't bear to speak to his neighbours. His kids are getting flak at school. His wife wants to take them away from it all and the only thing that's stopping her is that it will look like she sees him as the guilty man he's been painted. So while I understand and Tim understands that you meant no harm, you've done harm, Mrs Summers. You've done a lot of harm."

He reached across and spread the cuttings on the table, making sure she could see each and every one.

She stared first at Ray and then at the cuttings, her face deathly pale beneath its careful make-up.

"So let me try to find her," Ray said. He had not raised his voice one decibel during all of this. He realized she would have found it easier if he had. If he'd shouted, raged at her, she could legitimately have flounced out, slamming the doors and declaring that she'd been verbally abused.

But he had not. Long years of experience with assorted suspects when he had been a serving police officer had kept him outwardly calm. Concern for his friend had emphasized that necessity.

"Let me try to find her," he said again. "Look, Mrs Summers, I'm working this case anyway. For you, for Tim and for her sake because we all need to know what went on and if she is dead, then we need justice. Proper justice for her."

Slowly, she nodded. "I'm sorry," she said. "I was just so . . ."

The head was back in the beautifully manicured hands. Ray picked up both red mugs and returned to the coffee machine. This, he figured, was going to be a long and drawn-out evening.

CHAPTER 3

Tim Bennett looked at his friend, shock and betrayal in his pale blue eyes. "You're working for her?"

"No, I'm working for the missing girl. And for those that have been damaged by her going missing. Tim, if we pool resources—"

"But you know what she did to me."

"I know. And she's starting to realize. Tim, if you're to get through this then we need her on our side, trying to undo the damage she's caused."

"Like that's going to happen." Daisy's tone was harsh and she glared at Ray as though all the blame she had attached to Libby Summers had now been transferred to him.

"I think it is. At least let me try."

Daisy got up, crossed to the sideboard and poured them all another drink. Ray didn't bother reminding her that he was driving, he recognized her need for a moment's space in which to think. The need to do something simple and practical. From upstairs there was a sudden thump and a drawn-out wail. Daisy sighed.

"That'll be Ben falling out of bed again," Tim said. Ben, Ray knew, was their youngest. Two and a half now and just moved from the security of his cot to something larger. Daisy set the glasses down and headed towards the door.

"I'll go," Tim said and for a moment Ray thought she would argue. Then she shrugged and picked up their glasses once more. Tim disappeared upstairs. Daisy set Ray's glass beside the wine he'd still not finished and sat back, cradling her own. Ray waited. In this house it was Daisy that made the big decisions. Tim, bless him, Ray thought, could just about decide what colour shirt to wear. He was brilliant at his job but if it wasn't in his subject area, he floundered.

How he had ever made up his mind to ask Daisy out in the first place was a big mystery to all their friends. Most believed it was Daisy that had done all the running.

She sipped her wine, leaving a trace of deep red lipstick on the glass. She was small and dark and very beautiful, the post-baby roundness that her body had gained just adding to the appeal. She was about as different from Ray's beloved Sarah, tall, red-haired and slender, as it was possible to be. Except in one regard. If Libby Summers considered Ray was direct, he thought, then God only knows what she'd make of Daisy Hughes — or Sarah Gordon.

"So," she said. "When can I meet this bitch?"

"It that's what you're going to call her them probably never."

"Can you blame me?"

"Not at all. The woman has come close to ruining your lives. But, frankly, that's not the heart of the matter."

"Then what is?" she asked harshly.

"A young woman is missing. Her name is Ashley Summers and she's twenty-eight years old. And is very likely dead."

For a moment he thought she'd tell him she didn't give a damn. Instead, she set her glass on the table beside his and palmed her eyes wearily. "So what do we do," she said. "You think you can find her and this fake boyfriend of hers?"

"I'm going to do my best," he told her. It was just a matter of finding a place to start.

Driving home a little later on Ray turned the problem over in his mind. There were many puzzling and disturbing elements to this, but one that was nagging at him. Who were the two women in the café, the ones who had talked about a missing girl and Ray Flowers the private investigator. As he'd said to Libby Summers, one look at the Flowers-Mahoney website would tell prospective customers that the kind of investigations they undertook were more likely to do with corporate fraud and security issues. Ray's partner, the Mahoney part of the firm, had specialized in one sort of security or another all his working life and when they had started this business the blend of ex-police officer with ex government connections had been designed to be appealing to corporate customers.

They didn't handle divorces, cheating partners, lost dogs or missing people — or at least not on a regular basis. No, this was a mystery in its own right. Someone was maybe trying to draw Ray into this for purposes other than finding a missing woman. So, what and why?

The windows of the cottage were lit up when Ray turned down the little back lane and he smiled broadly. So, Sarah had arrived home. She must have heard the car because the front door opened and she stood, backlit, her red hair aflame and a big smile on her face. They had talked briefly about leaving this little stone house; a case Ray had been involved in had led to Sarah being attacked, here, in their own home and for a brief while she had been uneasy even with the doors locked and the new alarm. But that had passed. She loved this place with the walled garden and deep windows as much as he did and the idea of starting over somewhere else had soon lost its appeal.

"So," she said, as she welcomed him inside. "And how are Tim and Daisy?"

"Mad as hell," he told her. "Though I think I've convinced them that Libby Summers is not the enemy."

She smiled at him, set her head on one side as she regarded him thoughtfully. "So, who is then?"

Well, isn't that the question of the day, Ray thought.

* * *

He remembers the summer when they were all fifteen, exams over the sense of freedom. Kit was lying on the grass, a short summer dress rucked up around her thighs and her arms spread as though she had fallen backwards and landed spreadeagled. She was half asleep, listening to music and totally at ease. The three of them were always totally at ease with one another — then. Until she spoiled it all.

He and the brother were going riding and he knew that his body would ache when they got home, the only time he rode horses was in the summer when he came here. She was not keen, though she was actually the best out of the three of them. It was like so many things, she became good at something and she became bored with it, moved on to something new and fresh and interesting. He remembered that it was hot, that it had rained earlier and now the most delicious scents of grass and herbs and perfumed flowers rose up all around them. It felt perfect aside from the little tiny niggle in his mind that had grown over the past days. She was growing apart from them, she was changing.

The brother came out of the house and the two of them set off across the field to the stables. Paul always rode a horse called Ivan, a hard-mouthed brute of a beast that could be oddly gentle with small children but seem to take pleasure in challenging those who thought they knew what they were doing. Although it has been a year, he was sure the horse recognized him, snuffling at his hair and inhaling his scent and then pushing his great head into his skinny shoulder.

That, he thought, had been the final happy summer.

CHAPTER 4

A couple of days later Ray and Sarah were out for the evening at a country pub Ray was particularly fond of. They had been joined by friends, John and his wife Maggie. They'd got a babysitter for their wild tribe — just the two children and a couple of canines, but as Ray knew well, they could feel like half a dozen — and John was in civvies for the evening, his dog collar left on the bathroom shelf at home, he told them.

"So," Maggie asked. "Anyone we know playing tonight?"

The Red Dog was popular on the folk circuit and they'd seen some good bands in the past. Tonight was an open-mic evening, which, Ray knew, could be a bit of a mixed bag, but was usually enjoyable especially if the company was good, which this evening it definitely was. He'd never thought he'd be friends with a vicar and his wife but John and Maggie had come into his life four years earlier, when Ray, recovering from an attack that had left him badly scarred, had moved into a cottage left to him by his aunt. His aunt and this young curate, as John had been then, had been friends and soon it seemed that Ray had not just inherited the cottage but also the friendship.

They were seated in the beer garden at the back of the pub. It was a fine evening and there was a good turnout,

Ray thought, though looking around at the wooden tables it seemed that every second person had an instrument of some sort. The landlord had erected a large gazebo over an improvised stage and there was some basic amplification but not much else. Evenings like this were deliberately stripped down and mainly acoustic, to allow as many people as possible to play a set. Three songs per set. Max. No exceptions, which meant there was usually a good variety — and by a simple law of averages, some of the acts were generally worth hearing.

Across the table, Sarah and Maggie were discussing the running order and picking out familiar-sounding names. They had a first come first served policy at open-mic nights at the Red Dog and a rather unconventional way of logging the acts. You arrived, you queued up to use the computer. You wrote the name of your act on the list and when it had reached capacity it was printed out and distributed to both acts and punters.

Ray held up his pint to admire the colour against the evening light. Deep amber with a tinge of gold. Their food arrived and the first act took to the stage. All was right with the world, at least for the moment, he thought.

The conversation wandered, how the children were getting on at school, the conference that Sarah had just attended, what they thought of the music and were watching on the telly. The food was good pub food and the company was exceptional and the musical accompaniment was at least adequate and occasionally very good.

As the shadows lengthened the garden lights slowly began to come on, so that the whole was bathed in a soft golden atmosphere that seemed to be chasing back the darkness beyond the hedge and behind the stage on which new band were setting up. They were a three-piece that Ray vaguely remembered having heard before and enjoyed. The young female vocalist had a voice that reminded him of Judith Murray — and he was aware of how much that dated him. The stripped-down acoustic set was simple and pleasing. They played and Ray sat back, another pint in hand, glad that Sarah was driving so he could enjoy his evening.

The young woman stepped forward on the stage and adjusted her microphone and said, "We don't generally do requests but we made an exception in this case because it's a song we love to play." She looked out across the crowd as though expecting to find someone there and added, "And this one is a dedication. To Ray Flowers, from his brother, who is very sorry he can't be with you tonight but he's sure you'll get together soon and until then he's glad you've got John and Maggie and the beautiful Sarah with you."

Ray sat bolt upright and stared at the young woman on the stage who had now turned to the rest of the band, checking that everything was ready.

"So, for a song about demons and mayhem. 'Long Lankin', everybody."

"Ray?" Sarah was looking at him, clearly as confused as he was. The song began. A rollicking little melody that was at odds with the theme of child murder and a demon that could crawl through the tiniest crack in a window. A being it was impossible to shut out.

John was also looking at him quizzically. "A brother," he asked.

"I don't have a brother," Ray stated irrelevantly. Sarah and the others knew that. That sense that someone was trying to get his attention and doing so by strange means, a feeling that had been at the back of his mind since Libby Summers' visit, now seem confirmed.

Half an hour later he was talking to the band as they were packing away their equipment into a battered old van, but they were unable to tell him very much. The message had been left with the barman and as the song was part of their regular set anyway it was no hassle to fit it in. They were puzzled by his questions but could offer him nothing by way of explanation. Neither could the barman who had simply taken a phone call with a message to pass on. Apart from the fact that it had been a man's voice he could remember nothing of significance.

"So what's going on?" John wanted to know when Ray returned to the table. "I'd say you look like you've seen a ghost, but I've seen you after you've seen a ghost and this obviously bothers you a lot more."

Ray managed a weak smile. "I'm not sure yet," he said. "Only one person ever referred to me as his brother, and that wasn't in a good way. As far as I know he's still in prison but . . ."

He was conscious of his friends exchanging a glance with Sarah and that they were waiting for more information but he didn't feel that he was in a position to give them any right now. It was disturbing that the dedication had mentioned them by name. There were things he had to check on first. But the fact was if Paul Krantz was no longer in prison that would make a lot of sense of the strange things that had happened recently. Unfortunately it would make a really bad kind of sense, a really dangerous kind of sense, and Ray hoped fervently that there was some other explanation.

Something of what he was thinking must have conveyed itself to the others because Maggie said, "Ray, you know we will help with anything we can but I have to ask you, is there anything *we* should be worried about?"

The question hit him like a fist to the gut. It was a question that came from the knowledge that others had previously threatened Sarah and his friends in order to get to Ray. Maggie, conscious that she had family to protect, had a right to be curious and to be cautious. He reached out and took her hand, squeezing it tightly. "Truthfully, I don't know."

"This is something to do with Tim and that Ashley girl disappearing?" Sarah asked him, as always able to get straight to the heart of the problem.

"It might be. I have to make some phone calls before I can know for certain."

"Well, make them as soon as we get home," Sarah told him tartly.

"It's getting a bit late in the evening for that, isn't it," Maggie protested.

"If I'm guessing right about the kind of people Ray has to call, then they won't be in bed yet," Sarah told her. "Or at any rate they'll be used to being woken in the middle of the night. And in the meantime you better fill us in on what you do know. If there's a chance this might spill over and affect other people then we need to be prepared. We've all been through the mill before, best to know what we might be up against."

Ray nodded. The memory of Sarah being threatened in their own home, the knowledge that Sarah could have been killed was something that he would never be able to be at ease with. There were times when he thought he shouldn't risk having friends and relationships. He shook himself mentally; this was no time to sink into self-pity. Sarah was right, best be a Boy Scout and be prepared. Slowly he began to explain about Ashley, and Tim, and about the strange conversation in the café that had brought Libby Summers to him and about the man he suspected might just possibly be behind all of this.

"So how can we find out for certain?" Sarah asked. "Will Dave Beckett be able to tell you?" Unlike Ray, DCI Beckett was still a serving officer.

"He'll have the means to find out," Ray told them. "And he'll be my first port of call. But Dave was not involved in the original case. This was one I worked with Tony Nightingale, he's retired now and I have no idea where he might be."

"But presumably ought to find out," Sarah noted. "If this Paul Krantz character is behind it, then I don't imagine you'll be the only one he's threatening."

"I've not exactly been threatened," Ray pointed out. "Someone, as yet unknown asked a band to play a song for me. The brother bit might be a misunderstanding."

"Like you believe that." Sarah's tone was scathing enough to remove skin.

"And besides," it was John this time, "someone obviously knew you would be here this evening. Someone's been keeping an eye on you, Ray, someone has probably worked very hard to get you involved in this, that same someone was probably responsible for kidnapping this poor Ashley

Summers and for getting her mother-in-law to come to you and for sending that message tonight. Whoever that someone is, this Paul Krantz or someone else, you can be sure they are not intending to do you any favours." He glanced at his wife and Ray could see that both of them were deeply uneasy. "Maybe the kids could go away for a couple of weeks, stay with your sister."

"She's in the Bahamas, or did you forget? On holiday. You know that thing other people do?" Her words were softened by her smile but Ray could see the anxiety in her eyes.

"I did forget, sorry. Well, my mother's then."

"Only if you want a riot on your hands."

John winced but nodded.

"Why don't you ask Nathan? There's plenty of room at the cottage," Sarah suggested. "Nathan is as good a protector as anyone I can think of and a stranger would stick out a mile in the village. Presumably Ray can get hold of a photograph of this man so you can show it to Nathan. It might be a good idea for him to show it to Evie Padgett."

"And that information will be all round the village in half an hour if you tell Evie." Ray laughed. Their friend Nathan, a strange young man in many ways but one whose life had equipped him with the survival skills to take good care of John and Maggie's kids, now lived in the cottage that Ray's aunt had left to him. The redoubtable Evie came in and cleaned a couple of times a week, not that Nathan left much mess, but she had cleaned for Ray's aunt and Ray seemed to have inherited this arrangement along with the cottage. He had lived there for a while when he had first left the police force, before he and Sarah had set up home together, and Evie had also become a good friend. Somehow he was quite superstitious about breaking such a long-standing agreement. Evie and Nathan got along surprisingly well considering how absolutely different they were. Evie was matriarch to a large extended family and epitomized common sense and stability. Nathan had no family and had never known stability until he had settled in the cottage. Ray knew from experience that Nathan would move heaven and hell to protect those he cared about and in her own way Evie was just a fiercely protective of anyone she considered her responsibility.

"I don't think that's necessarily a bad thing," John said. "I know it feels as though we're overreacting but I would be happier if the kids were there at least for a couple of weeks. End of term is only a few days away, we can keep a close eye until then."

His wife nodded.

Ray looked at his friends and his beloved Sarah and felt his heart sink. It had not occurred to him, not really, just how much events in his own life had impacted on theirs. Not for one moment had they shown any lessening in their friendship for him, or their commitment, and yet it was now obvious that Ray's relationship with them had cost deeply in terms of peace of mind. They were now afraid, and not for the first time, and that was down to him.

He began to apologize, but Sarah held up her hand to silence him and then reached out and touched his fingers. She traced the scars that webbed across his skin. His hands and face had been badly scarred when he had been attacked while still a serving officer.

"Enough," she said. "The rest of us can take care of ourselves, and Nathan can take care of the kids. That's a safe pair of hands, and you know it, and it will give everyone peace of mind until you can sort this mess out. Besides, we don't even know if there is a mess to sort out until you phone Dave Beckett. It could just be somebody playing silly buggers to wind you up."

Ray tried to smile at her but looking around the table he could see that no one was any more convinced of that than he was.

CHAPTER 5

Dave Beckett was at home when Ray called and he listened in silence as Ray outlined what he needed to know and why.

"I remember the case," Beckett said. "And from what I remember it was messy and there were still at least two unsolved murders that Krantz didn't cop to."

"We had to get him on what we could," Ray said bitterly. "You know what it's like, you have to go with whatever has the best chance of a conviction. We knew there was more, we knew there were incidents we'd not yet even scratched the surface of but the main thing was he was inside."

Beckett promised he would contact Ray first thing the following morning, as soon as he had a chance to find out what was going on with Paul Krantz. He also said he would try and track down Ray's ex-colleague, DI Tony Nightingale. The Krantz case was the last he'd worked on, so he was at least ten years retired and could be anywhere. Beckett had never known him, having been a sergeant in a different division back then, but if he asked around, other colleagues might be able to offer a lead.

Ray thanked him and went up to join Sarah who was getting ready for bed. She was standing at their bedroom window looking down into the garden. "The fox is back," she said.

"Of course he is, you keep putting food out for him." He put an arm around her shoulders and looked down to the lawn where the fox, having finished his dogfood, was snuffling about. A high wall surrounded their garden with one small length of low fence, with a small gate set into it, between garden wall and house. After Sarah had been so seriously threatened they had put trellis all the way around the top of the wall, raising the height by another two feet to make it more difficult to climb without raising an alarm. Security lights, like the one that illuminated the fox and the lawn, now disturbed the peace several times a night usually as the local wildlife wandered through. The fox and hedgehogs and even the occasional rabbit gained access by going under or over that low bit of fence at the front of the house. *We should get a bigger gate and a higher fence*, Ray thought, but he didn't voice the idea. That would be to give in to what Sarah had called a siege mentality and which she had resisted violently once they had decided to stay in this house. Over the past months they had reduced the three security lights down to one and anything heavier than a cat approaching through the front garden or down the short drive where they parked their cars, could be heard crunching across the gravel they had laid.

Sarah turned from the window. "Come to bed, there's nothing more you can do tonight."

She settled down beside him, her body warm against his and Ray thought how lucky he was. Truth was he thought this every night and every morning and many times during the day and it hurt his heart that he had brought any kind of threat to this woman. He told himself that he was overreacting, that Paul Krantz was still locked up in jail and that all of this was a series of coincidences and somebody's idea of a joke. But as Sarah drifted off to sleep he lay on his back and stared at the ceiling and remembered.

It had been December almost twelve years ago now when he had first encountered Krantz. At first they had assumed he was the victim, not the perpetrator. He claimed to have come home to the flat he shared with his girlfriend and found her dead, her throat slashed and the place ransacked. He had seemed distraught and his alibi had initially seemed sound. He had found the body at 4.30 p.m., having left work early as he usually did on Friday. Arriving home he had found the door open and bloodstains on the handle. He had called out and then gone inside and found her lying in the living room, on her back, stretched out across a long, low coffee table. Her ankles had been bound to the legs as had her wrists and her throat was hacked so deeply another blow would have detached the head completely.

There was blood on the ceiling, on the floor, on the surrounding furniture. When Ray had arrived on scene, the CSI had laid plates across what looked to be the cleanest and least forensically sensitive area but it was obvious that they'd had a hard time finding anywhere where they might not be disturbing evidence.

The rest of the flat was a mess. There were items stolen — a laptop, some jewellery, some cash — but what first raised the alarm in Ray's mind had been two things. The nature of the killing; a burglar disturbed would lash out, certainly and might even kill but he would have expected a blow to the head with a blunt object, or stabbing with a kitchen knife, or, as he had seen on another occasion, death that had been caused by an overenthusiastic shove into a wall. That victim had cracked her head on the bricks and been killed instantly.

This death was different. It was brutal and deliberate and certainly, in Ray's view, not something carried out by a panicked intruder. Nightingale, then an older and much more experienced officer, had agreed with him. "It stinks," had been Nightingale's opinion.

The other thing that rang alarm bells was that although the place had been ransacked and there were items missing, other objects which would usually have attracted the attention of an opportunistic thief were still there. The dead woman had been wearing a large gold locket and that was still around what was left of her neck, the chain embedded in the wound and the locket, dripping blood but very obviously still there.

A clear plastic wallet had been thrown to the floor. A brief glance revealed that it contained passports, some cash, and travellers cheques in the days when people still bought travellers cheques. Could you still do that, Ray now wondered, did anybody bother?

And there was a small collection of pretty little silver snuff boxes miraculously untouched on a side table. It was almost, Nightingale had remarked, as though whoever had committed the crime could not bear to throw these tiny objects onto the floor. But why, if the perpetrator had been a thief, had they not scooped them up and taken them away?

Krantz had been in such a state that they had sent him to be checked over at the local hospital and an officer had been dispatched to his workplace to see if they could shed any light on who was next of kin. The night manager at the factory where Krantz had worked did not know him; Krantz was managerial, working in the offices above and the offices finished at around four o'clock on a Friday afternoon, the nightshift continued until ten. But he had a phone number for the day manager and they had put the police in touch with Krantz's supervisor. It was at that point that his alibi began to unravel. It seemed that Krantz had left a little early for lunch, in order to go to the dentist and had been back a little late. No one had thought anything of it; Krantz was a good worker, everybody liked him and if his dentist appointment had taken slightly longer than he'd expected it to, well, these things happen. The supervisor had noticed, however, that Krantz had changed his clothes and when he asked about it, was told that at the dentist he had got blood on Kranz's shirt and so he had gone home to change.

Later, when pressed on this, the supervisor had thought that Kranz had not just changed the shirt but his suit as well. At the time he assumed that the jacket too might have got blood on it and it was unlike Krantz to come to work in anything that didn't match, so he would not change the jacket but would have to change the trousers as well. That, the supervisor said, was just how he was. He liked to look smart, liked everything to be precise, his desk was a model of organization as was his work.

"You like him," Ray had asked and the man had looked as surprised as if Ray had uttered a stream of swear words.

"Everybody likes Paul, who wouldn't?"

And as the investigation proceeded Ray met with that reaction over and over again, even when the evidence against Paul Krantz mounted and it became apparent that there was no other explanation than that he had gone home at lunchtime, killed his girlfriend, staged the break-in, changed his clothes and then calmly attended his dentist appointment before returning to work. They never had found the clothes, though they had pulled out all the stops, knowing that the bloody clothes would have been a clincher and Krantz, after saying he'd taken them to the dry cleaners, changed his story and insisted he had no idea what had happened to them. In the end Krantz's undoing had been a tiny spot of blood on his watch band and another on his sock. He had tried to argue that he must have acquired them when he found the body, an idea belied by the spotlessness of the rest of his clothes. It seemed, Ray thought cynically, that Krantz had been prepared to sacrifice one decent suit on the murder but nothing more.

But even as evidence mounted — the threatening texts he had sent to his partner; her fear that she might come to harm, shared in other texts to friends. Texts she had deleted immediately for fear, perhaps, that he might see them — friends and work colleagues testified that he regularly examined her phone — it felt as though everyone was bending over backwards to find a reason why he couldn't have done it.

Dammit, Ray thought, looking back he had to acknowledge that even he had started to like the man. He had charisma, charm and utter, total self-confidence.

That death would only be the beginning. The murder of Ruth Edmondson, his partner at that point, had been the start of an investigation that had consumed Ray's life for the next fourteen months and which had necessitated him spending a great deal of time with Paul Krantz. He had interviewed the man initially, and then when he had been on remand, and then afterwards when he had been convicted of Ruth's murder and also the death of another woman, Polly Brown, an older lady who had signed everything she owned over to Krantz before her death. She had been found dead at the foot of the belfry stairs in St Nicholas' church, ostensibly an accident until the post-mortem had produced evidence of a struggle. There had been bruises on her upper arms and a faint line of finger marks appeared on her throat as post-mortem bruising emerged. Krantz had eventually confessed that this was his doing.

He had found him a very difficult man to get a handle on and, though Ray never lost sight of what Krantz had done, a difficult man to revile when he was face to face with him. It had been a conundrum. He recalled vividly one of his last interviews with Krantz.

"I always wanted a brother," Krantz said.

"You have no siblings."

"Blood siblings, no, but from time to time I have made connections that have felt like kinship." Ray remembered how he had leaned forward, looked Ray in the eyes as though this was significant.

"Like I have with you."

Ray had laughed, the idea was absurd. "I arrested you, charged you, I'm going to see you locked away. That's not kinship that's me doing my job."

"But you done it with the best of intentions, you believe you can cure me, make me a better person, don't we always want the best for our brothers."

This conversation was turning down right ridiculous, Ray had thought. The police officer assisting with the interview had been trying to hide his smirk. Ray couldn't really blame him; on one level this was actually funny.

"I know you can't show favouritism, I know you can't show how much you like me, but you do. You think of me like an errant child, like a little brother. You want to put me back on the right track."

"I want to lock you up and throw away the key," Ray growled.

Paul Krantz had just laughed then, as though Ray had come out with the funniest thing in the world. "Of course you don't," he said. "And you know, you can't."

And there were others too that had not received justice and Ray remembered them all. Victims who had lived but who had lost everything and victims who had died but whose death could not be conclusively tied to Krantz. And even after he had been convicted of the two murders which had put him in prison Ray had been left with the absolute certainty Krantz had been dangerous for much, much longer and the trail of destruction he had left behind was at least a decade long, even though Krantz himself was not yet thirty at the time of his conviction.

Ray recalled the days in court, Paul Krantz sitting in the dock or beside his solicitor, a look of deep concern on his face as he listened to the evidence against him, transmuting into a look of utter disbelief as the more serious accusations were made. *I did none of this, I am an innocent man*, that was the only thing he would say consistently and Ray had the impression, that even as the evidence against him piled up and became incontrovertible that Paul Krantz himself did not believe in it. That's how he had separated himself from his actions and become convinced, at least on some level, that he'd been set up by the police and more particularly by Ray and Nightingale.

Ray recalled the relief he had felt when the jury had eventually pronounced a guilty verdict. It had been a tussle, he recalled to get a unanimous agreement, some of the jurors having found it hard to equate the pleasant and concerned and obviously intelligent young man in the dock with whoever had perpetrated the appalling violence that had killed his girlfriend.

Ruth Edmondson, Ray reminded himself, that was her name. Ruth. Sometimes names and identities were in danger of getting lost in the blood and forensics and investigative minutiae but he could recall her parents sobbing in relief when the verdict was finally announced. Initially they had had hard time believing that this young man who had always been so attentive could have done such a dreadful thing. They had sat every day in court listening to the evidence and it had nearly destroyed them.

The foreman, Ray remembered, had been in no doubt of the accused's guilt and there had been a woman, late middle-aged, a teacher, if Ray recalled correctly. She had looked daggers at Paul Krantz throughout the trial. But there had been two or three others that found it just too much to believe, even though Krantz had never even spoken directly to them. Even though the evidence against him had piled high.

And the strangest thing was that even after his conviction . . . Well it felt almost like a contagion. Even some of Ray's colleagues had come straight out and asked him if he was sure that he'd got the right man. In prison Krantz seemed to have the ability to charm even the guards, even the toughest of convicts. Ray would almost say that he thrived. He kept track of Krantz in the first two or three years, obsessing about him for a while, until he had to give himself a good talking to and let go. He knew that Krantz had been moved on a half-dozen occasions because the worry was he was having too much influence on those who were supposed to be in charge of his incarceration. One guard was convicted of bringing in not one but three mobile phones, and of ordering takeaways because "Paul fancied Chinese". Of carrying messages to his supporters on the outside, mainly women, Ray noted, who harassed everybody on the enquiry and then after Krantz's incarceration did everything they could to have the enquiry reopened.

Occasionally even Ray had felt the doubts bubbling to the surface. Krantz seemed such a pleasant man and seemed so utterly bewildered by the accusations against him that if the physical evidence had not been so convincing and the history of his previous offending behaviour not been so damning, Ray would maybe have joined the ranks of those who doubted the man's guilt. As it was Ray had endured the flak; Nightingale had retired gratefully and Ray had spoken to him only a couple of times after, the man making it quite clear that he wanted nothing more to do with his former profession and simply wanted to be left in peace.

He had been so adamant about this that Ray had not been alone in wondering if something was seriously wrong. Was he feeling threatened, was he doubting himself, was something going on that he didn't want his former colleagues to know about?

"*I think of you as my brother, you know that, don't you. I told you that?*" Krantz had shouted to Ray as they had faced each other across the court, just after the guilty verdicts had been returned. "*I know that sometimes brothers have to do unpleasant things, just because they are siblings does not put them above the law, but, brother, I am telling you, I am an innocent man and you will regret this for the rest of your life.*"

The outburst had come out of nowhere and knocked Ray sideways. It had felt almost like a physical assault. Of course the press got hold of it, and all sorts of questions were asked. Ray had taken the opportunity to use leave owing to him and gone away for a few weeks. The truth was he had needed that time away in order to restore his equilibrium and by the time he had returned Krantz was in jail, the media had moved on to the next big thing and Ray was to a great extent able to get on with his investigations in peace.

Krantz was right, Ray reflected, as he turned on his side hoping to get to sleep. Krantz *had* haunted him, not because he thought he was innocent, far from it, because he felt he still did not know everything Paul Krantz was guilty of. And because there had always been this fear that somehow Krantz would get to him, one way or another. At first he had thought Krantz might start some campaign against him, seek to sully his name and reputation, make use of his rather fanatical supporters, especially when his right to appeal was denied. And indeed things were unpleasant for a while, but he'd been through worse and over time the anxiety faded to a soft nagging at the back of his brain and then to something he thought of only occasionally. Though the surge of emotion that accompanied those memories when they were triggered was powerful enough to take him by surprise whenever it happened. It was like a drench of freezing cold water; it left him breathless.

And now it seemed that very fear had surfaced big time.

CHAPTER 6

It was a while since Ray had seen DCI Beckett. They had arranged to meet in a small café close to where Beckett was based as neither of them was particularly comfortable with Ray coming into the police station. Ray had long since discovered that being a whistleblower, even when the officers were provably and extensively corrupt, probably earned you few friends among those who remained in the service after you left. Beckett, who probably thought he was a little weird, seemed to have no other objections to him apart from getting somewhat antsy that Ray kept turning up in cases he was investigating. He did seem sometimes to regard this as an inconvenience.

However the two men had come to like one another and respect each other's abilities. And Beckett had a definite soft spot for Sarah. How was she, he wanted to know. Had she recovered from the incident at the cottage when she had been attacked?

"We thought about leaving the house, I was afraid it would have some bad memories but in the end we decided to stay, we love the place and even if we moved you still take your memories with you. I think Sarah felt we had to deal with things where we were rather than try to run away. She had bad dreams for a while, come to that so did I, but we are settled again. Or we were."

"So tell me, and why the questions about Paul Krantz."

Ray took a deep breath and then launched into rather a long explanation. Beckett was aware of the accusations that had been made against Tim Bennett of course. He knew there was no foundation to them.

"And so you want reassurance that Paul Krantz is still safely inside," Beckett said slowly.

"He's not, is he?" Ray said flatly.

Beckett shook his head. "Ten months ago he was moved to a category C prison, he was considered low risk and his parole hearing was coming up. Now it's unlikely he would have been given parole, and he knew it, but there was also no reason to keep him in a higher security environment. So far as anybody was concerned he had been a model prisoner, made no trouble for anyone, taking his MA while inside, yada yada. So he does two months in this category C prison and then one day he's gone. It seems that he joined the group that were out on a day pass in preparation for release. He must've had help, both from inmates and from prison officers and two guards have been suspended, three prisoners returned to a higher category prison. But he must also have had help from the outside, new papers, somewhere to stay, some kind of cover story." He studied Ray carefully and then said, "You think this Paul Krantz is the mysterious boyfriend."

"I think it's likely."

Then you'll be needing this to show to anyone that might have seen him." Beckett dug in his pocket and removed a photograph. "It was taken when he was transferred so it's fairly recent. Of course he might have changed his appearance, but it's the best I can do. I can't do anything official, not until or unless we get confirmation of a sighting but if any of your witnesses recognize him, then I can bring resources to bear."

Ray studied the photograph. Krantz was now forty and most people who had spent the last decade in prison would have shown those years and more. Aggravatingly he looked little different from the man Ray had arrested and seen imprisoned. His hair had flecks of grey, the pale blue eyes gazed steadily from the image with just a hint of challenge in them and there was a trace of a smile, unusual in prison photographs. "He's still a cocky bastard," Ray said.

"By all accounts he was a popular cocky bastard," Beckett said.

"That I can believe. Thank you, Dave, I'll show this around and let you know what the results are."

"You think Ashley Summers is dead," Dave Beckett said.

"I think it's more than a missing persons case, I hope she's not dead but . . ."

Beckett nodded, he glanced at his watch. "Well, I must be going. Give my best to Sarah."

Ray watched him go, sipping the dregs of his coffee, his mind awash with emotions and impressions and fears.

* * *

He remembers the day Kit had competed in an event in the neighbouring village. She and her pony taking part in some kind of obstacle race, all quick turns and awkward jumps and she had to collect small plastic rings, hanging from the obstacles, that were decorated with coloured ribbons.

He and Rob had watched her cross the finish line, a half-dozen coloured rings hanging like bangles from her arm, bright ribbons against the subdued green of her hacking jacket. Her face flushed and her eyes shining. She had come in second, by the tiniest of margins but he and Rob knew she could have won. She outshone everyone else there. I did all right, *she had said when she came over to join them and he realized that she was happy with her second place rosette. That it didn't matter to her that another girl, a younger girl, a girl with an expensive pony of her own, not one borrowed from the local riding school, had crossed the line just a fraction of a second ahead.*

And she had turned to Rob, expecting praise, expecting him to be happy for her.

You should have won that *Rob had said to her.* You should have crossed the line ahead.

Paul knew that she had watched Rob as he walked away and that she had not understood his pain. The first time, Paul thought, that she had really not understood Rob's pain. The first time he had realized that she was less than he had thought.

* * *

Ray's first task was to get copies of the photographs. His next was to go and see Libby Summers on the off chance that this man had been hanging around or had appeared in social media Ashley might have posted. She didn't recognize him. She seemed chastened by recent events and Ray reflected rather grimly that although Paul Krantz did not seem to have aged more than three or four years at most, Libby Summers suddenly seemed to have acquired another decade. He explained who Paul Krantz was and watched as the lines seemed to deepen around her mouth. "He's killed her, hasn't he?" she said.

"We can't be certain of that."

The look she gave him was filled with contempt. "You, of all people know what this man is capable of."

* * *

He found only one neighbour at home in the block of flats where Ashley lived, the flats were not purpose-built but two adjoining Victorian houses that had been knocked through, so that they had a central hall and a single entrance and had been converted into six self-contained units. When he had visited Libby he had asked her to write him a letter of which he had printed several copies. He now enclosed a photograph with each copy and posted them through the neighbours' doors, together with his business card. The flats were of the kind occupied by professional people, being quite large and light and airy and in a pricey part of town, so he had not been expecting anybody to be at home during the day. The one neighbour he did encounter, Mrs Kathleen Caldwell, explained that she was retired.

"Do you recognize this man," Ray asked.

"Is this about the young woman who disappeared?"

"What makes you think that?"

"Well, why else would a private investigator be coming round?" she asked him tartly.

Why else indeed, Ray thought, reminding himself that old ladies were often very sharp and he should have remembered that.

He watched as she peered closely at the image and then nodded. "He was there the day the van came. I was at home. I hadn't realized that Ashley would be moving, of course, at that point we just thought she was moving not that she had disappeared. So yes, this man was supervising the loading of the furniture. I came out and asked what was going on and he said that Ashley was moving house. They were moving in together. Well, I was surprised, Ashley hadn't said anything and you'd think that would be the kind of news that friendly neighbours would exchange."

"Did you know Ashley quite well?"

"I thought I did. She was a lovely young woman. We'd often chat when we bumped into one another, and she'd sometimes come in for coffee. I dog sit for a friend once a week, on Wednesday, and she was often home from work early on Wednesday so sometimes we would go for a walk together. So, yes, I knew her more than just to say hello to on the stairs, which is all I know about the young man on the top floor. He's only here weekdays, he goes home on Friday evenings to be with his family and comes back on Monday for work, I do know that much. He's hoping they'll be able to move down here early next year, but his wife is a teacher and she has to give quite a lot of notice I believe and then find herself another job of course, so it isn't easy."

That's more than just say hello on the stairs, Ray thought, but he didn't comment. "Is there anyone else living here that she might be close to?"

"Well, there's the Langs, they live on the second floor on the other side, what was the other house before they converted. Nice couple, I go to dinner at their place once a month or so and Ashley is usually there. He is an engineer and she works at the university, in marketing I believe. He is not a proper engineer of course, he never gets his hands dirty, he just does things on computers. He says he is a design engineer." She rolled her eyes as if this was something too esoteric for words. Ray nodded sagely.

"And when might the Langs be in?"

"Well, it's Tuesday today so probably not until after seven. On Wednesday evening she usually gets home at about 5.30 p.m. and he's not much after that. But they don't know where Ashley went either, and they didn't know about the boyfriend, except that she had one but they were as surprised as I was that he'd turned up with that van."

"Was it a removals company?" Ray asked.

"Oh no, one of the self-hire things. Two trips it took, you wouldn't expect there to be that much stuff in one little flat, would you?"

"Two trips? And the man whose picture I showed you, was he driving?"

"The first time yes, then another man came back with him, to help with heavy stuff I suppose, the sofa, and so on. They had a right job getting it downstairs. Got it stuck on the dogleg, I told them they needed to turn it so that the back was angled towards the railing and that way they could pivot the whole thing around but of course they didn't listen. Young men rarely listen to old women, in my experience."

"Well, that's their loss," Ray said, commiserating.

"It most certainly is." She smiled at him, eyes sparkling with amusement.

"And the young man who was meant to be the boy-friend, how did he strike you?"

She thought about it and then said, "He was friendly and I suppose most people would have thought him pleasant and personable enough. But there was nothing behind the eyes,

39

there was an emptiness. You know some people who seem incredibly charming and everybody falls for them, and the only thing anybody ever says is what a nice person. But there is something about them that makes your skin crawl. Well, he was like that, do you understand what I mean. Usually I would have gone out and offered them a cup of tea, it's hard work moving furniture. But I asked him where Ashley was and he said she was at the new house waiting for them and that struck me as being wrong, you know?"

Ray waited.

"A woman might permit someone to move her furniture for her, but women in my experience prefer to pack their own clothes and personal items. They do not tolerate some man just throwing them into carrier bags and hoping for the best. When I saw him do that I decided that something was not right and I also decided that he was not a man I wanted to question. This is not in hindsight you understand, I spoke of this to my friend, the one I dog sit for. If you wish for confirmation that this is not hindsight, you speak to her."

"I think that was very perceptive of you," Ray said. "Mrs Caldwell, if this man does happen to come round again then will you let me know?"

"If this man comes round again I will phone the police," she said. "After that I will call you."

Ray agreed that would be a good plan. She assured him that she would talk to the Langs and make sure that if they had seen this man in conjunction with Ashley or otherwise, that they would also telephone him and let him know. Because the Langs lived in the other side of the converted house she thought it likely they would not have bumped into him on the stairs or anything like that.

Ray got back in his car and phoned Dave Beckett. "I got a very positive identification of Paul Krantz," he said. "He definitely seems to have been Ashley's boyfriend, and he was the man who moved her things in a self-hire van. He seems to have got somebody to help him move the bigger furniture, that someone might be quite innocent of course but it might be worth you sending a police artist round to see the neighbour, Mrs Caldwell on the ground floor. She is a bright old bird and might just be able to give us a lead."

Dave Beckett took down all the details Ray had gathered and promised him things would be set in motion. He sounded hopeful; up to now Ashley was simply a missing woman, old enough to have the right to disappear if she wanted to. Paul Krantz however had absconded from prison and if the identification could be made firmly enough, then this would be enough to give some impetus to the case.

Ray phoned Sarah next to let her know what he had achieved that morning. It wasn't much but at least it was something.

"I spent some time researching this morning," Sarah told him.

Of course she had, Ray thought. Sarah spent her entire life going through obscure archives and chasing stray facts down rabbit holes. Of course she would have looked at the Krantz case and Ray's involvement in it.

"I think we might reactivate the CCTV cameras at home," she said.

Ray felt his guts tighten. For several months after Sarah had been attacked they'd had CCTV cameras set up around the house. After a while they had simply lost that sense of necessity but they were still installed and linked to a sophisticated system that not only recorded on a home computer but also sent the recordings to a central database. One which Flowers-Mahoney, the company in which Ray was a partner, maintained for their high-end clients.

"I think that's a good idea," he said quietly.

CHAPTER 7

That evening, while Sarah settled down to watch something distracting on the television, Ray got out his old contact books and began phoning round old colleagues. Some he had not spoken to in several years, others he had kept in random touch with, exchanging the odd email or even the occasional text. But when Ray had stopped being a policeman that part of his life had receded into the background and he knew that, as a private investigator, they viewed him as quite a different animal. No longer quite one of their own.

Half a dozen phone calls in Ray noticed there was a similarity to the conversation. Yes, they all remembered the Paul Krantz case, how could they not. Even those who had not been in any way involved had followed it avidly. Two of them had heard about him absconding from the prison and Ray found himself slightly irritated that they had not thought to give him a heads-up. The first four could not remember where DI Nightingale might have gone, one thought he'd opened a pub somewhere down on the coast but the sixth person, who had been a DS last time Ray had caught up with her and was now a DCI, was surprised at the question.

"You are out of touch, aren't you? DI Nightingale was killed in a house fire about six months ago, a few of us went to the funeral."

"Really?" Ray had done an internet sweep that afternoon, looking for news of his old colleague and found nothing. He said as much.

"You were probably looking for Nightingale, right?"

"Who else should I have been looking for?"

"Well, that's the funny thing," she said. "He more or less dropped off the planet, as you know. Only kept in touch with a few of his old workmates." He heard her take a breath as though to prepare for a revelation. "The funny thing was that he also changed his name. His wife had died, you probably remember that, and a few years after he retired he changed his name to her maiden name. You'd have to have been looking for Billy Desmond, not Billy Nightingale."

"Desmond. Like the actress."

"Actress?"

"Never mind, you're probably the wrong generation. Where was he living?"

She provided him with a street address and told him to check out the local papers as they'd covered the funeral. Nightingale had moved a long way, Ray thought, the little village on the Welsh border not the sort of location he'd have expected him to fetch up in.

They exchanged a little small talk and then Ray put his phone down on the table and stared at it accusingly, before turning back to his computer. Now he had the right name to search for he found the media reports on the fire, and on the funeral but very little about the inspector's previous life. His career in the police force was not even mentioned. The media reports indicated that he had been popular with his neighbours, a member of the local gardening club, a quiet man who kept very much to himself.

What had frightened him so much he felt he had to change his name, Ray wondered. And did his death have anything to do with Paul Krantz? Had Krantz found him and killed him or was that too much of a leap?

On impulse he searched for the name of the foreman of the jury that had brought about the conviction. The foreman was a local businessman, Joe Capaldi, Ray had not known him personally, but had known who he was. He stared at the screen. Joe Capaldi had also died, also in a house fire, five months before. So a month after Nightingale, or Desmond, or whatever he had decided to call himself.

Ray did not like coincidences at the best of times, but this went far beyond random chance. He glanced at his watch, decided it was not too late to call Dave Beckett, after all it was only just after ten. "Nightingale is dead," Ray said without preamble, "and so is the jury foreman. House fires, the pair of them, a month apart. Now tell me that's not suspicious."

"I was going to wait till morning to call you," Beckett said, "but seeing as you pre-empted me—"

"Sorry, I know it's late."

"Considering it's you I should be glad it's this side of midnight. Anyway, I want you to consult on this case, we've assembled a team and we're working closely with the investigators looking into how Paul Krantz managed to abscond. As you seem to be last man standing from the original case it's thought your input might be valuable."

"You knew about Nightingale?"

"Desmond, he changed his name by deed poll. But yes, I found out a couple of hours ago. I did not know about Capaldi. I spent the last couple of hours persuading my bosses that you would be a good man to bring on board."

Ray paused, not sure this was news he wanted but then curiosity got the better of him. The chance to be officially involved was irresistible; he already was unofficially involved whether he wanted to be or not.

Beckett obviously knew him well enough to follow his train of thought because he said, "Can you be in for ten o'clock in the morning, we want to brief the troops first and then introduce you as an external adviser. There will be a few people who knew you from before, but there's also quite a lot of new blood since you left."

"You think they'll be any less prejudiced." Ray couldn't help but laugh.

"I think once they have familiarized themselves with the Krantz case and understand just how many offences we couldn't prove, and that he is almost certainly the abductor of Ashley Summers, they will forgive past indiscretions. You still have a good reputation, Ray, no one ever denied that you were a first-rate investigator."

Ray wasn't entirely sure that everyone would in fact agree with that assessment, police officers were supposed to catch legitimately recognized criminals, not other police officers. "I'll see you at ten," he said. "It might be a good idea to track the rest of the jurors down and check on witnesses." He paused. "Not that I have to tell you how to do your job."

"Until the morning then," Beckett said.

* * *

Sarah had decided that they needed supper before they retired for the night. The fact that she had chosen tea and cake told Ray everything he needed to know about her level of anxiety. Sarah only ate cake when she was either very happy or when she needed something comforting because she'd had a particularly lousy day.

"I think I'm glad you're involved," she said as she sliced her chocolate cake into slim pieces and then stabbed at them with the fork. He wondered who she was visualizing on the end of those prongs. "But it does put you in the firing line."

He noted that she did not add "again" to that observation. "You too," he said. "Sarah, maybe you should—"

The prongs of the fork were now aimed his direction. "Don't even say it. I'm not going anywhere. This is my home and I'm certainly not going to be chased out of it, not after all we've been through here. Besides, he managed to find

Inspector Nightingale even after he changed his name and moved well away from the area, where could I go and still be certain it was far enough or hidden enough. It would be too far away from you anyway. It could be we're making a mountain out of a molehill. And if we're not, well, I'm going to be with you, whatever happens next."

"You could go and stay with Nathan." His tone was edged with mischief and she looked at him sternly.

"That would make for a very crowded cottage. I promise, Ray, I will take every precaution and the situation has changed now, the police are actively looking for him and he'll very soon know that. He's not a stupid man, he'll keep out of the way. He's got what he wanted, that's you involved and you scared. No, don't deny it of course you are. I've only read about the man and I'm frightened of him, you had direct dealings with him. So he's got to be brought to justice and you've got to be part of that and I will be careful, we'll all be careful."

He nodded, there was nothing more to be said. But then he lay awake again, knowing that Sarah was only pretending to be asleep and by two o'clock they were both back downstairs watching old creature-feature horror films. Sarah finally drifted off during the return of the monster from the black lagoon. Ray covered her with a blanket and then wandered out into the walled garden, staring up at the sky. It was in his experience never fully dark at this time of year, there was always a hint of blue and now there was also a hint of dawn. He stood very still, watching as the fox drifted across the lawn again, presumably on his way back to bed, and the rising sun slowly brought the garden back into view. He had realized something earlier when he was talking to Sarah, something he did not like about himself. He had tracked men down, had to defend himself from violence, had to defend others and he had done so because he must but this time, he *wanted* to find Paul Krantz. He wanted — and he hated even thinking that this might be the case — to smash his fist into that smug face over and over again until it was obliterated. Krantz had got to him in ways that other criminals, even other murderers had not. Had somehow worked his way into Ray's consciousness so that even all these years later he could feel him squirming and wriggling inside his brain.

* * *

He remembered that final time. It was spring, not summer, not his usual time for visiting but this was different. They were all eighteen and preparing for exams and he was expected to go on to university. That would change things for them all, he thought, taking them all in different directions. Somehow, that didn't feel right.

When they had all been younger they had been dependent for communication on other people. The occasional phone call, sometimes even letters or postcards. As they got older, mobile phone, email, had made it easier to keep in day-to-day contact. And they had, rarely a day went by without three of them talking and though their families knew they were in communication, no one knew the depth of strength of their relationship or just how vital that daily communication might be.

How could they. This was kinship beyond anything any of them could understand.

He had passed his driving test at the first attempt, had been saving for the past two years so he could buy himself a cheap and probably only just roadworthy car. The insurance costs four times more than the car was worth and he paid for it on a monthly basis, his part-time jobs covering that and petrol but not much more. But it was worth it; another thing he did not have to ask permission to use.

When Rob had called him needing help he skipped school and went straight over. He helped the brother to bury the bodies close to where they had buried the fox all those years before. The brother had already cleaned up most of the blood and by dint of scrubbing and bleaching, the rest was quickly eradicated.

He had stayed there for a while, making use of the facilities until the money ran out and bills that needed paying attracted red letters and demands. By that time they had emptied the bank accounts, sold anything worth selling and when they all left in his car it was in such a fashion that they had left as much of a mystery as that of the Marie Celeste.

After that he had declared that he had no family and he had never returned to take his exams.

CHAPTER 8

On his way into the police station that morning, Ray stopped by Tim and Daisy's house. He had expected Tim to be home but was surprised to find Daisy there also. She had taken some time owed to her, she told Ray, and they were taking the kids off to stay with family for a while. She had parents who lived by the sea and as the school holidays were almost upon them felt no guilt about taking the older child out of nursery a day or two early.

"We'll be off tomorrow afternoon," she said. "I just need to get away for a time, we all do."

Ray nodded but made no comment. He showed them the photograph and Tim said, "A police officer called round last night and showed us this. So far as I know I've never seen the man, though Daisy had a feeling—"

"I don't know where I've seen him, but I'm sure I have."

"Is that when you decided you would go away, after seeing the photograph," Ray asked.

She looked slightly shamefaced but nodded. "I phoned work first thing this morning and told them I needed some holiday. They were pretty good about it really."

She bustled off upstairs to do more organizing and Tim offered Ray coffee. He declined, told Tim where he was going. "And she can't remember where she saw him?"

"She's been racking her brains, but she knows she has. Daisy wouldn't just imagine this, if she says she has seen this man Krantz, then she definitely has."

Ray nodded. "If I can pick you up this afternoon will you go to the university with me?"

"I suppose so, but what for? A lot of the staff will already have left, the students gone, the exams are over, there's just the last bits of marking to do and that's all online now."

"I'll bring the photo in case we meet any of your colleagues, anyone who might have seen Krantz but what I really want to do is get a feel for the layout of the place. Where Ashley said she had met Krantz. I need to walk the scene, I suppose."

"Well, I can give you a bit of time," Tim agreed. "I don't want to leave Daisy for too long, you understand that."

Of course he did, Ray thought. He promised to let him know if things changed, but suggested he picked him up about three o'clock and then left for the briefing.

* * *

It was quite some time since Ray had been inside the police station that had been his workplace and it felt very strange now, waiting in reception for Beckett to come and collect him. He watched as the familiar figure emerged from the rear office. Beckett was a little younger than Ray and, he reflected, a lot slimmer and fitter looking.

He looked tired, Ray thought. Then remembering his own face in the mirror that morning, realized this was probably mutual and would also probably not improve until Krantz was back behind bars.

The police station had changed since Ray had last been, the layout altered so that what had been three tiny offices, leading to a communal space was now a much bigger open-plan area. Large boards along one wall had already been laid out with images of Krantz, his victims, crime scene pictures — including images of Ashley Summers' now empty flat

— and the table beneath stacked with handouts and photographs. Ray looked around for familiar faces, spotted two. One skinny little elf of a man he remembered had been a PC last time Ray had met him. He was on the phone and raised a hand in greeting. The other, an older man with a head like a bulldog, who Ray recalled from another division, looked up from his computer and nodded in his direction. He looked wary as though not quite sure if he was glad Ray was there or not and had decided to withhold his opinion for a while.

Beckett called for everyone's attention and introduced ex DI Ray Flowers, who was going to be consulting with them. Ray found himself, coffee in hand, perched on the edge of the table and fielding questions from an already very engaged team. He felt himself relax, he knew how this worked. He might have been absent for several years, but the place smelt the same, and despite the building work looked the same. Stained grey carpet tiles on the floor, shabby flatpack desks, and air of intensity and purpose. That was something he had missed.

"What was he like to interview?" someone asked. "We've been watching through the interview tapes, and he seemed kind of cooperative on the surface but when you analyse what he says, there's nothing there. It's just fog."

Ray nodded. "We got expert advice from a forensic psychologist and that certainly helped, but it didn't make it simple. The psychologist recommended that we circle round the central issue, slowly work our way in by asking questions he was ready to answer and as you will know, if you've watched any of the interviews, this man liked to talk. It wasn't a case of no comment, it was a case of 'this is what I'm going to tell you', never mind what questions we happened to be asking. We began to realize after a while that he was actually giving us bits and pieces of useful information, but it was in a form that he wanted it delivered. We had to pull the strands out and if we figured out that he was giving us a clue it was like he gave us a round of applause and gave us a tiny bit more."

"When you asked him about Polly Brown," somebody picked up on this "he was quite happy to agree that she'd given him money, quite happy to agree that he persuaded her to change her will but when you asked him about her death, all he seemed to want to do was talk about the places they visited together. Is that the kind of thing you mean?"

Ray nodded. He recalled that particular interview as if it was yesterday, he realized he had stored these things up in his head and gone over them so many times that they were still almost in his present. "If you notice one of the places he told us about, places they visited, was St Nicholas' church where her body was eventually found at the foot of the tower stairs. She was into church architecture, she'd been a churchwarden for years, so they had spent quite a bit of time looking at medieval churches. If you noticed in the interview he gave us a whole load of detail about the architecture of the place and even details about the gravestones in the churchyard."

"So showing he had an intimate knowledge of the place and of her life and habits. He seemed almost proud of that, that he could remember the place and in so much detail."

Ray nodded. "And this was the same interview after interview. It was almost as though he was lecturing us, showing off his knowledge and, make no mistake, he is an intelligent man, and intellectual, despite the fact that he left school just shy of taking his A levels. That was something we could never get him to talk about, why he had left, but the psychologist who advised us suggested that there must have been some kind of traumatic event which changed his direction at that point and that may have impacted on everything he did after that. Thing is, we never found out what. We spoke to family and schoolfriends and teachers, but no one was able to pinpoint a particular precipitating incident."

"Would it have been useful to find out?"

"Possibly, anything I'd have to say in that direction would be just pure speculation. The fact is he left home at that point and his family never saw him again. Although when he was arrested, he still had living relatives but he insisted that he had no family. Whatever happened it was clearly traumatic or at any rate life changing, so it might have been useful to know, but we were a little more concerned with what he had done in what was then the here and now. It soon became obvious that we weren't going to get him on everything, that we had to pick our battles and getting him put inside for killing his girlfriend and Polly Brown seemed our best option. We did eventually manage that, but it was a sour victory in the sense that we knew there was more."

"This young woman that disappeared." This time the speaker was a rather young-looking, blonde woman. "Have you noticed how much like his girlfriend, Ruth Edmondson, she is?" She got up and crossed to one of the boards and Ray followed her over to look at the two pictures. Although he had seen photographs of Ruth Edmondson when her face had not been bruised and cut and battered, the overpowering image in his mind was of how she had looked when he had seen her dead. Now, looking at the image of Ruth and looking at the image of Ashley, he had to agree that this young woman had a point. He had forgotten the dark skin and the tight curls, verging on blonde and lighter than her skin tone. Though Ruth had shorter hair than Ashley, the resemblance was striking.

"No," he said. "I wasn't conscious of that. Now you point it out, they could be sisters."

"But Polly Brown was a good deal older," someone else commented. "And looked totally different."

Ray retreated to his perch on the table and reclaimed his coffee cup. He nodded. "When we looked at cases in which he had been implicated, those involved split into two types. Older women, who could benefit him financially and to whom he offered friendship and flattery, but with whom he didn't seem to have a sexual relationship. Then there were young women who were much smaller than he was, light hair colour though not always blonde. It was more a question of build than colouring but there was definitely a type he preferred. Two other young women he dated both came to unfortunate ends. One, Camilla Marsh, apparently fell down the stairs and broke her neck."

"The same way that Polly Brown was killed," Beckett commented.

Ray nodded. "Perhaps he found it worked once and so he arranged it again," *rather like the house fires, perhaps*, "but in both cases death was initially thought to be accidental. Both women were believed to have been alone in the house at the time and both had been drinking, despite the fact that neither were regular drinkers and in fact Polly Brown rarely had more than a glass of sherry, even when she went out. Bruising found at the post-mortem, that was inconsistent with an accidental fall, called this into question. Camilla Marsh had no obvious signs on her body, according to the PM and by the time connections had been made, she'd long been cremated."

"And then there was Olivia Campion," Beckett said.

Ray noticed the nodding around the room and understood that these cases had already been discussed at some length. Beckett was clearly using this opportunity to pull everything together and to emphasize just how complex the previous investigation had been.

"Olivia Campion was the youngest of the victims, she was just nineteen years old and she told her family that she found a new boyfriend, she confided to friends that he was somewhat older than she was and that her mother would not approve. It was only after she'd been found dead, having been bashed over the head and left for dead in a park close by her home that Krantz came into the picture. She died from her injuries three days later. Then a connection was made with Paul Krantz. He turned up at the funeral, apparently distraught and revealed himself to have been the mystery boyfriend. The family were not pleased, both at the scene he made at the funeral and that he'd been seeing their girl. He was investigated of course, but there was nothing to prove he had been anywhere near her on the night she died."

"You questioned him about this in the interviews, he said he felt it was only right that he should go to the funeral because after all he was in mourning too."

"He did," Ray said. "He had an alibi, as it happened. Another young woman. The family had been inclined to take his grief at face value until that came out. He did admit to feeling mildly guilty that he had been with someone else that evening, but said that Olivia was really far too young for him and that he was about to break up with her anyway.

"As to what he gained from these relationships, if you could call them that, well that's hardest to categorize. The older women provided him with financial rewards, the younger ones no doubt entertained him for a while, were a sexual outlet, and probably flattered him because they were all attractive, intelligent, and generally pleasant human beings. Maybe he thought some of that pleasantness would reflect well on him, I don't know, but there's no doubt he could be charming and there is equally no doubt that he left a string of broken, distraught and dead people in his wake. Those women that didn't die still lost financially and in terms of self-esteem. And I have no doubt they'll also be still living with the idea that he *could* have killed them. And if we make the leap and suggest that Paul Krantz was directly responsible for these unsolved deaths, then that leads us to another element that puzzled us when we were investigating. His decision-making seems almost arbitrary, who would live, who would die, who would simply be stripped of some of their assets and then dismissed. And dismissed is a word I don't use arbitrarily. It was a word that two of his previous victims used about him, older ladies who were charmed by him and thought he was their friend. One of them said that he had become almost like a son, he'd given her good advice, he'd listen to her, he had treated her with great respect until she trusted him enough to lend him some money. She phoned him the day after and he simply said, "I've done with you now I don't want to see you again."

"You have a good idea of the background," Beckett said. "Our concern now is for Ashley Summers, where she is, if she still alive, what happened to her. It's also relevant that the name Paul Krantz used when he was getting to know the young woman, is the name of a genuine lecturer at the university. That much you already know. But Tim Bennett is also a friend of Ray Flowers. And we have an increasing amount of evidence that suggests that Krantz deliberately implicated Bennett in order to draw Ray into this new situation. There doesn't seem anything to directly connect Ashley Summers to Ray or previous investigations, or any of the previous victims but there certainly seems to have been a concerted effort to trick Libby Summers into engaging Ray's services, after she felt the police had failed her.

"Ashley Summers is certainly the same type as Krantz goes for and he was almost certainly looking for a victim within the university setting, knowing that Tim Bennett worked there. This would have been convenient for him. So it's entirely possible that he just happened to see a young woman who fitted his preference and that was vulnerable enough to fall for what initially seemed his kindness. And make no mistake this man seems to be very good at reading what people need and what will allow him to get close."

"Something you should also think about," Ray added, "is the likelihood of Krantz having backup scenarios should this one have failed. Ashley Summers may simply have not liked him and though that would undoubtedly have annoyed him, he's flexible enough in his thinking to have moved on somewhere else."

"As I told you earlier, we are also certain that he must have had friends on the inside in prison and on the outside, in order for him to abscond and disappear, and there are a number of leads to follow up. Following the original investigation, Ray and DI Nightingale were made aware of Krantz's fan club, if I can call it that. Mostly young women but also a few young men who aspired to be like him and who tried very hard to get an appeal launched. There were even a handful of older women involved. We have good evidence that some of this group kept in touch with him, at least for a time, when he was in jail. While direct contact seems to have tailed off it's very likely that the support continued.

We know that for quite some time many of these people wrote directly to him and that he wrote back. Those we knew about have been interviewed and it does seem that most of the interest has tailed off over the years, especially after they failed to get the appeal. From those interviews we've gleaned a few other names. Krantz seems to have been close to three of them in particular, including an ex work colleague, a man called Philip Carstairs who still believed him to be innocent. And there's the barrister the group paid to try and get the appeal, Tom Beresford, though he doesn't seem to have maintained contact since that failed. There's also a woman, Suzette Preece, who used to be a prison visitor until she got too close to Krantz."

"Have they been brought in for interview?" Ray asked.

"At the time he absconded, yes. But attempts to contact them in the fast few days have been singularly unsuccessful. They seem to have gone to ground around the time Ashley Summers was abducted, which is a worrying development. They may be helping him."

"They may even be victims," Ray said. "Don't under-estimate him. If you are unfortunate enough to come face to face with the man, or, when you finally catch up with him, you interview him, bear in mind that he is slippery as a barrel full of eels. Superficially he can be charming and very pleasant." *And has the capacity to make you feel as though you're the only person in the room that matters*, Ray thought, but he did not say this out loud. Even thinking it still made him feel too vulnerable and vaguely ashamed.

* * *

Ray spent a little longer fielding questions and then hung around to bring himself up to speed on what was happening with the Ashley Summers case. Following his visit to the flat, the police had sent officers around and had spoken to the indomitable Mrs Caldwell who had seen Paul Krantz and another man moving Ashley's furniture. She had been able to give a police artist what they hoped was a reasonable description of the second man and Ray studied the image for a moment, hoping he would recognize the face. He decided in the end that it was quite generic, as these things often were. Still, it might jog somebody's memory.

Two other neighbours also identified Krantz as having visited Ashley Summers and one other happened to have glimpsed the moving van. Mrs Caldwell had only noted that it was a self-hire van but the second witness had added that it was the same self-hire company he had used when he moved into the apartment block. If this was the company in question, then it would save some legwork at least and they might even recognize the second man.

Having grabbed a quick sandwich at lunchtime he called to check with Tim that the trip to the university was still on and to ask if he could pick him up a little early. By two thirty he was at Tim's house. He showed Tim and Daisy the picture of the mystery man who had helped Paul Krantz.

"Poor girl," Daisy said. "Do you think there's any chance she might still be alive?"

Ray was about to answer but his attention was caught by Tim's sudden rigidity as he stared at the artist's impression.

"I think I know who this is," Tim said. He looked suddenly pale and Daisy took his arm.

She looked again at the picture. "Oh my goodness, that's Derek. Derek Fielding, he's one of the campus security guys. He's a lovely man, what the hell is he doing with Paul Krantz?"

Ray looked from one to the other. There was no need to ask either if they were certain. He took out his mobile and called Beckett. Somehow it seemed logical that Krantz should pick someone from the university. It was the kind of outrageous and audacious thing that he would do. Message delivered, he turned in puzzlement to Tim and said, "But if he knows you then wouldn't he know that Paul Krantz wasn't you, if you see what I mean."

"He might have seen me in passing but he wouldn't know who I was. I recognize him because I see him about the campus from time to time, and he's in uniform and with a name badge, but he doesn't look after the building that I'm in, he's up on the main site."

"Then how come Daisy recognizes him, she doesn't work at the university."

"No, I don't know him from there. I mean I know he works at the uni, but I know him from nursery. He has a little boy, Liam, he's in the same preschool as our two are. A lot of university employees use the same one, they can drop off on the way to work, it's just a short walk across the park."

An idea began to form in Ray's mind but Tim got there first. "Daisy, do you think the nursery is where you saw Paul Krantz?" he asked.

She thought about it and then shook her head. "No, I don't think so, I'm sure it was somewhere else. I'd have remembered if it was nursery, you get to know the usual faces. I do the nursery pick-up twice a week," she explained to Ray. "Tim does it the rest of the time. His hours fit better, and you've never seen him." She looked at her husband to confirm.

Tim shook his head. "No, like you say you see the same faces all the time, parents who pick up more or less the same time you do. And the nursery staff have CCTV all over the place and nanny cams, you can dial in from home or from your mobile and see what your kids are up to."

"Okay, so we have a little bit more of the picture. The chances are this Derek Fielding is innocent in all of this, he was probably just asked a favour." Though that implies, Ray thought, that he'd had enough interaction with Krantz that the request didn't seem strange. He could hardly have wandered up to him and asked him at random.

He asked Tim if he was still willing to go to the university with him and somewhat reluctantly Tim agreed. Ray promised he would not keep Tim more than an hour.

"Okay," Daisy said, "but I'm going to get everything packed just so we can load the car when you get back and then we're going."

Tim nodded.

"And I'm locking the door so you won't be able to get in with your key. I'll be putting the bolt on. You'll have to knock."

* * *

"Do you think we're really in any danger?" Tim asked they drove away.

"Hard to say," Ray told him as honestly as he could. "It's quite likely you were just a means to an end, he has no further use for you, so you won't be on his radar now."

"I feel like we're running away, and I don't even know if this is the right thing to do. I know Daisy will feel happier once we're gone, but what if he knows, what if he follows us?"

"I don't think that's likely, you and Daisy are now on the periphery of his gameplay. The focus has shifted. Like I say, you were a means to an end and this is not a man with infinite resources. He might well have friends, but they can't be everywhere at once."

Tim nodded but he did not look reassured. Krantz had found DI Nightingale, Ray reminded himself. He was in no doubt this was what had happened. The big difference of course was that Tim and his family had done absolutely nothing to interfere with Krantz or his ambitions, so from that point of view he was probably right in saying that they were not Krantz's focus and therefore not in immediate danger. And though Tim and Daisy were friends, Ray had many people much closer than they were that Krantz could target if it was his intention to hurt Ray. It was a thought that quite frankly filled him with dread.

They managed to find a parking space and left Tim's permit in the car and walked back along the main road to the university campus. A Victorian cemetery occupied the opposite side of the road, green railings separated from the pavement and the too narrow road, cars and buses squeezing alongside parked vehicles. The university campus took up most of the space on the other side and beyond that there was a park, beyond that the nursery both Tim's and Derek Fielding's children attended.

This was not the part of the campus on which Tim regularly worked. He usually taught in one of the large Victorian houses that the university also owned. They were not purpose-built for teaching and were often inconvenient and awkward spaces but Ray knew that Tim really liked the quirky old buildings. He dealt mostly with part-time and distance learners and also with lifelong learning and outreach programs. Ashley Summers in contrast worked in one of the main tower blocks, which housed lecture theatres, seminar rooms and tutor's offices. The campus was quiet at this time of year, most of the students having left and those still crossing the campus were mostly postgrads whose teaching semesters did not keep to the same term times as undergraduates.

Tim led him into the lobby. They had passed the café where Ray knew he often did his tutorials, the main restaurant seem to be closed or at least empty and the café was only occupied by a handful of students and what looked to be staff. The main lobby had a bank of lifts, a scatter of tables and chairs and noticeboards covered by several geological strata of notices.

Into the lift, up to the fourth floor. "They still have Paternosters here?" Ray was quite surprised, spotting the moving boxes as they exited the main lift.

"Yes, but we're not going up that high. In here, this big seminar room, this must have been where Ashley Summers met Paul Krantz because this is where the cross-curricular conference was happening, on this floor. Two of the smaller rooms would have been used as breakout rooms, but this would have been the main social hub and the presentations would have happened in here. I didn't attend that one, I've come to others and they all follow pretty much the same pattern. The really big conferences don't happen here, they take place at a repurposed hotel that the university owns or one of the dedicated conference centres. This was a fairly small and I expect quite a focused group. Most people would have known each other."

"So you'd have expected Paul Krantz to stand out."

"Enough to be memorable, enough to be noticed, but everybody would have assumed he'd just come from somewhere else or that he was maybe a new colleague. There were a handful of people I think from other universities but it was a kind of learning development conference, something put on by teaching staff for other teaching staff, not a big major thing."

"Were you invited?"

Tim shrugged. "I saw the memo go out, but it was a weekend, I wouldn't have got paid for attending or anything, frankly I felt like I'd got other things to do. Now I wish I had."

"A list of attendees, would that have been posted anywhere?"

"I wouldn't have thought so, it might have been available on the emails, so that people could see who was going, but I don't think it would be made public as such. I mean, some of the part-timers go to these things, and I do if it's something that really interests me, but if you wanted to choose somebody to impersonate then picking a non-tenured staff member would probably be a safe bet."

"There are many ways he could have found your name, I suppose," Ray said.

"My name could have come up in conversation with somebody who had attended a class, he could have wandered into our building and seen my name on the wall alongside my photo. We all have photos and general info up in the lobby. He could have looked on the department website and found it that way. I don't have a photo on the website. I just never got round to uploading one but I think if you take a look I'm not alone in that. Maybe he knew I was a friend of yours to start with, and then he did his research. Maybe he stumbled upon me by accident."

"Unlikely. He almost certainly knew you were my friend, he researched you. But how did he find out about the conference?"

"Noticeboards, downstairs or anywhere across the university, these things get posted out as emails but they also go on the boards. You see the emails aren't always universal, they get sent intra-departmentally and it's much more difficult to send out a global email to invite people from different departments, so the noticeboards are just easy. And everything goes on the library intranet, and anybody with a library ticket can access that. So anybody that studies here or anybody that previously studied here and has paid to keep up their library ticket. It wouldn't have been hard, and you said he's good at doing his research."

Tim fidgeted awkwardly and Ray could see he wanted to be away from there. Ray decided that he could always come back now he knew where that first meeting had happened. It somehow helped him visualize what might have occurred, now he had seen the location.

"Let's get you home," he said.

Gratefully, Tim headed towards the door.

CHAPTER 9

Once he had dropped Tim safely back with Daisy, Ray went to his own office to see if there was anything urgent he should be attending to, aware that he was neglecting his own work. Rowena, their secretary, handed him his mail and records of a few phone calls. George Mahoney, Ray's partner, sat at his desk reading something on the computer screen but he glanced up when Ray came in.

"So what's going on," George asked.

Ray got himself a red mug of very strong coffee, drew up a seat near George's desk and began to explain about Paul Krantz, about the disappearance of Ashley Summers and all of the odd circumstances that surrounded this. George listened without comment and when Ray had finished he said, "We reassess the security at your place, tighten it up. Any resources we have at Flowers-Mahoney, of course you must use and any strings I can pull, just say the word."

Ray nodded and thanked his partner. George, with his background in government and diplomatic security had access to resources that he did not. "I always knew he'd turn up again like a bad penny. That there would be trouble some-where along the line. You know when you get that feeling that there's unfinished business, that instead of putting a full stop, all you've done is add a comma or a semicolon. That sooner or later you will need to go back and finish the story."

George nodded. "I've met men like him," he said. "Some in the army, some in government, they are never good news."

Ray laughed, a small injection of humour made him feel better. He went across to his own desk, sorted through his messages and was about to leave when his mobile rang. It was Tim. Ray could hear the sound of a car engine and kids chatting in the back seat. So they had left home and were on their way.

"Daisy remembered where she'd seen him," Tim said without any preamble.

"Where?"

"You know Archie starts school next September? Daisy and the kids went along to one of the open days. I think I was working, anyway I didn't go, I'd been in to meet the teacher and all that before . . . Sorry I'm rambling. Anyway they did a bit of a sports day, and they put on all these displays on the school playing field and there was this man who seemed to be cheering one of the kids on, he was standing next to Daisy. She quite naturally asked him 'which one's yours'. He pointed one of the kids out and they exchanged a bit of small talk, you know 'what do you think of the school,' that sort of thing. It was no more than a minute or so, and she never thought any more about it, but she is convinced that was Paul Krantz."

Ray felt a sudden clutch of cold in his chest. "Which school, when was this, she'll have to make a statement."

"We're not coming back." Tim told him quickly.

"No, I understand that. Look, I'll talk to Dave Beckett and arrange it so that she can nip into a local police station and make a statement there, is that all right? But he might want to have a word with her first, it is okay to give him your number?"

Tim reluctantly agreed. Paul Krantz was following them, or at least that's how it must be feeling, Ray thought when Tim had ended the call. They were driving far and fast to get away from him, and still the man was hanging on. He knew how that felt.

* * *

That evening he and Sarah drove across to John and Maggie to have dinner with their friends. The children were due to break up from school in two days' time and they would then go and stay with Nathan. They were as excited about this as if they had been going on some distant expedition. There were plans apparently to visit Evie's grandchildren and great-grandchildren and although Maggie was clearly still worried she seemed relieved. There would be many pairs of eyes to keep watch.

"Mummy says we can't take the dogs," was Beth's only objection to the plan. "The dogs would love it there."

"And you know the size of the cottage," Maggie said. "Turbot would barely be able to turn around without knocking everything over."

Turbot pricked up his ears at hearing his name. He was a recent addition to the family. A tall, rangy, grey brindled cross, Ray suspected there was Irish wolfhound in the mix, with a tail that could start a dust storm and attitude to life that was exuberant as that of Beth and her brother. Sid, the older dog, was a little more staid, usually content to follow at a distance and amble along at his own pace.

When the children had been sent up to bed, or at least sent up to pretend to go to bed, Ray filled them in on new developments. He suggested that he should have George, or one of their employees, come over and install some kind of basic security system and to his surprise Maggie agreed. The house was old, somewhat isolated and although parishioners were always coming and going, could not be seen from the road and backed onto fields.

"It's not that I'm scared," she said quickly. "It's just that I'd feel happier."

Ray nodded, he promised he'd arrange a visit for the next day.

As they always did when they came over, they helped clear the table and all washed up together in the old-fashioned kitchen. "What did you tell the children about why they were visiting Nathan," Sarah asked.

"That part was easy, they've been nagging about doing that all this last term. They stayed at Easter and Evie's great grandkids and Nathan helped them build dens in the wood. You'd have thought they were the first kids to ever build a den. So all we're doing is giving in to what they already wanted."

Maggie turned to Ray. "You really think they'll be okay there?"

"There's nothing to suggest Paul Krantz has turned his attention your way," he reassured her. "But as they'll be staying with Nathan they've got an entire village looking out for them, Evie seems to be related to most people."

But as they drove home Sarah was unusually quiet.

"Penny for them," Ray said.

"You don't need to pay to know what I'm thinking. Ray, do you ever consider that this is just the pattern of our lives. One damn thing after another, I really am sick of it."

"I know. Sarah, if you want—"

"I've already told you, whatever comes up we face it together. It's just not knowing what direction it's coming from. He could be anywhere. He turned up at university, he turned up at the school open day, he almost certainly arranged for those women to be talking about you in the café just when Libby Summers was there, so he must have known what her habits were. And that poor young woman that's disappeared and is probably dead. Your DCI Nightingale is dead, the jury foreman is dead. I'm seriously thinking of getting a shotgun."

He laughed. "I can just see you blasting seven shades out of him, that would be very satisfying."

"You're not supposed to encourage me. You're supposed to be saying, Sarah, violence is not the answer."

He reached out and touched her arm before returning his hand to the steering wheel. The scarring on his hand felt particularly sore today. Sometimes it happened like that, the skin would get dry and uncomfortable and on occasion even some of the heat felt as if it was returning, deep within the muscle and tendons. It was not lost on him that if it had not been for violence he would never have met Sarah. It was as though their relationship had been born out of the aggression and pain he had endured. He pushed the thought aside, knowing it to be nonsense, knowing it to be the result of stress and tiredness and guilt. Knowing also that he had nothing at all to be guilty about but that didn't make it any better.

"I can't make it right," he said.

It was her turn to reach out and touch him. He felt the gentle pressure as she squeezed his arm. "It isn't yours to make right," she said. "You have done nothing wrong."

CHAPTER 10

It had been another night with very little sleep though exhaustion had won in the early hours and they had both almost overslept.

Sarah went off to work as usual and Ray to the office. Checking his emails he discovered that Dave Beckett had sent over the reports on the house fires that had killed Nightingale and Joe Capaldi, the jury foreman. In each case arson was suspected. Each man had been alone in the house, Nightingale because he lived alone, Capaldi because his wife was away. Did she just get lucky, Ray wondered, or was this another one of Krantz's random choices.

In both cases the fire had started downstairs, an accelerant poured through the front letterbox but also used to soak the back door. The fire had taken hold quickly. Nightingale hadn't even made it out of bed but had died of smoke inhalation, Capaldi was found halfway down the stairs.

There had been no suspects, nothing to suggest why these men had been targeted, the police had no leads. Both cases were open but had moved little beyond what the investigation had found out in the first two days; that they were well liked and had no obvious enemies.

Looking at the paperwork, someone had mentioned that Capaldi had been on the jury when Paul Krantz been convicted but it was observed that this was ten years before, and Ray could find no suggestion that this had been followed up. The investigation had focused on minor disputes with a difficult neighbour, one who had caused problems with others in the street but who had an alibi for the night in question, and on the possibility that business rivalry might have given rise to some kind of revenge. That angle had died a death within days.

Ray called Beckett. "Dave, why did nobody follow up the Krantz connection when they were looking at the Capaldi case? It's mentioned; if they'd found out he was on the loose, that would have opened up the enquiry."

"It was only ever seen as a faint possibility, the officer tasked with following it up fell ill, and was off for the next month. By the time he returned the Capaldi case had been shelved and he was onto something else. The irony is, he sent an email to the prison and the response was in his inbox."

"Then how come nobody else picked it up?"

"The email was read, and the response was logged but the focus of the investigation at the time was on the troublesome neighbour. He'd made threats, he'd caused problems, he'd poured paint over Capaldi's car. So they dropped the ball on Krantz. In mitigation, this all happened when the division was dealing with yet another lockdown and a massive counter terrorist operation."

Mitigation, maybe, Ray thought, but was aware that Dave Beckett did not sound happy. However it had happened, this was a massive error.

"Anyway," Beckett continued, "as usual you called me just as I was about to call you. Are you free later on this morning? I've got permission to take you to Willingham Grange. I'm going to speak to the prison officers and some of the inmates. Not of course the prison officers who have been suspended, or the inmates who have been assigned to different prisons, that would be too much to hope. But we do have recorded interviews with them which you can look over later. But I'd like to get a general feel for how Krantz was regarded, now everyone's had time to get over the shock and think about it."

Ray told him that he was free and Beckett arranged to come and collect him at eleven.

George Mahoney wandered in to find Ray sitting at his desk, looking thoughtful. "What do you know about Willingham Grange," Ray asked him.

"Category C, with additional housing as a Cat D, preparing men for release," George said. "It generally has a good reputation for rehabilitation and getting work placements. The previous governor was a woman called Julia Khan and I *did* know her, and liked her. She left about eighteen months ago. I don't know the new incumbent."

"The current governor is on extended sick leave," Ray told him. "It's presently being run by his second-in-command, Roland Griffin. He looks good on paper."

George came round and studied the screen. "And was he in charge when Krantz went AWOL?"

"No, that was the governor. Griffin stepped in a few days after that, when the governor went on sick leave. I suspect you can read into that whatever you want. Anyway I'm heading out there later on with Dave Beckett."

"Have fun." George smiled at him. "I'm having the security system sorted at the vicarage today and I'll double check yours at the cottage."

Ray thanked him.

"So what else is bothering you?" George asked him.

"If I knew I'd tell you. No, I do know but I don't know what I can do about it. When Krantz was eighteen, just about to take his A levels, he suddenly dropped out, left home, lived on the streets for a while. Refused to acknowledge his family after that. We were never able to find out why or what happened. I'm wondering how relevant it is. At the time we were so busy looking at the crimes committed we maybe didn't look closely enough at how he got to that stage. Did we miss something, something that might have helped us to understand what moves he would make next?"

"Possibly," George said. "Or it could be unrelated, or it could be that the man is just a complete bastard and didn't need an excuse. No, all right, there is always history, no one ends up at the finish line without a history that dictates the direction they took. You want me to do some digging?"

"You might be wasting your time."

"It's mine to waste. And what else should I be looking at?"

Ray couldn't help but laugh. "Am I that transparent? Actually there was a real cock-up when Joe Capaldi was killed."

"That's the jury foreman."

Ray quickly filled George in on how information had been missed. "It happens," he acknowledged. "Beckett mentioned that there was a big counterterrorism operation going on at the time and this was taking resources and attention from other cases. I don't know, it just seems very convenient. Or maybe I've just been out of the job long enough to forget what the pressure was like."

* * *

Beckett arrived just before eleven. Ray was waiting for him on the pavement, knowing it was hard to find a place to pull in near the office. Beckett eased into the bus stop and Ray scrambled in.

"We interviewed Derek Fielding," Beckett told him. "The man who helped Krantz move Ashley Summers' stuff from her flat. We've nothing to prove that this wasn't an innocent act on his part, it seems that he thought Krantz was Tim Bennett, and on the face of it he had no reason to think anything else."

"So how did Krantz get to know Fielding?" Ray asked.

"Well, it started with just a casual exchange of good mornings, Fielding assumed that the man who introduced himself as Tim Bennett worked on the main campus, he had no reason to question that, Krantz had ID and seem to know where he was going. Over a period of several weeks the conversation transitioned from a casual good morning to discussions about the local football team. Fielding is a season-ticket holder."

Ray had to laugh at that. "The real Tim Bennett knows absolutely zilch about football," he said.

"Well, anyway, another case of Krantz having done his homework. He probably overheard Fielding chatting to somebody else. One thing led to another, they ended up going to the Black Horse to watch a match, I wouldn't say they became friends, but friendly acquaintances. Fielding certainly seems to have been at ease with the man, introducing him to his friends and so on. He says he thought it was strange, because the teaching staff don't normally have a lot to do with estates and security, unless they actually need something doing. But it's been his experience that the part-timers are generally more friendly so he didn't really think a lot of it. Krantz, in the guise of Tim Bennett, chatted about his family — Daisy and the kids — and Fielding talked about his. Something he's now very worried about. It's quite likely that this is how Krantz knew about the open day when Daisy Bennett encountered him."

Ray nodded thoughtfully. "It would have been a logical school for Daisy to select," he said. "There are two close to where they live but that one is closer to the university, so would have been easier for Tim to do the school run. Maybe he went to open days at both just to be sure, always assuming the other one had one. It might be worth showing his photograph around."

"Oddly enough, we had a similar thought," Beckett said.

"Sorry, old habits. Of course you did. So how did a trip to the pub to watch the match transmute into helping his girlfriend to move, which presumably is what Krantz must have told Fielding."

"Apparently so, he approached Fielding in something of a state, apparently, spinning him a yarn about having been let down by a friend last minute and not knowing how on earth he was going to get the sofa downstairs. He told Fielding that

Ashley had sprained her ankle and gone to stay with a friend over the weekend, that she would be moving in with him the following week, but had too much furniture for his little place, so they were putting it all into storage."

"Which they did?"

"Took whole lot to a self-store. We now have CSI down there crawling all over it, but I doubt if they'll find anything useful. Krantz is too careful for that. I expect there'll be fingerprints, but they won't tell us anything we don't already know."

"And that was all Fielding was able to tell you?"

"Well, there was a bit more detail about what Krantz liked to drink, and how the match went, and how friendly this Tim Bennett seemed to be, but in essence yes. He is now deeply shocked and rather scared. Fielding is a solid bloke, into his boxing and his martial arts, so I don't think he's especially scared for himself but he does have a wife and young family."

"With luck Krantz will have got what he wanted done, he won't be interested in Fielding any more," Ray said.

"We told him that he must call the nines first sign of any trouble, anything that worries him or his wife. It seems they were due to go on holiday this weekend, we've told him to go and informed the local police. They're staying on a big holiday campsite down south for two weeks, so security there should be reasonable, and we've informed the camp security. Fielding will check in with them when he gets there."

"But it's still another score for Krantz, more people scared, more resources used," Ray observed dryly.

"If that's all it is, then I'll be well satisfied," Beckett responded. "From what I've seen looking through the records, anyone Krantz comes into contact with is a potential victim. That's not a pleasant thought, the man is a user, and utterly without conscience."

That about sums it up, Ray thought.

* * *

Willingham Grange had been a farm and the farmhouse remained and was now the admin building on the very perimeter of the prison campus. In a separate compound on the left-hand side, as they approached the Grange, were two purpose-built, two-storey houses, surrounded by a perimeter fence and hedge, to which the gate was open. Ray remembered from the website that this was the category D section where prisoners were prepared for their release, a minibus taking them daily to external training centres or work experience. Willingham Grange had an excellent record when it came to rehabilitation. He wondered how much Krantz's disappearance would impact on that reputation.

They paused at the checkpoint and the guards perused their ID and radioed ahead. The single-storey buildings occupied by the prisoners were arranged around a central structure that reminded Ray of an air traffic control building. It bristled with cameras and aerials and all the paraphernalia of surveillance and massive windows on the upper story did nothing to reduce the similarity between this building and something that might be found at an airport. He remembered from the website that beyond the prison buildings were gardens and allotments and workshops. This central tower seemed at odds with the more relaxed atmosphere — Ray could see little knots of people wandering around, some with spades and garden tools, two inmates exchanging a joke with a prison guard, and he wondered if the compound had originally been intended to house a much higher security prison and that plans had been changed.

A woman emerged from the central building and directed them to a parking space and then came over to greet them. She was dressed in the black trousers and pale blue shirt that seemed to be the uniform here with a breakaway lanyard around her neck from which hung her identity card. She introduced herself as Nadine Carrington, checked their ID once more as though, Ray thought, it might've morphed into something else on the short drive from the gates. She then spoke into the radio attached to the epaulette on her shoulder.

The door to the tower buzzed and they were led inside.

The ground floor lobby was quite small, with a number of doors leading off marked up as storerooms, server room and gender neutral toilets. Nadine Carrington led them upstairs onto the second floor, it must be the third floor where the surveillance was carried out, Ray thought, because the second floor seemed to be occupied by normal offices, with normal windows and not the floor-to-ceiling selection he had spotted from the yard. He was quite surprised to find that the acting governor had his office on this floor; somehow he had expected this to be in the admin block, in what would surely be nicer surroundings.

Griffin must have noticed his surprise or maybe he was just used to explaining this to visitors. He told them that this was *his* office, as deputy, not the governor's office.

"You didn't fancy a move then," Ray asked.

Griffin, a man with a round face and grey hair shook his head. "When Ty went on sick leave we assumed it would just be for a couple of weeks so it didn't seem worth moving. When the sick leave extended, well for one thing it didn't feel quite right, it would be like occupying his space when he might come back at any time and for the other thing, quite frankly I couldn't be bothered. I'm well settled here, it's quite literally central, and I know where everything is. We've not long moved house, and I'd had enough of packing and unpacking boxes and not being able to remember where we left the kettle. Speaking of which, tea, coffee?"

Once settled with beverages, Dave Beckett said, "I expect it had quite an impact, this business with Paul Krantz?"

"Unfortunately yes. Oh, we've had occasional prisoners abscond of course, which always seemed so counterproductive when they're so close to release, but there's no accounting for the way some minds work, I suppose. But they've always either come back, or been brought back within a few hours, at most a few days."

"Come back?" Ray was curious.

"On a couple of occasions that I can remember, yes. One man had spotted a local pub when the minibus brought them back, fancied getting there and buying himself a pint. He didn't realize it was actually about five miles away and got completely lost. The other lasted an hour and then it started to rain, peed it down, he was soaked to the skin. He tried to sneak back in without anybody noticing, of course that didn't go too well for him. Both got returned to higher security prisons, which was a great shame because they were doing well before that."

"How has it affected morale, knowing that at least one prison warder and a couple of inmates helped him get away?"

Griffin pursed his lips. "For a while we all found it very hard, but you have to move on. Two officers are still on suspension, as you know, one has accepted the consequences, the other is insistent that Krantz set him up and I'm inclined to believe him. They certainly didn't get on when Krantz was here, Tom Pollard is inclined to be a tad old school, thought Krantz was a cocky bastard — his words — tended to come down a bit hard on him at times."

"And you, how did you feel about him," Ray asked.

"I didn't know him that well, there are around three hundred men here and some draw more attention to themselves than others." He paused and added, "Krantz drew attention to himself, he was very aware of what was expected in terms of behaviour, knew what answers to give, the odd times I did have contact with him my feeling was that he was arrogant, very self-possessed, a narcissist, I suppose. He was able to manipulate people and he made full use of that, knew what buttons to press."

"But some people were resistant, like Mr Pollard."

"With Tom, what you see is what you get, he's a little old-fashioned, could be a bit sharp but if you toed the line he would bend over backwards to help. Unlike some older prison officers he really did believe in rehabilitation and that if we didn't send people out with life skills that they'd just bounce back into the prison system. Yes, he was resistant to Krantz's charms, but he also resented the way Krantz manipulated not just other inmates but some of the officers as well.

He felt that they were taking things too much at face value and that just because Krantz appeared to have changed his behaviour and caused no problems that they were reluctant to look more deeply. He'd persuaded the governor to get another psychological assessment done before Krantz came up for release. Krantz was less than happy about that."

"And had that taken place?" Beckett asked.

"Yes, about a week before he absconded."

"Interesting."

Griffin nodded. "I can set up a video call with the forensic psychologist if you'd like. I'll get that sorted before you leave today. I've already raised the idea with her and she's happy to oblige."

"That would be very useful," Becket told him.

"Other officers thought that Tom Pollard was being unfair, too much of the disciplinarian, too regimented. I think with hindsight that Krantz must have just sat back and enjoyed the show."

"So how come he is also suspended, this Tom Pollard? How was he implicated?" Dave Beckett asked.

"Because he was responsible for giving out the day passes and checking the list. Krantz should not have been able to get hold of the pass, he should not have been able to get on that bus. The simplest and most straightforward implication drawn was that someone had given him a pass and turned a blind eye when he got onto the bus. And as Tom Pollard was in charge of the passes, was the one to keep them under lock and key until they were given out on the morning for day release, then his job to double check as the men got onto the bus, then . . ." He spread his hands as though there was nothing more to say. "There was no clear evidence, but if Krantz had chosen any other day, Tom Pollard might not have been on duty. Had we had the normal level of staff then there would have been a second officer with him. Usually we operate a buddy system but we were short staffed already that day and then when another officer called in sick that morning, well, that put things under even more strain. The irony is that Tom hated having to cancel day release at the last minute. He thought it was unfair to those inmates who were trying their damnedest to get back on track. He was an experienced officer and the job was routine, he would not have thought twice about just getting on with it.

"He feels that Krantz dragged him into this because he resented his attitude towards him. In any prison you will find Paul Krantzes, people who manipulate others because they are cleverer, slicker, more determined. Prisons, as you know, are full of people who underachieved in the world, who fell through the cracks, who have problems with literacy and with mental health and with poverty and prejudice. We can't do anything about why they ended up here, all we can do is try and help them get their best shot at making it in the so-called real world once they leave here."

He laughed a little self-consciously. "I sound as though I'm making a mission statement, but I do happen to believe it. Julia Khan set all of this up, hired me ten years ago and I came here feeling very sceptical but I became a convert. Education matters, rehabilitation and feeling valued matters. Of course there are some people for whom nothing matters apart from whatever it is they want and therefore consider they have a right to. In my opinion there's very little you can do for people like that."

"And Paul Krantz was one of those." Ray nodded.

"So how come you didn't go for the governor's job when Ms Khan left?" Dave Beckett asked.

"Because I have less than two years to go until I can take early retirement. I'll lose a little bit of my pension, but not much. My wife is due to retire at the same time, she's a teacher, we both want to have some fun before we get too old to bother. Just say I've seen what it takes to be a governor of a place like this and now, this last eight months or so, I've experienced it. I don't have that kind of ambition left in me."

Seemed fair enough, Ray thought.

"So I've arranged for you to talk to a half-dozen prisoners who were close to Krantz, or at least shared the accommodation block with him. And also the prison officers who had most to do with him, those not on suspension. If anyone else's name comes up in conversation, will see what we can sort out."

"Thank you," Beckett said.

A few minutes later they were following Nadine Carrington over to one of the single-storey buildings that surrounded the central tower. "Did you have dealings with Paul Krantz?" Ray asked.

She frowned, and it occurred to Ray that this was the first time he had seen anything but a quiet smile on her face.

"Unfortunately yes. He could be charming, seem to think there wasn't a woman born who wouldn't fall for him and I think it's easy to see why women did. He had this way of talking to you as though he saw something special, you know what I mean?"

Ray nodded. "I do indeed. But you weren't charmed?"

This time she laughed. "No, he soon realized I wasn't going to be so he moved on to someone else. Nora was far more easily influenced, unfortunately."

"Nora Blaine, the other prison officer on suspension," Dave Beckett said.

"Unfortunately." Nadine sounded bitter this time. "She was a good friend, I liked her a lot, I couldn't believe she'd fallen for it."

"And why didn't you?"

"Because I've met his type before. Got burned, it was a painful lesson but it stood me in good stead, I suppose. Men like him might seem convincing but their strategy is to make you feel that you're the only person in the world that they need, and then make you feel that *you* don't need anyone else, so you slowly get separated from everything else that might influence you in the opposite direction. I had a boyfriend like that when I was younger and it took me a long time to get out of that relationship. Krantz reminded me of him."

She held the door open for them and said, "I set up a table and chairs over there, in the communal area. We've asked people to come and talk to you, but you have to understand there's no compulsion. I think you'll find that everyone's a bit sick of hearing about Paul Krantz, so you might find that there are a few who are more reluctant than others. There's a list on the table. Everyone's out on work or education, but they're all on site, they're being released to come and talk to you then they'll go back to their groups. Approximate times are on the sheet, and the two prison officers you want to talk to, one will come in after the third appointment and the other at the end. That way we don't have to find extra cover for them. They're already booked on activities but they'll be due a break at those times."

Beckett thanked her and Ray glanced at the list.

"There's tea and coffee stuff over there, and spare mugs and biscuits. I'll make sure somebody brings you some sandwiches at lunchtime. If I can ask you to wash your mugs and stuff at the end, everybody has to clean up after themselves here, no exceptions."

When she had gone, Ray took the opportunity to wander around. The single-storey buildings were bigger than he had at first realized, this recreational and communal area was at the end of the building, housing the basic kitchen, comfortable seating, small tables with chairs for dining and a half-sized pool table.

They had entered the building by a door set in the middle of the longest side and he had noted that there were two fire escapes, one at each end of the building. At the other end of the corridor, as they came in to the building, he had spotted doors labelled toilets and showers. The rooms occupied by the inmates all stood with their doors open, all had viewing panels on the doors so he guessed that even when they were closed the idea of privacy was slightly illusory. These men were being trusted to manage their affairs within the setting, but there was still this implied warning that they were also being observed. He did not go into any of the rooms, but from what he could see they were clean and tidy, single beds made, surfaces dusted and notices set around the building exhorted their inhabitants to clean their spaces and leave everything as they had found it. It reminded him a little of an army barracks.

He wandered back to the table that had been set up for them and accepted the cup of coffee that Beckett handed to him.

"It's incredibly quiet here," Beckett observed.

Ray nodded, knowing what he was getting at. Both of them had had reason to go into prisons from time to time to interview inmates and staff and the noise and the smell was what Ray remembered. The cabbagy smell all institutions seemed to build up over time, overlaid by sweat and whatever they used to clean the place, sometimes lemon, sometimes pine, though whatever it was it never quite covered the other odours. But the noise was constant, footsteps, the rattle of keys, metallic sounds from prisons that were usually old, and usually had a lot of bars and rails and locks in their construction. This place was aurally more like a monastery, or somewhere you might go on retreat.

The silence was suddenly broken by the sound of footsteps. A person walking fast, walking confidently, along the gravel outside then in through the door. They saw him as he turned into the hall, a tall man in jeans and a grey shirt, he smiled when he spotted them both sitting at the table and that in itself was unusual, Ray thought. He was used to being viewed with overt suspicion.

"You must be Andy Jones," Ray said.

"I am indeed." He held out his hand to shake. Another unusual formality, Ray thought. "All right if I get myself a coffee?"

"Kettle's just boiled," Beckett said.

They watched as the man flicked the switch again to bring it back up to the boil, spooning coffee into a mug, then he seated himself at the table.

"So you want to know about Paul," he said. "Only one thing you need to know about him is he doesn't have a sane bone in his body. Whoever catches up with him could do us all a favour and put a bullet through his brain." He smiled pleasantly as though this was a very ordinary idea, one with which they could not disagree.

Beckett raised an eyebrow and Ray asked, "What brings you to that conclusion?"

Andy Jones leaned forward across the table as though what he was about to say was confidential. "Takes one to know one," he said. "Difference is I know just how screwed up I am and am doing something about it. But him, he relished it. Seeing someone scared, that was like meat and drink to him. He liked power, and he didn't care who it was over, or how he got it."

"And did he have power over you?" Ray asked.

Jones leaned back and laughed, but there was a small shift in his gaze that told Ray his laughter was hollow. "Over me, no, never. But just about everybody else here was shit scared of him, including the staff."

* * *

Paul knew he had always had the capacity for making people feel what he wanted them to. Mostly he found it useful for people to like him. At school, in other situations where he had to deal with adults, it was usually better if they thought he was likeable and easy going. But sometimes it was better to show that other side.

He remembered an incident at school, when he was younger, before he really understood what he was and that he could turn on the charm or turn on that other side, when he was just beginning to discover that other half, before he really got to know the brother and the sister and his life began to make sense. Before he had anyone to share this knowledge with.

He was small for his age when he was nine or ten. Skinny, awkward, not good at team sports, not so good at making friends — though that skill was developing. He was discovering that in the tribal environment of school, one little act of what was seen as kindness could act as major currency, could build major regard among the staff and among those of his fellow pupils who were not completely obnoxious and stupid — and he regarded most of his peers as either or both. He was beginning to learn that a small investment could reap great rewards.

It was autumn, close to the half-term break and half the walls of the school were decorated with pictures of pumpkins and cats and witches flying high on broomsticks. The other half were dedicated to scenes of harvest festival abundance and collection points had been set up in the reception and the main hall for donations of groceries to be made up into hampers for local charities.

He had brought some things from home. His mother had supplied him with the usual tins of beans and soup, some packs of sweets and one of biscuits and he was in the process of depositing these in the collection boxes when the boy came up to him and demanded the sweets that he had brought in.

I didn't care about giving, he told the brother long years after. It didn't matter to me who got them, but they were mine to give, not his to demand. And the boy had never expected resistance. He was in another class, he was bigger, stronger, older, used to getting his own way and he saw in this other just another potential victim, another boy with a reputation for being nice. For being weak.

He demanded I give him the sweets, he snatched them from me and he stood back laughing and I turned around to face him and I let the other half of me come through so he could see. And he stopped laughing and he looked at me, like he was seeing something strange and then like he was seeing something that disturbed him and then like he was seeing something that scared the shit out of him. And I can remember hearing him scream and then the teachers came running and they find him on the floor and I'm just standing there with a tin of beans in one hand and a pack of biscuits in the other, like I've no idea what's been going on and I tell them that he's just collapsed in a heap and that he hit his head as he went down, on the bench that the donations box is sitting on. I suggest that he must have had a fit. That I saw him shaking and writhing and falling down and that I didn't know what to do. And then he screamed and of course so did I.

God, but it was funny. Funnier still when they realized he'd pissed himself and they were all concerned that I might have been traumatized because of all the blood on his face from where he hit his head.

It had taken bare seconds to grab him, to smash his head down against the corner of the bench and it had happened too fast for him to react. He was unprepared for the nice boy to take him on, for the sweet *kid who was always so helpful to grab him by the hair and smash his face against the wood and even when he told the staff later what had happened, he never was believed.*

As he had told Rob later he had learned a lot of lessons that day about what he was capable of and what fear could achieve. He relished it all and he especially relished the understanding, later shared with Rob, that the human eye is such a fragile thing.

CHAPTER 11

Beth and Gavin Rivers were dropped off at the cottage that evening. John and Maggie sat with Nathan in the garden, drinking tea and eating one of Evie Padgett's cakes. The back gate to the cottage garden was open so they could watch as the kids paddled in the little stream beyond. After a while John wandered off to join them, rolling up his trouser legs and gasping a little at the cold water.

"I love this place," Maggie said. "It's always so peaceful. Do you still see your ghost?"

"Kitty? Yes, occasionally. We don't bother one another," Nathan said. "And Beth and Gavin aren't bothered by her either, so you needn't worry."

"I'm not," Maggie said. "Thank you so much for looking after them, I do feel better with them here."

"I will do everything to keep them safe," Nathan told her. "How frightened are you?"

Maggie thought about it. It was typical of Nathan to be so direct. "I'm very frightened if I'm honest, once we knew who we were dealing with. I looked him up on the internet. He's got a fan club, did you know that? There are all these people analysing his crimes and his possible crimes, he's kind of legendary. It's like this man has . . ."

"Created a glamour," Nathan said quietly. "The old-fashioned use of the word glamour, something so powerful people used to think of it as magic."

Maggie nodded. "I suppose you could call it charisma, but that doesn't feel right. You're right it is a kind of glamour, something almost mysterious. What makes people like him the way they are? What makes other people want to flock to people like him? I've never quite got it."

"Your husband is a vicar," Nathan observed. "Religion creates its own glamour. It doesn't have to be evil, though it can turn that way, even with the best of intentions. People seem to want to be a part of that. I suppose it's a kind of reflected glory."

"Is that what Harrison Lee had?" Maggie asked a little cautiously. "Glamour?" She rarely spoke about Nathan's childhood and youth, feeling this might be painful to the young man.

Nathan considered the question. "Something like that," he said. "He also had a mission, something he believed in implicitly and explicitly. Nothing was going to stop his mission."

"But you walked away from him."

"He never believed I'd gone. He always thought I would come back. He believed that it was destiny. When somebody gets an idea into their head, and they believe that they are right and everybody else wrong, then it becomes impossible for them to think that anyone can think differently or would go against them. They might accept that something could be delayed, but not that they would fail. How can they fail, their thinking is perfect."

"And you think Krantz has a mission? So what's his ultimate goal?"

"The ultimate goal is always power," Nathan said.

"Power over what? Power over whom?"

"Everything, anything," Nathan said. "Harrison Lee acknowledged he wanted power over everything, Krantz probably believes he wants power over his enemies but as everyone eventually becomes his enemy it probably amounts to the same thing. Some he will kill, some he will damage, some he will leave alone because that is a kind of power too. Making a judgement, being merciful. He probably enjoys that too. He can decide if someone lives or dies, is hurt or walks away unscathed, as long as people are aware that he has this power, I think at the moment that's what matters to him. Even those who have been loyal to him will fail him in the end because no one can attain the level of perfect obedience that he expects. If they fail then then they become the enemy too."

"At the moment you think he's focused on those who put him in prison. Who punished him? You think that will change?"

"I think for men like him the goal always changes." Nathan said. "There is no such thing as enough."

* * *

They arrived back at the vicarage, where the dogs greeted them with their usual exuberance. An envelope containing the flower-arranging rota and suggested dates for Ladies Guild meetings lay on the doormat. By tacit consent they walked through the house, checking doors and windows. Maggie paused at the entrance to Beth's room, and then glanced across at Gavin's, which was opposite. Should she have kept the children here? Were they any safer with Nathan? Was she letting her imagination run away with her?

She walked into Beth's room and straightened the covers on the bed and then stood for a moment by the window looking across at the now twilit fields. Beyond the sheep, the ponies and the crows, nothing moved. The evening was peaceful and calm.

Irritated with herself, Maggie went back downstairs to where John was now checking the recording made while they were out. *Is this life from now on*, Maggie wondered, *CCTV cameras on a rural vicarage*. John had the recording on fast forward. Mrs Atkins from the Ladies Guild scuttled up the path, posted her missal and scuttled off again.

"What was that?" Maggie asked a moment later.

John stopped the recording and reversed frame by frame. When Mrs Atkins had come through the gate she had cast a shadow across the left-hand lawn, now another shadow impinged upon the path, stretching out, tall and Maggie felt, menacing. The shadow was noticeably larger than that which the woman had cast though that had only been a few moments before, so it was the shadow of a larger person, not the result of a lowering sun.

"There was someone there," Maggie said. The shadow had been present for only a couple of frames then had gone as though whoever had cast it stepped away.

"Ray said if we were worried about anything we should alert the IT guy at Flowers-Mahoney," John said.

Maggie nodded. "Can you remember how to do it?"

"Yeah, and George left instructions just in case. Maggie, you get the kettle on, I could do with a cup of tea and maybe some of that cake we brought back with us." Evie, as usual, had left enough for an army.

Maggie glared at him for a moment. She felt dismissed but then she looked at his face and realized that he was worried too and was just trying to inject a little bit of normality into the evening. She turned and went through to the kitchen, the dogs following her; Turbot leaned against her leg as she filled the kettle, the weight of his massive head comforting against her hip. She set the kettle to boil and absently fondled the dog's ears. It was nothing, she told herself. Just someone walking by. But she was glad that the camera was there, and that the downstairs alarm could be set when they went to bed. The dogs would be sleeping on the landing tonight.

CHAPTER 12

Nathan needed very little sleep and long after the children had gone to bed he sat in the kitchen with his laptop, finding out everything he could about his enemy as he had now designated Paul Krantz. This man was threatening people that Nathan cared a great deal about, and that was something he could not countenance. Maggie's mention of Krantz's fan club, as she had called it, had interested him. Nathan had enough experience of cult leaders to recognize Krantz for what he was, a man who set up a congregation of worshippers, people whose needs he met in return for their sacrifice and help. Nathan, who had grown up in such an organization and been groomed for leadership in his turn knew all about how this worked. The one mistake that Harrison Lee, the original leader of that cult, had made had been in his assumption that Nathan would simply follow where he led and acquiesce to whatever it was he wanted him to be or do. He had never understood the way Nathan's mind worked.

Nathan had in some measure been his downfall and if there was anything Nathan could do to bring this Krantz to justice then he would do so and Nathan wasn't much bothered whether that justice was imprisonment or the termination of Paul Krantz in some other way.

He was not making a particularly moral judgement here, he had heard people say that such and such an individual had no place among decent society though he had long since decided that his version of decent society didn't necessarily match up to the exploitative and unfair set-ups that most people seem to accept as normal. It was a problem he had long since set aside as one he could not immediately solve.

He heard quiet footsteps on the stairs and a moment later Beth appeared in the kitchen doorway. "Gavin's asleep, I woke up and my brain wouldn't go quiet. Can I get some milk?"

"Of course you can, do you want hot chocolate?"

She nodded and Nathan decided that he would quite like a chocolate too and put two mugs of milk into the microwave. He wondered if Gavin would wake up and be concerned to find his sister gone, but decided that Gavin usually slept like the dead so it was unlikely.

He turned around to find that Beth was staring at the computer screen. "Is that the man Mum and Dad are so scared of?" she asked.

Nathan considered. He should probably have closed the computer down as soon as she came into the room and he reflected that he was not always very good at doing the things he *should* do. At least not without someone reminding him. Instead he asked, "You know about him?"

"I knew Mum and Dad and Ray and Sarah were worried about something, so I sat on the stairs and listened. I couldn't hear everything but I know they were really worried and that's why we are here. We wanted to come anyway, but that's why we're here right now. Do you think he might hurt them?"

Nathan set the hot chocolate on the table and wondered how he should answer that one. It was Nathan's default position to always tell the truth but he had realized in a vague way that adults did not always approve of this, not when it came to discussing things with children. "So what do you know about him?" he asked.

Beth blew on the surface of her chocolate. She had curled up in the rocking chair that stood in the corner of the kitchen. It was really too big to be there, but whenever Nathan had moved it elsewhere it had felt . . . uncomfortable. This was the chair people sat upon to think things through when they had a problem, curled up in when they wanted to talk, snoozed in when the old range was lit. The kitchen had a modern cooker but the black-leaded range that was probably several centuries old had been preserved and in the winter was used every day to heat the ground floor of the house. That Beth had chosen this chair signalled to Nathan that she wanted and needed to talk about this and that he had to take that need very seriously. Not that Nathan ever took what Beth had to say or what she was thinking less than seriously. She and her brother were very different creatures, he thought. Gavin was a delight, seizing every moment, whatever he was doing with absolute enthusiasm. Except when he was asleep, he was never still and Nathan knew that this had caused problems at school. Beth was far more thoughtful, now in secondary school she had grown more perceptive, more self-possessed and he glimpsed the woman that she would become, a woman not so unlike her mother. So how should he approach this? He changed his question.

"What do you want to know about him?" he asked and then added, "and what do you think your mother would tell you about him? I'm not sure those things will match up very well, so we might have to compromise about what I can say."

He watched as she considered this and then she nodded. "I know he's killed people, I know he's hurt people, I know he's escaped from prison and that Ray was one of the officers that put him there. I know Ray thinks he killed the other policeman, the detective that Ray was working with. I know that my mum and dad are scared."

He was aware that she was studying him, watching his face to see how he reacted to this. Nathan had been told that he was very hard to read, because his expression didn't change very much but he also knew that Beth had become very good at gauging his reactions. He nodded. "All of that is true," he said. "Because they don't know where he is, and because he is very good at persuading people to do things, they are right to be frightened of him and what he might do. Men like him are very unpredictable because they work with their own rules. They decide what they want and they try to get it or try to make it happen, but the way they think about the world is different to the way most people think about the world and so most people find it very hard to guess what they might do next."

"Do you think he knows what he is going to do next?"

It was a very good question, Nathan thought. "I think he has an idea of what he wants, at least at the moment. But that might not be the same as what he wants tomorrow. Just now he wants revenge because he was locked up in prison, but I think that his ideas about who is really responsible for doing that might not be what we think it is. He might want to punish Ray by hurting someone he cares about or he might want to punish Ray by hurting him. It's hard to know."

"Are you scared of him?"

"I think being worried about what someone like him might do is sensible," Nathan said. Was he afraid of Paul Krantz? It would be more accurate, he thought, to say that he was wary. Like an animal that knows there might be a trap. Like a soldier that has survived one battle and so can believe they might, with luck, survive another. He wondered how he might convey this to Beth.

Finally, he said, "Being aware of what might hurt you helps keep you safe. But it doesn't have to stop you doing things. You know you should be wary of, maybe even a bit afraid of fire, because fire burns. But that doesn't stop you liking the fire here or bonfires or the range when it's lit. But you know not to put your hand in it and if you see someone else playing with fire you know to keep away and maybe go and tell someone else what you've seen."

"Maybe?"

Nathan realized he had slipped there but then he nodded. "*Usually* you should go and tell someone what you've seen. But there are occasions when the best thing you can do, the best thing to keep yourself safe, is to creep away and not be seen and only tell someone when you're in a safe place."

He watched her face, trying to read the emotions that flickered momentarily before shifting again.

She nodded. "So if I see something or someone that I'm not sure about I should make sure me and Gav are out of the way first, that we're in a safe place, and then tell someone or get help." She grinned at him, suddenly. "So we don't run off screaming!"

Nathan managed a rare smile. "Screaming might not always be the best idea," he agreed. "You'll have to decide if it's a screaming opportunity or a time for creeping away."

She nodded as though satisfied and then finished her chocolate and slipped out of the chair, and Nathan figured his answers must have been good enough — for the moment, anyway.

Beth came over and kissed him on the cheek. He submitted to her quick, affectionate hug.

"Night, Nathan. Love you."

"Love you too, sleep well." He watched as the small figure wrapped in her red dressing gown crossed the living room and opened the door to the stairs. Having people to love was a wonderful thing, Nathan thought. But it scared him too, scared him far more than the likes of Paul Kranz.

CHAPTER 13

A video call had been arranged with the forensic psychologist who had been brought in to assess Paul Krantz, before he had been transferred to Willingham Grange. Ray had read the summary of her reports and it was clear that the psychologist had not been in favour of this move. He hoped to get a clearer picture when they spoke to her later.

Before that however he was going to view the interviews with Tom Pollard and Nora Blaine, the two suspended prison officers. He had read the transcripts of the interviews but long experience told him that this was only part of the story. Body language, facial expression and the general demeanour of the person being interviewed could add to that; words only told the interviewer so much.

He sat alone in a tiny side room watching the interviews on a laptop and taking notes and now feeling frustrated because the camera angle only gave him a partial view of the room. It was hard to see the reaction of the interviewer and others in the room at the same time as the interviewee and to see what prompts the interviewer was taking from the attitude of the accused. But, he supposed, it was better than nothing. The one thing that struck him forcibly was how angry both of the prison officers were, not just because they had been accused, he decided, but at Paul Krantz and also, he felt, at the series of decisions that had allowed Krantz to come to Willingham Grange.

"He should not have been sent to the Grange," Tom Pollard had insisted on more than one occasion.

"He's a dangerous man, he shouldn't be mixing with men getting ready for release." This was Nora's opinion and in Ray's view was at odds with a woman accused of being his patsy.

He looked up as Becket came to the door. "What if this was just a distraction," he asked. "If Pollard really was set up. If Nora Blaine had nothing to do with Krantz absconding but was too vocal about him being at the Grange at all. That would be enough to make her a target."

Beckett pulled up a chair and glanced at the screen. "It's been raised as a possibility," he agreed. "Krantz made a play for all the female officers he came into contact with. He was subtle about it, apparently, nothing that couldn't be put down to them misunderstanding his intentions. Nora Blaine said she didn't like his attitude towards her and the governor intervened. Krantz, by all accounts was abjectly contrite. Blaine let it pass, but . . ."

"So how did the accusation arise, that she'd aided and abetted? I get the circumstances around Pollard, though if you ask me the accusations are based purely on the authorities having to blame someone. There's not a whole load of evidence that Pollard was complicit."

Beckett nodded. "Blaine was seen having what were termed private conversations with Krantz in the weeks before his escape. He had dropped hints to his fellow inmates that she was interested in him, that the fuss she'd made with the governor was just a ploy to throw her colleagues off the scent. And after he had left and his room was searched, her home address was found scribbled on a piece of paper, in what looked like her handwriting. The clincher was that the paper had her fingerprints on it."

"So, he could have picked the paper up from anywhere, taken it out of a bin. Forged her handwriting."

"He could have. But proving that . . ."

Ray nodded, conceding the point. "And the conversations they were supposed to have had. What does she say these were about?"

"She insists that there was nothing private about them. The fact that they were in full view of anyone who happened to be passing, in her opinion shows just how private they were not. She does say that Krantz seemed to seek her out on occasion, asked her opinion on various things, but that was all."

"Her opinion on what? I've not had time to look at all the transcripts." The written reports ran to many pages in the fat folders that sat on the desk.

"From memory, Krantz got involved in many of the activities on offer at Willingham Grange, including the drama group. Blaine was quite involved with that and with the choir and various of the art therapy sessions. Krantz, as you can imagine, was full of ideas for 'improving' these sessions. Nora Blaine swears this was all they were discussing and admits that it did get a bit intense at times. She remembers that on a couple of occasions he even touched her arm. She reprimanded him and he apologized. But it's quite possible he made this play so that witnesses would see it."

"Sounds like something he would do."

"Anyway, the appointment with Eloise Barnes is only a few minutes away. We should get ready for that."

* * *

The forensic psychologist, Eloise Barnes was in her early forties, Ray guessed. She had neat, dark hair and wore heavy spectacles that looked too big for her face. She was a few minutes late joining them, having taken an opportunity to grab a much-needed coffee.

"Meetings since first thing," she told them. "And the afternoon isn't looking much better."

Beckett thanked her for sparing them some time.

Eloise Barnes snorted. "If I'd had my way this would have been discussed a long time ago," she said. "In fact if I'd had my way there'd have been no opportunity to abscond. He'd have been transferred back to a maximum-security psychiatric unit and that would have been that."

It was a forthright opinion, Ray thought. But he picked up on something he'd not been aware of. "Krantz had been in a psychiatric unit?"

She nodded. "Started off in a maximum-security prison but his behaviour was causing concern. About eighteen months in, there was a suicide attempt and sometime after that he was formally diagnosed with a personality disorder. He became violent and distressed, according to my records, and was eventually transferred to a psychiatric unit where he could be properly assessed. Anyway, he seemed to make progress after that, was transferred again back to the general prison population and once more attempted suicide. On both occasions he attempted to hang himself but this second time he'd also attacked the prison guard who intervened." She paused.

"So someone was on the ball then. He was on suicide watch, I presume."

"You presume right and you and I both know that there's a fifteen-minute window between checks. More than enough time for an act of self-harm. Even with safeguards in place, if someone is determined enough there's not a hell of a lot anyone can do to stop them. Anyway, Krantz seems to have timed his action for the moments just before the next check. He was blue in the face but not unconscious. As soon as he'd recovered enough he attacked the guard and could have done him serious damage. He'd got his thumbs pressed into the man's eyes when he was dragged off."

"That must have extended his tariff," Ray said, referring to the length of Krantz's prison term.

"Oh, it did, but it also ensured he'd be transferred back to the secure psych unit. He was no more trouble after that, so for the past seven years he's been a model patient, taken every class, therapy initiative and self-help group available. Passed every test. Until me."

"And you were called in to approve his transfer."

"His doctors were convinced he was ready for transfer back to the general population, but only if he could be sent to a less traditional establishment. Willingham Grange has done well with long-term inmates, who are no longer seen as a threat. If he did well there he'd have been up for parole again in three or four years." She glanced at her watch and then said, "Anyway, long story short, I assessed him and counselled against the transfer. I didn't believe he had tackled the roots of his offending, he'd just learned to give the answers everyone wanted from him. But everyone else said what a good boy he'd become, so . . ."

"So he was transferred to the Grange."

"No, not immediately. He was sent to a small unit within a higher security establishment, just to see how he coped. Once past that hurdle he was sent to Willingham Grange and the rest you know."

Ray nodded thoughtfully. "I remember from my interviews with him that there was something that happened when he was about eighteen or nineteen. He dropped out of school and left home, denied he even had a family after that. I spoke to his parents but they said they could shed no light on what had happened but that he changed suddenly and violently. Though they were reluctant to say what exactly they meant by that. But did he tell you anything?"

She shook her head. "No. As I said, he never came close to exploring the roots of his offending. Resisted all attempts I made to get him to talk about his childhood or school or adolescence." She frowned. "It struck me as odd at the time, and I did try and challenge him on it, but all I could get him to say was that he was different person back then, so none of it was relevant."

"We're all different people, to some extent, at nineteen compared to who we are at thirty or forty, I suppose," Ray said.

"We develop, certainly, but core values and behaviours are often laid down when we're young. And I came to understand that he didn't mean it figuratively. It was as though he meant it quite literally. That, to all intents and purposes, he was someone else."

"So what did you make of him?" Beckett asked. "I don't mean in terms of him having learned to play the game, exactly, more, what did *you* make of him?"

"Well, he's outwardly charming. Intelligent, genuinely curious about any subject you care to mention. Tried to turn the discussion onto me and what I thought every chance he could, but the thing is, I believed he genuinely wanted to know. In part because it might give him leverage but also because of that curiosity. That need to know. I spoke to prison officers and other inmates and the thing that came up time and time again was that he was a good listener. That he paid attention and he remembered. There was no such thing as casual conversation with Paul Krantz; he listened, he stored that knowledge away, he'd know if you contradicted yourself later and he'd take great pleasure in saying so. He was no physical coward, he'd stand up to anyone and usually get them to back down. On the odd occasion that didn't work then he'd fight his corner, even if he came off worse. None of it seemed to matter to him so long as he was scoring points and in prison, even in a secure psych unit, you score points for standing your ground or for facing someone down. You've got a mix of egos in prison, all jockeying for position and he was determined to be top dog."

"And yet he played the victim, if you want to put it that way," said Beckett. "The suicide attempts . . ."

"The first one may have been genuine. The subsequent attempts I believe were manipulative. Krantz is capable of deferring gratification, of playing the long game. He might have to be seen to lose something in order to gain later. To manoeuvre himself into position for a strike."

There was a knock at the door behind Eloise and she turned and spoke to a young man who stood for a moment in the doorway.

"I have to go," she said.

Beckett and Ray thanked her for her time. Beckett said, "You realize that—"

"That I'm a potential target. Yes, of course I do. Believe me it won't be the first time and I take my personal security very seriously."

"So, what do you think," Ray asked when the call had ended. "You think he will target her?"

"I think he's enjoying the game," said Dave Beckett. "He's already killed, if you're right about Nightingale and Capaldi, and he's already created trouble for a number of others and frightened a whole lot more. He must be relishing all that. I think he'll go after whoever might cause the biggest headlines or he might just choose to pick away at everyone's nerves until he spots the most obvious cracks appearing. Either way I'm with the psychologist. They should have sent him back, locked him up and then lost the key."

* * *

When Evie Padgett arrived to clean the cottage that afternoon she brought two of her great-grandchildren with her and the sound of the four children playing in the little brook was, Nathan thought, a rather glorious noise.

"So how is everything?" Evie asked as she bustled into the kitchen. "The children seem settled enough."

"They are, though Beth has asked some interesting questions. I am just hoping I've answered them well enough."

Evie put the duster and polish in the cupboard, took off her apron and settled down to drink the tea that Nathan had made for her. The removal of the apron marked the switch from professional transaction to good friends sitting down to have a chat. Nathan wondered if this was a habit with all her clients.

"Beth is a bright child, she'll have a good idea of what's wrong. Of course she'll be asking questions."

"She says she listened on the stairs while her parents talked," Nathan said.

"Sounds about right. I can remember doing that when I was a little thing. I'd have got a good walloping if my parents had caught me, mind. And just because Gavin hasn't said anything doesn't mean he isn't wondering. That boy might seem like a scatterbrain that can't settle to anything but he takes it all in just the same. My Lynn had one like him, the school had him statemented and got him all sorts of labels, which is all well and good because it got him some extra help, but he's now married, got some kids, he's holding down a decent job. Some of us take a bit longer to get settled in the world. Some of us never do, but that's not a problem, is it."

Nathan had a sneaking suspicion that she was referring to him.

"Now you need to know that the Prices have their niece and her husband staying and that Mrs Richardson has some new guests at the B&B, but they're a family group, so probably nothing to worry about. Just so you know what unfamiliar faces might be around."

Nathan sipped his tea and then asked, "Does everybody in the village know that there's trouble?"

"Only those that need to know. But there are plenty that have made the connection between Krantz going missing and Ray, with him owning this place. Everybody knows he was an inspector involved in that investigation, and a fair few remember the Krantz case all too clearly. People draw their own conclusions."

Nathan supposed that was the case. He glanced out of the back door to where he could see the children. A while ago Nathan had given Gavin a little clear plastic pot with a lens on top and a book on insects, including the kind of weird creatures that might be found in water. He took the portable magnifier everywhere with him and Nathan could see that he was now examining something that he had found. The others were inspecting the pictures in the book, trying to work out what it might be and the debate was getting lively.

Evie had reached across the table and, to Nathan's surprise, she patted him on the hand. He sat very still, trying not to pull his hand away. When he looked up at her, he could see that her expression was slightly challenging and she nodded in acknowledgement that he had accepted what he realized was her simple expression of affection.

"It will all be fine," she told him. "You see if it isn't."

Nathan nodded, wondering if the universe would dare to go against Evie Padgett.

CHAPTER 14

There followed a week of such quiet, calm and lack of significant events that Ray found himself wondering what all the fuss had been about and if they had all been overreacting. The investigation was getting nowhere, but nothing new seemed to have happened and he began to hope that Krantz had perhaps gone to ground and was simply intent on not being discovered.

Then something totally unexpected happened.

The news came out of the blue that Ashley Summers had been found and not only found, but was alive.

"She was wandering, dressed in nothing but a man's shirt. She was barefoot and totally confused. She turned up outside a pub on the outskirts of the village of Carlingford, that's about fifty miles from here. The landlord called an ambulance and I'm about to head over to the hospital, I thought you might want to come with me. Libby Summers and her husband should already have arrived by the time we get there. She was going to call you, but I said I'd handle that."

"And she's all right?" Ray could hardly believe it.

"Well, according to the landlord she was a bit of a state, very confused, didn't know where she was or how she got there. I'll pick you up in fifteen minutes."

Ray just had time to call Sarah, shut his computer down and pass various tasks on to Rowena and George. He stood on the pavement outside the office and waited for Dave Beckett to arrive. He felt profoundly relieved, almost light-hearted, but with a nag at the back of his brain, wondering what on earth was really going on, and what Krantz had planned. If Ashley Summers was alive it was because Krantz had decided she was more useful to him that way. It was not an act of mercy, but an act of utility.

Beckett arrived and Ray hopped in the car, the satnav had been programmed and the journey time was something over an hour. Mentally, Ray added a half hour to that just for getting out of the city and he was proved right as they followed the one-way system into the slowly building rush-hour traffic. Beckett was able to tell him just a little more, that Ashley Summers had undoubtedly been kept drugged, there was still a good amount of sedative in her system and she seemed to have little recollection as yet as to what had happened to her. She had been minimally fed and watered and had lost a great deal of weight, which indicated that she had not been fed regularly, perhaps just enough to keep her alive. But at least she was alive and that was more than anyone had hoped for.

* * *

Ashley Summers looked in really bad shape. Ray recalled the photograph he had seen of her, the pretty young woman with tightly curled, shoulder-length, mousy blonde hair, dark skin and a very beautiful smile. She had clearly lost a lot of weight, but she also looked older and as though in the last few weeks she had gained lines around her eyes and mouth. Libby Summers held her hand and a man that Ray guessed must be Dan Summers sat on the other side of the bed, stroking Ashley's fingers and trying to avoid the cannula in her hand.

"Ray." Still clinging to Ashley's hand, Libby got to her feet and reached out for him. She pulled him into an awkward embrace. "She's alive, she's going to be all right. I can hardly believe it."

Gently, Ray freed himself and introduced DCI Dave Beckett. "Has she been able to say anything?" Beckett asked.

"Not much, the doctors think she's been sedated most of the time that man had her. They say the sedative must have worn off enough for her to walk, for her to get away, but we still have no idea where she came from. She keeps crying in her sleep,"

This, Ray thought, seemed to be distressing Libby most of all.

She indicated the drip. "She's really dehydrated, they're hoping that as she rehydrates, and the sedative wears off, she'll be able to talk. The local police have been lovely, and arranged for some accommodation for us, not that I want to leave her at the moment. And there's a really sweet girl who is acting as liaison. And they've said there will be somebody outside her room all the time."

Ray was conscious of the reproach in her voice; the implied comparison between the local police and those she had originally contacted who had told her that Ashley was an adult and therefore not really their concern if she wanted to move without telling her mother-in-law.

She turned back to Ray and said, "Do you think he'll come after her again?"

"I don't know. It's possible she's served her purpose and he's now done with her, so he'll leave her alone. The problem is we don't exactly know what that purpose was, if it was just to draw me in then the chances are . . ."

"It was a very elaborate way of getting you involved." It was the first time Dan Summers had spoken.

"It was, but unfortunately Krantz thinks in elaborate ways. He doesn't seem satisfied unless his actions are as dramatic as possible, as distressing as possible. His methods are rarely simple and straightforward. I'm so sorry you've been through this, all of you."

He was aware that Dan Summers was considering his words, the man's eyes were hard and cold and he was clearly simmering with anger that he was trying hard not to express. Ray had no doubt there were things Dan Summers had to say to him or to the police or to anyone else he felt might bear some of the responsibility for what had happened to this young woman and that he would create the opportunity to say them. Ray didn't feel he could blame him.

There was a light knock at the door. Beckett opened it, listened to the officer outside and then turned to Ray. "They think they've found where she was held," he said.

"Already?"

"The SIO wants to know if we would like to go and view the scene now," Beckett said.

"Go," Libby urged. "We'll be staying with her, if she wakes up and says anything at all, I promise I'll text you."

A few minutes later they were in a police car and heading for the house in which it was likely Ashley Summers had lost the past three weeks.

"How did you find the house so quickly," Beckett asked one of the officers taking them there.

"As you'll see, when we pass the George and Dragon, there's a limited number of ways she could have come. The landlord and some of the locals took a walk back up the road and they found blood on the grass, probably from a cut on her feet. They had the sense not to go any further, fortunately, but once we arrived they took us up the path, and suggested a couple of possible locations, it stands to reason she couldn't come far, she was barefoot and woozy and it's a miracle she made it to the pub."

They passed the George and Dragon, where Ashley Summers had arrived so unexpectedly and the car took a side road between high hedges and grass verges sporting the last of the cow parsley.

A few hundred yards on, the car turned left onto a farm track, the paintwork being scratched by hedge on one side and tall, but still green, wheat on the other. They pulled up onto the verge behind another police car and a scientific support van. "Got to walk from here," they were told.

Through a gap in the hedge and up another track, this one leading through a spinney, Ray spied a house. It wasn't derelict, but it clearly hadn't been lived in for quite some time. Whitewash flaked from the walls, two of the upstairs windows were cracked but the door was solid enough and a fresh padlock had been attached to the outside. The officer led them round the back. The back door was also solid, but this one locked with a standard Yale. The door stood open and the familiar scene of white-clad CSIs and the floor set out with square raised plates, marking the designated pathway, met Ray's gaze. He paused before going in, glancing around the overgrown yard, the outbuildings, the rising ground beyond. Through gaps in the hedge he glimpsed another road.

Dave Beckett gave voice to what Ray was thinking. "How did she find her way from here down to the village? She'd have to get out of the house, through that little wood, walk alongside the field, then down the hill. It's less than half a mile but it's not a straight half mile, how come she didn't get lost and in the middle of the field?"

"He must have taken her to the road, even in the state she was in she could probably have made it down the road to the pub. She didn't escape, he let her go, he made sure she was found. He wanted us to know he could have killed her but he didn't. Not yet anyway."

"That's pretty much the conclusion we reached," a voice said.

Ray turned to greet a tall, heavyset man. "DCI Blatchford," the man introduced himself.

"You're the SIO?" Ray asked.

He nodded, introductions were made. "The locals know about this place, guessed the girl might've been held here because there isn't really anywhere else. The man who farms the adjacent fields lives a couple of miles away. As you saw there is a public footpath, but it's not much used and besides this house is well screened by the wood. No one is likely to have seen anything. But to find your way out of here, especially in the state Ashley Summers was in, is in my view nigh on impossible. So," he looked speculatively at Ray and Beckett. "What are we dealing with?"

* * *

In a room at the back of the house was a mattress on the floor, covered by an old duvet and a couple of blankets. A hospital-style commode chair stood in one corner, suggesting that someone had been present to help her from the bed to use the pot every now and again. There was also a small Primus stove, a couple of saucepans, and an assortment of soups and instant noodles and easily prepared food. There had been apparently no sign of the clothes Ashley must have been wearing when she arrived here, and no bag or phone or any other personal possessions. Had Krantz stayed here, Ray wondered, or had someone else been helping him. Something made him think the second option was most likely.

"What do we know about this place?" Dave Beckett asked.

"Not a lot, it's not been lived in for perhaps twenty years. Amazingly the outside toilet still is usable if you flush it with a bucket and there's a pump in the yard that still works as well, and from the look of it somebody's maintained it recently. We spoke to the farmer and he tells us it's fed from a well that's filled from a deep spring. He's got a similar arrangement up at his farm and there's another one down outside the George that used to supply water for the whole village."

"Ray?" Ray was suddenly aware that Beckett was staring at him. "What is it?"

"Something I remember from the interviews. Krantz would rarely talk about his childhood but there was one place he mentioned, a place that mattered to him. Something about there being a pump in the yard and a well that was fed from a spring."

"Do you recall who it belonged to?" Blatchford asked.

Ray shook his head. "A cousin maybe, or a distant relative of some sort. He rarely talked about his childhood, he was extremely resistant to talking about his early life at all but there were one or two details that I do remember. If this is the place then he rode horses when he stayed here."

"There's a riding stable about a mile away, been in the same family for donkey's years."

"And I think, I'd have to go back over the interviews to check, I think he mentioned kids of his own age that lived here, and they were distant relatives of some sort, maybe on his mother's side. But the thing about the well was what stuck in my mind because Krantz was so interested in it. Apparently they got the water tested once or twice a year. He was here one time the chap came over to test it, Krantz told me all about his test equipment, and what he was looking for, amoebas and that sort of thing. He said it got him interested in microscopes and he wanted a microscope but was unable to have one."

He shook his head. "Sorry it's been a while, this only stuck out because it was one of the few times he ever talked about memories of his childhood, normally he just refused point-blank."

"Any idea why he made an exception," Beckett asked. "What sparked the memory?"

Ray thought about it. He was surprised at how vivid the memory of these interviews with Krantz still was, how much it still impinged on his consciousness and caused him discomfort. So how had this conversation about the house and the well and the spring water come about?

"Bottled water," he said. "It was a hot day and a constable brought us bottled water. Spring water that had been chilled. Krantz said he thought it was obscene, the amount of money that was charged for something that just bubbled out of the ground. He made some joke about police budgets and then he started talking about spring water and wells and when he was a kid about eleven or twelve, about this place perhaps, or one very like it. I don't remember him giving me any names, I would have asked, but I don't remember him giving me any. He talked about the well, he talked about the technician that came to test the water, he talked about a horse called Ivan. I think that's about it."

"Well, it's one more bit of the puzzle," Blatchford said. "Like I say, the stables have been in the same family ownership for several generations so it's possible someone might remember Paul Krantz or that they once had a horse called Ivan. Local knowledge will provide us with information about who lived here, and that's often more accurate than looking up who was paying the council tax or who was on the electoral roll. Places like this were often used as temporary accommodation for seasonal workers." He paused. "So do you think he was here, that it was this Krantz that kept Miss Summers here?"

"It's likely," Beckett said. "It's as good a place as any to hide out."

Ray was shaking his head. "There's a commode in the room where she was kept, which implies that someone took from her bed, let her use a commode and then emptied it presumably into the outside toilet. Krantz wouldn't do that. Blood never bothered him, but other kinds of mess did. He liked his flat tidy and abhorred bad smells and mess. Early in their relationship, just after she'd moved in with him, his girlfriend was once really sick with a stomach bug and he sent her home to stay with her mother for the week. He said he couldn't bear the stink of vomit, couldn't bear the idea of the mess of cleaning up after her. He said that before he killed her they'd been fighting a lot, arguing about the future. She wanted kids, he didn't. I asked him why and he quoted something about a noise at one end and a lack of discipline at the other.

"He didn't much like children, in his view they just took up a lot of time and effort and energy for very little reward. And they were messy. Snotty and pukey and the idea of changing nappies just completely put him off."

"The girlfriend, she really didn't see it coming, the violence, the threat?"

Ray shook his head. "Every time I asked people about their relationship I was told that he was kind and considerate and that they seemed happy. He seems to have been very good at preserving this facade. Even her mother liked him; Ruth's mother could not believe that he was responsible for her death, even after we'd charged him."

"So there were no warning signals about the murder."

"No, they were arguing about the idea of having children, but there was no indication that it got physical, and those friends that recalled the disagreement, when we talked to them, were sure he would come round to the idea in the end. The fact is, it seemed inconceivable to most people that he could have had anything to do with Ruth's death and it was only when the evidence piled up until it couldn't be ignored any longer that people began to remember little things that seemed off in his behaviour. She'd never told anyone about the abusive texts, took the controlling behaviours to be evidence of his affection and when he expressed jealousy, which it seems he did increasingly often, just suggested he come with her when she went out, which seemed to work for a time. Though there was increasing evidence that he was simply persuading her not to meet other people. Even her parents were seeing less and less of her, but the process was gradual and subtle and he always had an excuse for everything. Of course hindsight is twenty-twenty, and there's no way of knowing if the things other people then claim to remember were exaggerated because of what they knew he'd done."

One of the CSIs came down the stairs and told them it was all clear for them to go up now.

"Something interesting to show you," Blatchford said.

They followed him up the stairs and entered the bedroom at the front of the house. Through the window Ray could see the edges of woods and then the gently rising land going up towards the road. But his attention was held by what was on the walls. He stood in the doorway and took it in, the newspaper clippings, the string linking names to events, the photographs, the children's drawings.

"What is all this?" Dave Beckett asked.

"It seems to be the career of Paul Krantz," Blatchford said dryly. "I'm hoping with the experiences the two of you have had, that we can all put our heads together and try to make sense of it."

Ray's eye was caught by something that flashed on the ridge and he looked out of the window to see a man with what seemed to be a pair of binoculars looking down at the house. His first thought was that this was a journalist who had got wind of events and was trying to get a jump on his peers. But then the man lifted a hand and waved and Ray knew immediately who it was. "Krantz."

Everyone moved at once, Blatchford speaking into his radio, constables running from the yard towards the hill, Ray thundering down the stairs driven by an impulse to chase after the man despite logic telling him that Krantz had a head start and he'd never reach him.

The figure on the hill had gone, and a car engine could be heard already receding into the distance by the time anyone got there. Ray stood in the gateway through which Krantz must have accessed the field and stared down the road. The feeling of vulnerability was overwhelming and inside he quailed. He forced himself to breathe deeply, to stay calm, he sensed that today's events presaged a new move in the game.

Who's next, Ray thought. *Who is that bastard going after next?*

CHAPTER 15

Ray and Sarah had eaten dinner late. He'd picked up a takeaway on his way home and Sarah had opened a bottle of wine, an unusual occurrence for a weekday, but somehow it had seemed appropriate. He had been in to see Ashley Summers again before they had left and she was showing signs of recovery, a little more alert, remembering fragments. She clung to Libby's hand as though afraid that if she let go she would be back in the nightmare.

"So you'll be going back in in the morning," Sarah said. "Any idea how long you'll be gone?"

"No, it should just be a few days but I don't like the idea of leaving you on your own."

"I'll be all right, and if I'm worried I'll go and stay somewhere else. I can book into a hotel, or camp out in your office and sleep on the sofa."

Ray laughed, they both knew just how uncomfortable sofa was. If a piece of furniture had ever been designed to create backache and a numb backside, that was certainly it.

"Eloise Barnes, the forensic psychologist I was telling you about, she's coming up to join the team. We'll be forming a kind of subunit with Dave Beckett and a couple of others, hopefully between us we can sort out whatever message it is he's left for us in that room."

"You think it's a deliberate message and not just something he had to leave behind?"

"It was meant for us," Ray said.

"Meant for you, you mean." Sarah's tone was harsh. He didn't bother to contradict her.

When Ray had left, the whole display was being photographed, catalogued and thoroughly recorded in preparation for it being laid out in the incident room that was being prepared. A Major Crimes team was in the process of being assembled and though Ray would take no part in the actual investigation, it was hoped that whatever insights he could produce could feed back into the enquiry. Beckett would act as liaison between Ray, Eloise and the main enquiry team but also, by virtue of the fact he'd had training earlier in his career for the role, would act as a family liaison between the team and the Summers family. It was expected they would travel home as soon as Ashley was well enough. A lot of emphasis had been put on keeping lines of communication as short and direct as possible and the team itself, though substantial, was also being kept deliberately compact. DCI Blatchford would report directly to his superiors but would retain his role as SIO, coordinating the enquiry. It felt strange to Ray, to be involved like this but to be standing a little outside. He wasn't entirely comfortable with this position.

"I'll be travelling up with Dave tomorrow afternoon," he said. "They should have everything and everyone in place by then and the first full briefing will be at four."

"And in the meantime he could be anywhere."

* * *

At around midnight, Ashley grabbed Libby's hand and then began to talk. She had managed to eat a little and had drunk tea as though she anticipated a shortage. A little colour had returned to her cheeks and the doctors had suggested that another day of observation would probably be sufficient.

She had been quiet that evening, drowsily watching the television with either Dan or Libby as they took turns to go and eat and to stretch their legs. But just before midnight she began to talk about Paul Krantz and what she remembered had happened to her and it seemed that once she had begun she couldn't stop. Libby gripped her hand tightly and leaned in close, hanging on every word.

The young police constable, Rose Morton, who had been assigned to look after the family was summoned. Libby had the presence of mind to switch on the recorder on her phone and then, because her battery had run low, Dan had taken over. By the time Rose had sorted out a proper recorder, Ashley had been speaking for over an hour. Not all of it was coherent and she backtracked and corrected herself but under Libby and Rose's gentle questioning, she managed to convey how Paul Krantz had come into her life and what had happened on the day he had abducted her. Libby was horrified by what she had to say.

"He said he had a surprise for me and took me by the hand and led me down to his car. I got in. I was laughing, I can remember that. He was joking about a big surprise. I got into the passenger seat and then I realized there was someone in the back seat. He'd been lying on the seat and then he sat up and the next thing is I had something round my neck and he was pulling it tight and I could hardly breathe and he said 'told you it would be a big surprise, didn't I' *and then the man laughed and he pulled the scarf tighter and I realized it was one of my scarves, that silk one you bought me for my birthday a couple of years ago. The big one like a shawl I had for that thing we all went to in London. When Dan's team won that award. He tied it round the headrest so I couldn't move. It was so tight round my neck and I was so scared and I kept saying* 'Tim, what are you doing, Tim you're scaring me' *and he just said* of course I am. That's what I want to do. *And I was struggling and fighting and trying to hammer on the window. We were driving through town and I thought I could make*

115

*someone see me but then I felt a sharp pain in my arm and I realized
the man in the back had injected me with something and the next thing
I remember is waking up in a strange room and it was dark and there
was just a little lamp and I could smell paraffin and I could hear voices
and I tried to get up but my legs were so shaky I just fell onto the floor
and then they both came into the room . . ."*

She trailed off and Libby slipped an arm around her
shoulders and gave her some water.

"His name isn't Tim," Libby said. "He took someone
else's name and, God help me, I'm afraid I made the poor man's
life a complete misery. The real Tim Bennett, I mean."

"Not Tim?"

"No. His name is Paul Krantz." Libby practically spat
the words.

"Paul Krantz." Ashley closed her eyes and drifted for
a few minutes, her head against Libby's shoulder. Then as
though coming up for air from some deep depth, she gasped
and pulled away, her breathing rapid and panicked, the
words falling over themselves again.

*"I could see his face but the other man stood by the door and he was in
the shadows. He lifted me from the floor and put me back on the mattress
and then it all went dark again and I don't remember any more but when I
woke up the other man was there and he gave me water and I still couldn't
see his face. He was wearing a mask, like a surgical mask and I could only
see his eyes but he had eyes like Tim . . . like the man who called himself
Tim. Though I knew it wasn't him, this was someone I didn't know."*

In short bursts of panicked energy Ashley told them how
afraid she had been. How she realized the man had undressed
her and her clothes were gone. She was dressed in a T-shirt
and then in a man's shirt and then in a T-shirt again. The
man fed her soup and gave her water and washed her. She
remembered fighting him when he touched her but her limbs
felt heavy and she couldn't coordinate enough to resist.

And then she said, "He read to me."

"He read to you?" Libby asked. "What, from a book?"

Ashley shook her head. "Notebooks," she said. "He had
a stack of them. It was like a story of three siblings, a sister

116

and two brothers and it was kind of fantasy but not a good kind." Her eyes widened and her face paled. One of them was called Paul. Do you think it was about him?"

Then it was as though the energy had drained from her body. She sat very still, Dan holding her hand, Libby's arms around her and Rose sitting at the foot of the bed and it was evident to them all that she had exhausted herself.

"I don't think I can talk about it just now," Ashley said.

"It's all right, you should get some sleep now," Libby told her gently. "That's enough for now." As Libby felt Ashley grow limp and unresisting, falling quickly into a deep sleep she met Rose's gaze. The police officer turned off the recorder, her face pale and her eyes concerned.

"You got all that?"

"Yes, I'm going to need you to send the recordings from your phones. I need to go and talk to my boss, will you both be all right? There's still an officer outside the door."

"Go," she said. "We'll be fine."

Rose left and Libby turned to her husband. "There are two of the bastards, in this together," she said. "I'd tear them apart with my bare hands."

CHAPTER 16

At 10.20 a.m., there was a knock at the vicarage door. Maggie was unsurprised by this as she was expecting the steering committee for the children's playgroup at ten thirty and just assumed that some of them might be a few minutes early. The only thing that warned her this might not be the case was a low growl from Turbot and what she interpreted as a quizzical look from his canine companion. It was this that caused Maggie to check the camera before opening the door.

After the incident with the strange shadow, a camera had been positioned higher so that she could see down into the street and she could see three members of the playgroup committee coming along the road. The second camera showed who was at the door, a man turned away at an angle so that she could not see his face. Deliberately, Maggie waited until the committee members were in sight of the gate and then, putting the door on the chain, she opened it slowly. She tried not to react as she recognized the face of the man standing on the doorstep. Paul Krantz.

Maggie had the button for the panic alarm in her hand and she pressed it now, knowing that an alarm would sound both at the local police station and the Flowers-Mahoney office. "What do you want?" she asked.

He smiled at her. "Nothing at the moment, I just wanted to get a look at you. I just wanted to let you know that I'm around." And with that he turned on his heel and walked away bidding a cheery good morning to the members of the committee who were now waiting for him to come through the gate.

Maggie opened the door fully and ushered her guests inside, aware, from the glimpse she caught of herself in the hall mirror, that she must look both pale and scared.

"Whatever is the matter?"

"Maggie, are you all right? Who was that?"

The telephone was ringing Maggie knew she must answer it. It would either be the police station, or George Mahoney, or actually both — her mobile had now started to ring as well.

"I'll get the kettle on," someone said and Maggie nodded. The vicarage was a very informal place and this was quite a normal thing to happen, she reminded herself. Two other committee members now made their way in through the open door, shouting good morning to the rest. Maggie answered the telephone, then briefly responded to George's call, then went back to speaking with the police officer. A few moments later copies of the recording were being sent to both and a marked car sent on a drive-by. Maggie went through to the kitchen and sat down at the head of the table, determined that this committee meeting was going to go ahead as normal.

"Are you all right, love? You don't look too grand." The enquiry was one of the older committee members, one of those capable ladies Maggie had encountered in every parish she had ever known, that were at the heart of the community, knew everything and everyone, and were one of the last people you could ever tell a lie to.

Maggie didn't even try. Suddenly there were tears pouring down her face and she was aware that her hands were shaking so much that when someone handed her a mug of tea she spilt some of it on the scrubbed pine kitchen table.

This will be all around the parish in no time, Maggie thought and the arrival of two police officers in a marked car a few minutes later put paid entirely to any hopes she might have of recovering the situation. In fifteen minutes, Paul Krantz had gone from a secret Maggie had kept to a piece of gossip that no amounts of pleas for discretion would contain.

The thing was, she reflected, as the meeting was finally called to order and the routine problems of financing the playgroup, replacing damaged toys and adding an extra morning in the church hall took over, this actually made her feel better about the whole thing.

* * *

At about the same time Beth and Gavin were helping Nathan in the garden at the cottage. Nathan had taken to vegetable gardening, initially under direction from his neighbour who was something of an expert, but now very much under his own steam. He'd taught Beth how to use a hoe to weed between rows and although the implement was taller than she was, she was doing a pretty good job. Gavin had been weeding too, but he was now looking for interesting insects and was showing them to the neighbour, Mr Markham, who had come into the garden to chat to Nathan. Their chat, Nathan thought, was often one-sided, but he liked to listen as the old man told him about his early life and about the village as it had been in his younger days.

Markham had once asked him how he had spent his childhood and Nathan had told him quite honestly and simply that he'd grown up in a religious cult that suspected he might be the next messiah.

Edward Markham had nodded wisely. "That would put the mockers on things for you," he said and the conversation had moved on to other subjects, never to return.

Nathan looked up from his pruning, sensing that someone was standing close to the back gate. He opened it and looked out. A youngish man with dark brown hair stood there and Nathan knew at once who he must be — though it occurred to Nathan that he did not look exactly like the photograph Ray had shown him.

It was not in Nathan's nature to panic. He looked quizzically at the stranger, waiting for him to say something. He sensed that this was not what the man had expected; that he had anticipated a more dramatic reaction.

"I seem to be a little lost," the man said. "I thought this was a short cut through to the high street."

"I suppose that depends on your start point," Nathan said. "If this way ends up being shorter or longer."

"I suppose it does," the man agreed. He shifted position so he could see into the garden through the partly open gate. Nathan could hear that the children had fallen silent and knew that they and Edward Markham were probably all staring back at this man by the gate. He noted the way the man was standing, his body at a slight angle to Nathan.

"You need to go that way." Nathan pointed.

"Annoying, I've just come from that direction."

"Then it didn't turn out to be a short cut after all," Nathan said softly. He could sense the man assessing him, judging if he might be a threat. Assessing him against some measure of his own. Nathan reached out suddenly and grabbed the stranger's arm, twisted it behind his back and the next instant the man was on the floor, Nathan's knee in his back, the knife he had been holding lying on the ground.

"Well, I never," Edward Markham said.

"I'll call the police," Beth said.

The man on the floor was shouting that Nathan was hurting him. "What the fuck! I only asked for directions. But what the hell!"

Nathan made no answer, he held his position for the time it took for the police to arrive. Edward Markham had helped both children over the fence and into his own house. He stood guard at the back door.

"You saw what happened?" one of the police officers asked him.

"Said he was asking directions," Edward Markham said. "But it's a funny sort of person asks for directions with a bloody great knife in his hand."

* * *

121

"So it's not Krantz," Ray confirmed when he spoke to Nathan just a little later.

"No, but at first glance he looked very like him. The distance between the eyes was wrong," Nathan explained. "I knew there was something different and that was what it was."

"But he had a knife. Nathan—"

"Beth and Gavin are fine. The police want me to make a statement later. Mr Markham will be making a statement as well, he saw what happened." Nathan reflected for a moment and then added," I think he found it all exciting. I suspect he thinks that life is boring sometimes."

Ray took that in. "I'm on my way to join the Major Crimes team," he said. "If you want me to come back I can."

"There's no need, Ray, Maggie told me what happened this morning and we think it might be best if we go back to the vicarage and stay there for a while. There's less chance of anyone having to be on their own if we do that."

"Sounds like a good idea," Ray said. "But Nathan, be careful, this shows Krantz has the resources to keep track more closely than we thought."

"So it's better if we are together. John and Maggie are collecting the children and then I'll collect Sarah from work."

"On the bike?"

"I have a spare helmet," Nathan assured him.

He rang off shortly after and Ray was left with the interesting image of Sarah riding pillion on Nathan's motorcycle. He wasn't sure what to think about that.

* * *

A third incident would take place that same day. Tom Pollard was driving home from doing the weekly shop when he became aware of a four-by-four tailgating him. One thing Tom hated was tailgaters.

"Damn you, back off." He glared at the driver in the mirror, reflecting that he really was bloody close. He drove on, deliberately slowing down, touching his brakes regularly intending to signal to the driver that he was not going to be intimidated.

Evidently neither was the driver of the four-by-four.

"What the hell does he think he's playing at?" He had slowed down but the driver of the other car had held his ground and now, as Tom reacted by slamming on the brakes, the car behind had accelerated, ramming into the back of Tom's car.

"Fuck!" A tight bend was coming up ahead. Tom tried to accelerate, turning the wheel hard so he could make the bend but the four-by-four seemed fixed to the back end of his car as though stuck by magnets. As they reached the bend Tom realized that maybe both cars would be ending up in the ditch. At the very last moment the second vehicle must have slammed on the brakes and swerved sideways. Unable to react in time, Tom's car hurtled across the verge and his car slid side on into the dip beneath the hedge and came to rest at an angle, with the passenger side wheels fully in the mud. Unhurt, but badly shaken, Tom clambered out of his car and ran after the vehicle that had put him there. The vehicle was red, he had a vague idea that he might recognize the model but the number plate was covered in mud and the vehicle now moving off at speed.

CHAPTER 17

Post briefing, Dave Beckett, Ray and Eloise Barnes found an Italian restaurant and took some time to weigh up what they knew. News of the incident with Tom Pollard had filtered through to them late in the day. The driver of the recovery vehicle had reported the incident to his boss and the police had been notified. Tom Pollard's name had been flagged as a person of interest in the Krantz case and DCI Blatchford been informed.

"So, three incidents and the time and distance between them preclude it being the same man. No one was hurt, this time, but any of these incidents could easily have had a different outcome. I've seen the CCTV images of the man who called at John and Maggie Rivers' place and I'm satisfied it's Krantz. The man Nathan restrained does look a lot like him, but Nathan was right, there are differences when you look more closely."

"And this man is in custody?" Eloise asked. She dug a fork into her bowl of pasta and then chewed thoughtfully. She had a side order of salad and the curious habit of alternating between the two. Ray wondered if she was conscious of doing so.

"In custody and refusing even to say 'no comment'," Dave Beckett confirmed. "They tell me he sits staring at the same point on the wall and refuses to speak."

"He'll get bored, sooner or later," Ray said. "I'm assuming for now he's one of Krantz's followers. Any reason I shouldn't make that assumption?" This to Eloise.

"It seems reasonable," she said. "Unless you reckon there are just a lot of random people roaming little villages with ill intent." She paused. "Of course that might be the case. How would we know?"

"No one was injured today," Dave Beckett sounded weary. "But we're all certain this will escalate. This is just the opening volley."

Ray nodded. It was not a good thought. "One other thing," he said. "I managed to have a quick look at the stuff Krantz left at the house." It had taken the CSIs several hours to ensure that everything had been re-posted in the exact positions it had been in the house where Ashley had been held. "And something really doesn't make sense."

"Only one something?" Beckett wanted to know.

"Ok, so more than one something. But we reckoned at first this was Krantz just crowing about what he'd done. There were obvious references to his girlfriend, Ruth Edmondson, and to Polly Brown and also to other incidents we knew about but had not been able to tie to him. But a quick look showed other stuff that Krantz can't possibly have been responsible for, because he was inside at the time."

"Interesting," Beckett agreed. "Such as?"

"Such as the murder of an elderly couple just outside Boston in Lincolnshire. Money and jewellery were stolen. This was two years ago and there are a series of armed robberies referred to in the clippings. The child's drawings, well, I've no idea what those are about but they look freshly done and if we assume there's some kind of timeline represented, then they are in the more recent section."

"So, are you thinking that the anomalous events represent actions by his followers? The armed robberies, I suppose they might be useful in terms of financing what's going on now. It would take money to provide accommodation, transport, bribes . . ."

Eloise was nodding. "It could still be part of his power play," she said. "Not just 'look what I've done' but look what has been done because I commanded it. The man that turned up at your friend's house today, armed with a knife, who knows what he'd been told to do. And we can be fairly certain I suppose that it wasn't Krantz that ran Tom Pollard off the road. The timing doesn't work, not unless he had a helicopter and I think that might have drawn too much attention."

"And what do you make of what Ashley Summers has had to say?" Ray asked.

"Very interesting indeed. She says the man read to her, but from a series of notebooks so presumably something he'd written or something Krantz had written. She doesn't seem to think the man set to guard her was Krantz himself and, let's face it, she'd have recognized him immediately. There were no notebooks found at the house?"

"Nothing like that so far no. So presumably whatever it was he took it with him, whoever he is."

"What do we know about who lived in the house before, and does anybody remember Krantz visiting?"

Dave Beckett dug in his pocket for his notebook. "We don't have much as yet, the riding school definitely had a horse called Ivan, he passed to the great stable in the sky over a decade ago, at the grand old age of twenty-four. Is that old for a horse? I know nothing about horses. A family lived at the house about ten years ago, but apparently didn't stay long. They complained to the council that it was damp and the landlord wasn't doing anything about it. Before that it was used for casual labourers to bunk down, so I can't imagine it was kept in a particularly good state. The last registered tenant is a Roger Denison, the house by the way was the farmhouse of a place called Woods End, presumably a reference to that little spinney or whatever it is. Denison was known to sublet mostly on an unofficial basis. The landlord at that point was a guy called Beale, that's the family on the next farm over. They reckon the house has not been in use for more than a decade."

"So do they still own land?"

"They say not. But they're not sure who does. The Land Registry bears that out, they have the owner down as someone called Terrence Brown, but they don't have a current address for this Terrence Brown and although I know it's a common name, it does make you wonder if there's any link to Polly Brown, the woman Paul Krantz conned out of most of what she owned before she conveniently fell downstairs. Apparently her husband was called Terry. He died about three years before Krantz came into her life."

"Which suggests this is more than coincidence. It would make a kind of sense for him to want to own the place that meant something to him," Ray said. "If that's what happened of course."

"It also begs the question if he targeted Polly Brown because the family owned this house and he wanted to get his hands on it. Or if he acquired it using that name. We'd have to clarify the timeline on that. This of course is only a connection if this is the house talked about in the interview with Ray all those years ago. It's not the only rural property with a well in the garden. My aunt and uncle had one, I'm sure they were once quite commonplace."

Ray nodded and for a few moments they all ate in silence, then Eloise rubbed her hands together and said, "Who's for dessert?"

"You're going to be one of those annoying people that can eat anything they like and not gain any weight at all, aren't you," Ray said.

She grinned at him. "My mother was the same, she said it was because she had so much nervous energy."

He watched as she studied that dessert menu and then asked, "So how do you think Ashley Summers is going to cope with all of this?"

"I think it's very hard to say. I would like to talk to her, and I would like to know more about the story she was told because I think that will prove to be at the heart of this matter."

"Why would you think that?" Dave Beckett wanted to know.

"Well, it's quite obvious the second man is very close to Krantz; he is trusted and potentially he is just as violent. I can't help but wonder if they were both in some way connected to this house, and if they'd known each other since childhood. We also have to wonder if this was the same man who came to your cottage. The knife he carried suggests he was there to do harm, not merely to reconnoitre."

"We believed that Krantz had cut all ties with friends and family when he was in his late teens," Ray said. "He left home in the January, was due to take his A levels that summer but he just up and left."

"Perhaps this was an exception. Perhaps this came later. Perhaps this friendship was the reason he broke contact with his family."

Ray nodded, perhaps any of those things. Perhaps none. "Ashley talked about the man who kept her prisoner reading from notebooks, a story relating to two brothers and a sister. One of them she was certain was referred to as Paul."

"Which is one of the reasons I think they may be so important. Though we know he was an only child, so could the idea of siblings be symbolic? If so, who is the sister? Or could the story in the notebooks be nothing whatsoever to do with the real Paul Krantz?" She frowned as though displeased at the thought. She was, Ray knew, looking for a way to tie everything together and frustrated by not having all the pieces.

"Have you spoken to the family since all this started?" Eloise asked.

"They moved, I didn't know where to, Dave was tracking them down."

"And we've had no luck so far," Beckett told him. "Enquiries were made at their old address, none of the neighbours seem to know where they've gone. But they moved out when Krantz went to prison, so again you are looking at a decade ago."

"The case attracted a lot of publicity, and though they'd had no dealings with him, obviously it came back on them. I wouldn't be surprised if they just wanted to get away, so they could be anywhere."

"And did you get any sense of how the relationship was with them before Paul left home?"

Ray thought about it, truth be told he had thought about it a lot at the time and he couldn't remember he'd come to any strong conclusion then either. "They seemed like an ordinary family, working class, he did something in a factory, a knitting-machine mechanic, I think. She had a job in an office. Paul was an only child, I got the impression that they had hoped to have more but it hadn't happened. They described him as shy and quiet but he seemed to have done all right at school, and the school always said that he was popular, that he had friends, that he joined in after-school clubs and that sort of thing. Everyone claimed to have been surprised when he just ditched his A levels and disappeared. We had no reason to disbelieve them, and by that time it was eight or nine years since anyone had seen him. The only reason we contacted the family was that he still had his mother's address in his address book and you know what it's like in a case like this, we simply go through all of the addresses we can get hold of."

"So he had dismissed his family as irrelevant, but still kept the address."

"At the time we thought it was odd. They had no idea where he was. He told Ruth's family that he no longer had any dealings with his parents because they had been abusive, we found no evidence of that but who knows?"

"Who knows indeed? Was this brought up in court, was it claimed that he had been abused as a child? In mitigation perhaps."

Ray shook his head. "It was suggested to him, but he wouldn't have anything to do with it. He said he had no family, he didn't want to know anything about them and he didn't want them to know about him. Of course they saw his picture on the news, recognized him, and so did their neighbours. The thing I remember is how shocked everyone was, I think there was a feeling that he had gone off the rails in some way, hence the disappearing act he did, but no one seemed to suspect he would do anything as violent. Everyone said what a nice boy he was, or had been."

"And he had no history of offending as a juvenile?"

"There was nothing that came to police attention, of course that doesn't mean there *was* nothing. But those who had been close to or seemed to be close in school, they've gone on to live perfectly ordinary lives and none had a criminal record, not even as juveniles. You'd expect there to be some bad apples in the mix that he could have associated with but nothing came up. One of his old classmates was a doctor, one I think was a receptionist, a couple had kids and all of that sort of thing, so far so ordinary, and although I don't think any of them were questioned in any depth, it had after all been years since he last went home, the general consensus was that he had been very unremarkable."

"No girlfriends? Most kids have had a few relationships by the time they get to eighteen or nineteen."

"Nothing serious, nothing anybody recalled. No one came forward and said they'd been his girlfriend or his boyfriend though friends remembered there were plenty of girls interested. He doesn't seem to have done anything about that though. And as I say by and large he refused to discuss anything that had happened before he left home and he wasn't that keen on discussing anything much before he was about twenty-five. That's when he started seeing Ruth, they'd been together about a year when she moved into the flat, he'd lived there for a couple of years before that. The relationship seemed stable and the landlord reported that they were quiet tenants, paid their rent on time, never bothered anyone. At work he was described as conscientious and meticulous, he was outwardly friendly and would occasionally go to the pub with his colleagues after work. Ruth's family liked him. They thought he was a little peculiar at times, a little over fussy I think was how the mother described him, he liked everything neat and tidy, but he didn't seem obsessive about it."

"So who is this friend, and I'm also wondering, as Ashley's account of the story included three characters, a brother, a sister and another brother, if there is a woman involved in all of this."

"You honestly think this story is relevant, that these notebooks mean something? Maybe this other bloke is just a wannabe novelist."

"Of course that's possible," Eloise said. But it was clear she didn't think so.

* * *

Ray called Sarah from his hotel. She was fine, she told him, but she was also glad that she was not alone.

"How was the motorbike ride?"

"Surprisingly pleasant, I could get used to that. Nathan's gone back to the cottage, I think he wanted a word with Evie and to check on his neighbour, I don't know if he'll come back to the vicarage tonight. Maggie was very badly shaken but she's feeling better now, and I think I'm going to throw a sickie for the next two or three days. I seem to have picked up a stomach bug."

Ray laughed. "What, with your iron constitution. Do you think anyone will believe you?"

"That's their problem. And what about you, how are you feeling?"

There were many answers that he could have given but he gave her an honest one. "Like I'd like to be a million miles away," he said.

* * *

They had been allowed to take Ashley out of the hospital and Libby had ordered room service at the hotel organized by the local police. They had adjoining rooms, with a connecting door. The hotel said it was usually booked by families, with two single beds in the second room. Libby had made sure the outer door was locked, demonstrating so Ashley would not have to worry. She knew Ashley felt it unlikely she would get much sleep, but Libby recognized that all three of them were so exhausted it was likely they would simply crash in the end. Dan was pretending to watch television, but she could see him nodding, the only thing preventing him going to bed was the feeling that he should be staying up to look after his wife and daughter-in-law.

"Don't be such a daft sod," she told him gently. "Go to bed."

She went back through to the other room. Ashley sat on one of the beds, staring at the door. She had wedged a chair under the handle. "I know it's not going to do any good, but isn't that what they do in all the films?"

"Well, it won't do any harm," Libby said. "I fancy another cup of tea. I told Dan to get some sleep."

Ashley nodded. "You know what? I'm not so scared now, I mean, I am, but not as scared as I was. But I am so bloody angry. With myself, with *them*, with . . . Well, I don't know who with. Being angry feels better than being scared."

"I suppose it's something to do with the stages of grief," Libby said. She looked at Ashley and they both laughed.

"Do you remember that counsellor I saw after Aidan died? She went through all of that, how grief has stages, and I have to work my way through it."

"I remember you were very rude about her?"

"I was, wasn't I? And I did tell her I was sorry. You know, it didn't work like that. It's not like it goes through all these neat stages, the grief doesn't go away, I still miss him like my heart's been torn out and I know you do too and yes, I was angry, of course I was angry. I was angry because we didn't know what was wrong with him, because we couldn't do anything about it, because he just dropped down dead pushing a supermarket trolley. My God that's no way to go is it, pushing a bloody supermarket trolley. It was just so stupid, so absurd, so . . . So I don't know what it was. I just knew he would have hated that, I just know I still miss him. And the first time I get interested in somebody else he turned out to be a bloody psychopath. So, yes, I think angry is a good feeling right now."

"It is definitely better than just scared," Libby agreed. She looked at the kettle, wondered if she could really be bothered to make tea, went to the bathroom to fill it with water and by the time she got back Ashley had collapsed onto her pillow and was fast asleep. She pulled a blanket over her and was painfully reminded of when Aidan was a kid and she went in last thing at night to tuck him in, knowing his bed would be a mess because he always was such a restless child even when he was asleep.

Dan was snoring softly, spread out on the bed looking as though he'd been dropped from a great height. Quietly she got into her pyjamas and, leaving the television on low so the sound of it would be soothing, she got into the other single bed and within minutes she too was sleeping.

* * *

Outside the hotel a man watched, he was dark-haired and of average height and his face would have been very familiar to Ashley Summers. He didn't trouble to try and go inside, it was enough that he knew where she was. If he decided he wanted to reach her then it would be easy enough but he had not yet made up his mind.

He had become concerned when the other had not reported back and being somewhat irritated when, on making enquiries, he discovered that he'd been arrested. That this Nathan, whoever he was, had disarmed him and handed him over to the police. That was not good, that was not part of any plan, but he would resolve that one later, for now there were other things on his list.

He turned and walked away, collected his car from the side street and was soon driving back south again.

CHAPTER 18

Dan had woken in a state of hypervigilance. He could hear Ashley crying softly in the other room, and his wife trying to comfort her. He remembered when their son had died, the overpowering, overwhelming, all-consuming grief that had broken like a tsunami. He had felt helpless then and he felt helpless now, what could he do to change this?

"Absolutely fuck all," he told himself.

He tapped gently on the connecting door and went over to where the two women sat on the bed, wrapped around one another, limbs locked so tightly he wondered how they could ever untangle. He sat down on the bed and hugged them both but it felt as though there was no room for another pair of arms in such a tight knot.

He drew back, Ashley was going to be interviewed this morning and the police had said that they could be there, but it was still going to be difficult.

"You have to eat something," he said to both of them. "I'll order room service."

Libby nodded. "I know you don't feel like it, but you must eat something Ashley, we all must. It's going to be a long day."

Ashley nodded, she wiped her eyes with the heels of her hands and Dan, glad to find at least a tiny thing to do, fetched her some tissues. He was grateful when she took his hand and squeezed his fingers. He wanted to be included in her grief and in her pain but he didn't know how to ask.

They watched television while they ate breakfast, avoiding the news and instead putting on a cartoon channel. Bright colours crashed and flashed on the screen and the voices of the characters seemed as though they were speaking another language, the screen jittering and jabbering, and Dan could barely take it in.

The phone rang, informing them that the police escort had arrived and they made their way downstairs. Rose and a couple of constables they recognized stood in the foyer waiting for them. Outside the day was grey and dreary, looking like anything but high summer.

As they made their way down the steps towards the car, a flash of movement attracted Dan's attention and, he realized, that of one of the constables. There was a man standing across the road watching them, and one Dan instantly recognized.

"It's him," Dan shouted and then before anybody could stop him he was hurtling away from his family and the police officers and heading towards the figure he had identified as Paul Krantz. Krantz ran. Dan was fast and angry and driven by a desperate need to do something and he caught up with Krantz as he turned into a side street, grabbing him by the shoulder, the police officer who had followed was only a few steps behind.

Krantz turned and lashed out and Dan felt pain.

He looked down to see blood pouring from his abdomen and instinctively he pressed his hands against his stomach before collapsing onto the pavement.

Dimly, he was aware of the police officer beside him and that he was summoning assistance and that Paul Krantz had turned and run. He wanted to tell the police officer to get after him but he couldn't seem to speak, he could feel his body going into shock, feel the darkness and feel himself slipping down into it.

* * *

Dave Beckett arrived at the hospital to find the two Summers women accompanied by two police officers, in the family room.

"How is he?" Beckett asked.

"They say he'll survive," Libby told him. "The constable administered first aid and the paramedics got to him really fast. But what did he think he was doing? Why didn't he just get in the car?"

"I think he just reacted," Ashley said. "I don't think he could help himself." She paused. "He's been watching us, hasn't he. Maybe all the time."

"Not all the time, but he certainly seems to have been keeping watch, yes," said Beckett.

"How do you know not all the time?" Ashley's eyes widened, "Because he's been somewhere else? He's been seen? What else has he done?"

"Nothing as bad as this."

"Yet," Ashley finished for him. "Nothing as bad as this yet."

Beckett didn't feel he could correct her.

"Ashley, I know it's a lot to ask, but would you feel up to coming to the police station? Anything else you can remember might really help. And a man was arrested yesterday, I want to show you some interview footage of him, see if you recognize him."

"The man from the house?"

"We don't know that yet, but if you could take a look."

Ashley looked at her mother-in-law. "Go," Libby said. "I'll call you as soon as I have any news. Like Dave said, anything might be helpful. We have to catch this man, Ashley."

Ashley was wary as they left the hospital and Beckett couldn't blame her for that. They were joined by a constable who had been waiting by the main doors and who fell into step beside them.

Ashley eyed him with suspicion. She looked left and right as they crossed the car park, examining faces. "I feel like he's everywhere," she said. "I feel like I'm never going to feel safe again."

"Ashley, we've got a forensic psychologist working with us, trying to guide our understanding of Krantz and what we're dealing with here. Would you be willing for her to sit in on the interviews?"

She nodded. "If it might help."

He watched as she checked the back seat of his car before getting into the front passenger seat. He tried to imagine what it must have felt like. To be at ease and relaxed one minute, to have a ligature tightly round your throat the next and your head and neck pinioned to the headrest, hardly able to breathe. To know that someone you had trusted was responsible for the terror and the pain. Believing that you were about to die. He saw her flinch as the constable got into the back seat.

"Would you rather sit in the back?" Beckett asked.

"If you don't mind."

She seemed to settle a little once they were underway but he noticed she was staring intently out of the window as though Krantz might suddenly appear.

"We've got a detective from the original enquiry working with us," he told her. "Libby might have told you about him?"

"Ray Flowers? Yes, she did. She said he got involved because he was a friend of the real Tim Bennett. Are they doing OK, by the way, him and his family? Libby's so ashamed of what she put them through."

"They'll be fine," Beckett told her. "Just relieved the truth has come out, I think."

Watching through the rearview mirror he saw her nod and then return to her surveillance. Was anyone really going to be fine, he wondered. How long did being fine actually take?

"Do you mind if Ray observes? He might recognize something you talk about as having come up when he interviewed Krantz."

"Sure, why not, the more the merrier." She paused and he saw her take a deep breath. "Sorry, that came out wrong. I mean, of course. Look, none of this feels quite real, you know?"

Dave Beckett didn't think there was an appropriate response to that. She was right, none of it did seem real.

"Libby said he had followers, people who tried to get a retrial."

"That's true. Yes."

"Have you talked to them? Do they know what's going on?"

Beckett laughed a little bitterly. "His fan club seemed to have dwindled to a hard core of about twenty," he said.

"Twenty! That's crazy. No, but it's not, is it. I liked him, I thought he was a nice man. And I wasn't actually looking to get involved with anyone, it wasn't that I was keen to find someone or putting out desperate vibes or anything." She laughed at herself. "He just seemed OK, you know and I get the feeling now that he hadn't really turned on the charm. That he knew he had to be a bit subtle, a bit careful not to come on too strong because I'd have run a mile. It was only because he took it slow and he was just the right kind of friendly that I even agreed to have coffee with him. Then it kind of grew from there. It took weeks before I was prepared to get any more involved. He's a man who knows how to be patient, I've got to give him that."

"He seems to be able to read people exceptionally well," Dave Beckett said.

"So, these followers of his . . ."

"We've interviewed about a dozen so far, but they've told us nothing useful apart from the fact that he seems to have become particularly close to three people. I have to say this caused a fair amount of jealousy in what you might term the rank and file. But this inner court seem to have been picked for their loyalty to him but also because they have no real family ties. They are all people who could leave home and not be immediately reported missing."

"And that's what they've done," Ashley guessed.

"Inasmuch as we can't locate them, it would seem so. I have to be honest and tell you that he may have contact with other people and they might also be working with or for him, certainly under his direction, but we know about these three."

"Does that include the man at the house? At Woods End? The man who . . . stayed with me?"

Beckett shook his head. "We don't think so," he admitted. "That would be our fourth person of interest. We have a man in custody, as I told you. I want to see if you recognize him. Don't worry, it will just be a matter of showing you a photograph and perhaps some video, if you feel up to that."

They had pulled up outside the police station and Ashley got out cautiously, flanked by Beckett and the constable. Again she was glancing around, searching for hidden corners and shadows where someone could hide. Scrutinizing the expressions on people she passed as they went inside. Looking, he thought, for escape routes.

He took her to the room that he and Ray and Eloise were using as their base of operations. Ashley stood in the doorway and surveyed first the room and then the two people seated at their desks. Ray had stood up, ready to greet her but Beckett noticed that he took one look at Ashley's face and stayed where he was. Beckett made his introductions from the doorway and for a minute they all maintained their personal space until Ashley felt ready to move.

She looked curiously at Ray's scars, her hand moving to her throat as though recalling her own pain.

"Ok then," Ashley said at last, her voice shaking a little. "Let's get started, shall we?"

* * *

Ashley had recognized the man in the photograph. She had covered the lower part of his face with her hand and then studied the eyes intently. Finally she had nodded. "It's him," she said. "I never saw his whole face, but I know that's him. How did you catch him?"

"He went after someone with a knife," Beckett said briefly. "Fortunately someone else intervened."

"And has he told you anything?"

"So far he's refusing to say a word."

They showed her some video of the man in the interview room, staring at the wall. Ashley watched carefully, her body very still, her hands clenched. "He would sit like that," she said. "Sometimes I'd half wake up and he'd be there, just sitting totally still, like he was meditating or something."

Ray said, "What interaction did you have with him? Did you get a sense of how often he drugged you, of passing time, of any pattern to the day?"

She thought about it and nodded. "It was like he sometimes wanted company," she said. "I'd wake up in the morning and he'd give me a drink and sometimes some soup. It was mostly soup. I don't think I'll ever be able to eat soup again. Evenings it was some kind of malty drink, I think there was something in the drink because I'd always lose consciousness straight after.

"I was never really awake, if you know what I mean, but sometimes I'd be less awake than others and at night . . . I don't remember ever waking up at night."

"So he'd give you a drink and then what?"

"He'd help me to the commode thing. God, that was embarrassing. I must have been conscious enough to think that! Isn't it weird where your mind goes to? It wasn't, oh, this man might kill me it was oh, this man is going to watch me pee or whatever."

"The mind protects itself any way it can," Eloise told her.

"And then?"

"And then he'd give me breakfast, I suppose. I mean I'm assuming this was early morning but all I can tell you is that I think it was the earliest thing that happened in the day."

She paused, something surfacing, Ray thought. Something she wasn't sure she wanted to deal with. He watched as she decided just to get it out there.

"Twice I remember waking up and he was washing me and changing my shirt. I felt the water on my skin. I was naked. It was like, so personal, I felt so vulnerable, I mean I was only wearing a shirt the rest of the time but this was like the final bit of protection being stripped away."

She was shaking now and Ray watched as she seemed to take a conscious hold on herself. He knew instinctively that she needed to be moved past this moment. "And after breakfast," he said.

Ashley tensed. He watched her throat clench, momentarily blocking the air going into her lungs, a tic he was all too familiar with. "Try to breathe through it," he said. "You have to be kind of conscious about taking the breath."

She looked at him in surprise and he found himself breathing with her. Taking air into his lungs, holding it, releasing it, finding an artificial rhythm until the natural one could reassert itself.

"He'd talk," she said. She sounded as though she'd been running, the breath in short spasms.

"Breathe again and just focus on that. You're in control of all this," Eloise's voice was quiet and calm, picking up on Ray's instructions.

A breathing therapy tag team, he thought. "So he talked. Is this when he read to you?"

She nodded. "He had all these notebooks, a stack of them. They looked like school exercise books, you know, the ones with the slightly faded-looking covers? He would choose one and he would read and sometimes I'd sleep and when I woke he was still reading."

She closed her eyes, visualizing. Ray wanted to warn her not to try to go too deep, to keep a hold on the here and now. Instinctively, he reached out and took her hand. Ashley gasped but then gripped his fingers hard. Her thumb made contact with the scars on his hand and unconsciously, she explored the web of thicker tissue.

"I can remember the shadows crossing the room," she said. "I can remember the light changing. I'd wake up and it had shifted and he'd still be talking."

She opened her eyes and let go of Ray's hand. Everyone seemed to realize that she needed to be left alone for a few minutes and Ray filled the kettle and set about making drinks.

"Could I have hot chocolate," Ashley asked, coming up behind him. "Oh, what's that you're making?"

"It's what Eloise likes in the morning. A spoon of coffee, a spoon of chocolate and one of sugar. Then a dash of milk and the rest hot water."

"Can I try that? How did you get your scars? Sorry, you don't have to say."

"Someone mistook me for a man he'd got a grudge against."

"Did you catch him? I mean, was he caught."

"He died," Ray said. "Actually, his was a sad story. He's not someone I can hate."

"Not like *Him*."

"Paul Krantz? No not like him. I don't know his story but it's hard to envisage one that can justify what he's done."

"Why take me to that place?"

"We think it's a place he knew when he was much younger. We think he might be the brother that your captor talked about in his stories. That would make sense anyway, since you remember him mentioning Paul by name. Of course, we can't be certain the notebooks were referring to Paul Krantz, but it does seem worth considering."

"There was a sister," she reminded him.

"There was. According to the stories he told you. Ashley, do you feel up to looking at something else?"

She sipped her drink, blowing gently across the surface when it proved too hot. He knew it bought her thinking time. "OK," she said. "I'll bring my drink."

In the office next door, the room at Woods End had been reconstructed. Ray stood in the doorway and watched as Ashley moved around the room, examining the press cuttings and the photographs, the drawings, the red string linking events.

"Did he do all this?"

"No, not all of it. When some of these things happened he was in prison. We think the other one might have been responsible for the rest or at least some of it. We're still trying to unpick things. But does anything here remind you of anything the man said? Anything he might have told you in his stories?"

She shook her head. "I'm not sure. I think the stories were mostly about when they were younger." She came back to the door and began her perusal again. "So what did Krantz do?"

She had spoken his name with more confidence, Ray noted.

"This was his girlfriend," he said. "Her name was Ruth and he murdered her."

Ashley studied the picture. "She looks a bit like me," she said. "The curls, the shape of her face, the—" she frowned then pushed whatever else she had noted aside. He could see the strain on her face, knew he was stressing her. He pointed again. "This is a woman called Polly Brown. She gave him money, she signed her possessions over to him. She thought he was a friend but he killed her by pushing her down the stairs and then staged an accident, making it look as though she'd just fallen. We are certain he killed others but we could never prove it. This girl here, she was just nineteen and she thought Krantz was her boyfriend."

"Just like me — except I was older and should have known better."

Ray did not respond to that. Instead he pointed to two newer clippings. They had not been certain about Krantz's involvement in the deaths of DCI Nightingale and Joe Capaldi until seeing the room at Woods End, but they knew now.

"This was Tony Nightingale. He was my boss on the first Krantz enquiry. He was killed in a house fire just after Krantz absconded from prison. And this is Joe Capaldi, foreman of the jury that convicted him."

"My God! And he's probably after you too?"

"Probably. He's already harmed people that I care about. Not physically as yet, but I believe the intent is there."

"And the things he can't have done?"

He pointed out the armed robberies, the thefts from a vet's surgery of ketamine and a pharmacy of barbiturates. "We think that's what he used to drug you."

"And you don't know what this man is called?"

"Not yet, no. He's telling us nothing."

Slowly she paced the room again, pausing to sip her drink, her hands folded tightly around the mug, struggling to keep calm, though he could see that panic was close to the surface.

"I think it might be Robert," she said finally. "But Krantz called him Rob. I can't be certain but that first night at the house, I woke up and I heard them talking and Krantz was getting annoyed about something. He said something like, Rob, when this is done you can do what the hell you like."

"Rob," Ray said.

"And in the notebooks, when he was reading, I think he mentioned the name Rob." She rubbed her eyes, a look of frustration on her face. "It's possible I'm getting things mixed up, isn't it. That someone in the stories was called Rob, so I think that man might be called Rob too."

"It's possible, it's also possible they are one and the same person."

She nodded but he could see she was becoming distracted.

"Sorry," Ashley said. "I don't think I can tell you anymore. Ray, do you think I can go back to Libby now? I think I've had all I can take for today."

CHAPTER 19

Across town Beckett had joined the interrogation of the man arrested after Nathan's intervention. The man Ashley had identified as being her captor at Woods End. DCI Blatchford had been told of this development and that Ashley thought the man's name was Robert — perhaps more usually known as Rob.

Beckett had arrived while they were taking a scheduled break and watched the recorded interview that had just taken place.

Rob, if that was in fact his name, listened impassively while they told him about the attack on Dan Summers, his face expressionless, eyes fixed on that one spot on the wall. They had tried to disorientate him by shifting his position in the room, by turning the table and chairs, by moving into another room but it made no difference. He still found his place, that one object of interest and focused on it intently. Interrogators sensed that he was listening, that he did hear them, but he had trained himself not to respond.

A constable, who was in the TA and liked to think he knew about these things, said confidently that this man was probably ex-special forces. That he'd been trained to withstand interrogation and torture. He tried out his theory on anybody that would stand still long enough to listen and DCI Beckett had been tolerant enough of his enthusiasm and willing enough to explore any idea, under the circumstances, and had told him to contact the regiment in Hereford and see if they had anybody missing. It was no great surprise when a negative answer came through.

"He's not dead," Beckett told the man Ashley had identified as Robert. "I've no doubt that was the intent, but he's not dead and with luck he'll survive, so your friend Krantz didn't get what he wanted." He paused. "Or should I call him your brother? That's how you think of him, isn't it. In the story you told to Ashley Summers, he was your brother."

To Beckett's surprise Rob shifted his gaze and turned his attention to his interrogator. "Did he slash or stab?" he asked.

Beckett was taken aback but he said, "He slashed with the knife. Why?"

Robert nodded as though this was the right response and then turned his head away and gazed once more at that spot on the wall.

Slash, don't stab. To stab you have to get in close and if something goes wrong it's too easy for them to turn on you. If you use a slashing movement with the knife, you can keep your distance, the knife at arm's length and your body even further out of range. See?

And they had practiced, slashing their blades against the line of dead rabbits until the guts were falling to the ground and the blood dripping from the black bin bags they had used to protect their clothes.

At the end, when the corpses of the rabbits had been shredded into unrecognizable, bloodied lumps of meat, Paul had smiled at them and announced himself satisfied.

Except, of course, he remembered, the meat had been ruined. Once they'd tidied themselves up and removed the evidence of their practice, they had to shoot more for the pie. But that was never a problem. Rabbits there were in plentiful supply and the local farmers happy enough for locals to shoot them for the pot.

* * *

Later, Beckett returned to the hospital to see the Summers women. They came out into the hall to see him, the surgeon having just arrived to check on Dan.

Beckett asked Ashley. "When he was reading to you, telling you the stories, did he ever mention rabbits? Rabbits and knives?"

He saw Libby Summers flinch. "Rabbits?" she asked. "What the hell?"

But Ashley nodded slowly. "One day . . . it was summer. It always seems to be summer in his stories. They'd shot some rabbits in one of the neighbouring fields. To eat, I think, but instead of eating them they hung them up in a row and practiced stabbing things."

"Stabbing the rabbits?" Libby asked, her face a picture of horror but Beckett could see that Ashley was already correcting herself.

"No, not stabbing. Using a blade to slash," she turned pale, "like he did with Dan."

"Oh my God." Libby's hand flew to her mouth.

Clearly uncomfortable, Ashley continued, "It was to do with keeping your distance in an attack, so the victim had less chance of fighting back. So it was easier to hurt someone without putting yourself in so much danger." She glanced anxiously at Libby. "They practiced on the rabbits," she said. "So they would know what to do when they did it for real."

CHAPTER 20

A call came in from the forensic teams at Woods End at three in the afternoon. They had extended their search to the yard and what had been the garden, noticing evidence of recently disturbed earth at a point where the old garden met the corner of the field. It was an overgrown space and covered with brambles and nettles and, where the edge of the plot was in brighter sun, cow parsley.

The area of disturbed ground was quite small but it was distinctive enough to stand out. The CSI who had noticed it began to scrape back with her trowel and had only gone a few inches down when the smell rose up to meet her. There was definitely something dead in there.

A few more inches down and fur began to appear, brown and white and mottled grey. Then smaller bundles of brown and black and grey fur. "It's a dead cat," she told her colleagues. "A dead cat and four kittens."

The crime scene manager stared down into the hole. "Bag and tag," he said at last. "Who knows what the hell might be relevant in a case like this."

Slowly she began to lift the furry bundle from the shallow grave. "Its neck's been broken," she said. She examined one of the kittens. "Its mouth and nose are full of earth. Do you think—"

"That someone killed the mother and just dumped the kittens into the same hole. Wouldn't surprise me at all."

The CSI stood and together they stood looking at the little corner of field, this remnant of what had been garden. The crime scene manager was not known to be an imaginative man, but she knew he was currently speculating about what else might be down there.

"Maybe just do a bit more digging," he said. "Just in case. I'll get you some heavy gloves so you can wrangle those brambles."

The first bones emerged a couple of hours later. First a fox's skull and then small bones from a human hand.

* * *

"How many bodies do we have?" Blatchford asked.

"So far, two. Adults and possibly a man and a woman."

A tent had been erected over the site, lights brought in. It was almost midsummer and the light would last until late, but the dig might continue well after it had faded.

"How long have they been in the ground?"

"I can't be definitive. At a guess, a decade or so. They were buried deeper than the cat and the bramble roots have grown through them. A botanist might be able to tell you how long it takes for a bramble to get to the size of a tree," he added, eyeing the offending plant with extreme prejudice. "There are remnants of clothing and we also found these."

"A wedding ring and a heart-shaped pendant. It's quite distinctive, someone might recognize it."

He signed for the piece of evidence, they both checked the seal, signed that this had been done. "Where are you taking it?" The crime scene manager wanted to know.

"Over to the riding stables and to the next farm along the track. Both have been in the same families for years, and the Beales, the farmers, once owned this place so it's possible someone might know who the necklace belonged to.

"You could send a constable."

"I could, but it's a glorious evening and it's nice to be outside for a bit."

The crime scene manager looked down at where the bodies lay. "I suppose it is," he said. "Though that sort of depends on what you happen to be doing."

* * *

The riding stable was now owned and run by the third generation of Merricks. The older generation had retired and moved a few miles down the road but Jenny Merrick reckoned that if anyone knew anything then it would be her grandparent. "He can't remember where he put his house keys but he's got a memory like an elephant for anything that happened years ago."

DCI Blatchford wasn't sure that was particularly encouraging but, Jenny having called ahead, he followed her directions along a particularly twisty country mile to a small hamlet. Sid Merrick was waiting for him in the garden, in a shady spot just beside the front door. It was well after seven in the evening, but warm and light and the garden smelt of roses and lavender.

"The last years it was used, it was just casual labourers there," Sid told him. "Then the Beales switched from soft fruit to oil seed rape and some fancy type of wheat. Spelt, they call it, fetches a good price. Some say the Romans brought it in. Anyroad, they didn't need the summer labour after that so they let the place go to rack and ruin and then I heard they'd sold it on. No one lived there though. It's a shame to let the place go like that."

"And before that?"

"Before that was a young couple only stayed six months or so. Had some idea about self-sufficiency. Watched too much old telly, I reckon. Lasted the summer but come winter they complained about the damp and off they went. Back to town, I reckon, tails between their legs."

"When was that?" Blatchford asked. Mrs Merrick had come out to join them. She had a jug of lemonade and biscuits on a tray. She brought a folding chair and settled herself close to her husband.

"Be about fifteen years ago," she said, helping him out. "It's been empty for ten, near enough. Before the *Good Life* couple it was rented out to an older couple. He was a retired doctor or something."

"Oh yes, I remember him. Drank at the George, played darts."

"He did not, he played pool. Competed for the pub."

"And about twenty years ago?"

"Now you are going back. Now that would be the Holts. Stayed for a long time they did, rented from the Beales and it was such a shock when they just up and left. They'd been such good tenants but it seems they had money troubles that no one knew about."

"They just left?"

"Oh yes, something of a nine day wonder it was. He was an average sort of man, I can't recall what he did, can you?"

Her husband shook his head. "Not much of anything I don't think. Didn't he claim to be an odd job man, did some painting and decorating and gardening and that sort of thing. She worked as a receptionist somewhere in town, I think."

"A hotel maybe?" They looked quizzically at one another. "Oh, but she was such a pretty woman. Exotic, I always said. She spoke with an accent. French, I think. Had the most wonderful halo of hair, all these little ringlets and the daughter was the same. Her skin was quite dark but the hair was paler, and her daughter was almost blonde though still with the same dark skin. Very pretty, the pair of them. She was a sweet soul, but I don't think we liked him all that much. A bit of a layabout if you ask me."

"And their name was Holt? And there were children."

"Two. One was his and one was hers. I suppose it's what you'd call a blended family today?" She looked uncertain as though the term was unfamiliar. "But the odd thing was that

151

the children were the same age. Birthdays within a couple of weeks of one another. Now if I recall correctly they were nine or ten when they arrived. The boy was Robert, like his father. The little girl was Kit, it might have been short for something, I don't think I ever asked."

"And the mother?"

"Oh, she was Celeste. Such a pretty name for such a pretty woman."

"And there was another boy who came to stay in the summer. Paul?"

"Well, yes, there was. A relative. He used to come to the stables, didn't he?"

"Liked to ride Ivan, very few people did. He was a bit of a brute."

"What's this all about anyway? I hear you've had people digging and searching at the old house since that poor lass was found wandering. You found something up there?"

Blatchford took the evidence bag from his pocket and showed them the wedding ring and the heart-shaped pendant. "Do you recognize these?"

They shook their heads. "Well, a plain wedding ring is just a plain wedding ring," Mrs Merrick said, "and a lot of people wear heart-shaped pendants."

"So why are these all muddied up?" Sid Merrick asked pointedly. "You've found someone buried up there, haven't you?"

It took a moment for realization to hit and then Mrs Merrick said, "You mean they didn't just leave the place. You mean all these years they've still been up there? The children too?"

"They weren't children by then," her husband reminded her. "Almost grown up they would have been."

"Even so."

"We're not certain who or what we've found yet," Blatchford said carefully. "But bones have been found."

"And you think it might be them."

"We think it's possible," Blatchford said.

CHAPTER 21

DCI Blatchford and a sergeant from the Major Crimes Unit sat opposite the man they now believed to be Robert Holt and the duty solicitor. It was almost 10 p.m., but the prisoner had been well rested and Blatchford was tired enough already that another hour or so would make little difference.

"So, your name is Robert Holt," Blatchford said quietly.

No response.

"We know you lived for about nine years at Woods End Farm, a place where this young woman was held. She's identified you as her captor."

He laid a picture of Ashley on the table and then two pictures of the house and grounds. "And just here, in this spot, we found something buried. A tortoiseshell cat and her very young kittens. Was she sheltering in the house? Was she in your way, Robert? Her neck was broken and we think the kittens were buried alive."

Again, no response, though Ray, sitting next to Beckett and watching on the view screen, thought he saw a twitch in the man's cheek.

"And when they dug further they found other bones. What we think was the skull of a fox and then human

153

remains. A woman and a man. The woman was wearing these. Were they your parents, Robert?"

He had just laid the evidence bag on the table when something utterly unexpected happened. Robert Holt broke out of his stillness and launched himself across the table at Blatchford. Seconds later the two of them were on the floor, Blatchford struggling beneath the smaller, slighter man. A man who was making up, in rage and ferocity, for any disadvantage he had in size.

Ray and Beckett were out of the viewing room and racing down the corridor. Someone had pressed the alarm and others were running too. By the time Ray made it through the door there were a half-dozen people in the small, cramped room. Four of them were now restraining Robert Holt, his hands were bloody and he writhed in their grasp with such violence they could barely manage to hold on.

Two others piled into the melee and Ray turned his attention to Blatchford. The man lay on the ground, moaning in pain. His face was covered in blood. His left eye ruined.

"His thumb," the duty solicitor, kneeling at Blatchford's side, said. Ray could see that the man's mind could barely cope with any of this. "He was pressing his thumbs into Inspector Blatchford's eyes. He was trying to blind him."

Ray's stomach turned. He felt sick. Six men now wrestled Robert Holt out of the door and the duty first aiders knelt beside the DCI.

"Best get out of the way," Beckett said. "Fuck's sake, did you see his eye."

* * *

Later Ray called Sarah. It was much later than anticipated — the interview had not begun until nearly ten and the aftermath had occupied them all for some time after that.

"I was getting worried about you."

"Sorry, there were developments. I got a bit caught up. How are you all doing?"

154

"We're all fine. I've just come up to bed. This is a rambling old place. I'd hate to go through the winter here. Maggie says they close a lot of the rooms up in winter; it's just too expensive to heat. So, what developments? What's upsetting you?"

Ray sighed. "It's been a bit of an eventful day."

"So tell me."

He began with the attack on Dan Summers and then Ashley being brought to the incident room and the rabbits and the knife and the discovery of the bodies and then the interview that had ended so dramatically.

"Will they be all right?"

"Dan Summers is still in ITU but they are very hopeful for him. Blatchford is in surgery, but he'll lose one eye and they're worried about the other one. I've not seen anything like that, Sarah. It was like he was possessed. It took four of them to drag him off and they needed two others afterwards just to hold on to him."

"Where is he now?"

"In a secure psychiatric unit pending assessment."

"Was he on something? You hear about drugs, things like PCP that seem to give people super strength."

"Most drugs like that just act to inhibit pain, so the person acts like nothing can hurt them. But no, he was searched, how could he get access to anything like that? Besides it wasn't like he was high. He went from totally detached, totally controlled to totally wacko in a split second. There was no warning, no wind up to it. Frankly, if I never see anything like that again it'll be too soon and we both know I've seen some terrible things."

"And how are you?" she asked.

"Tired, frustrated, I want to be home and leave all this behind. And I'm worried, Sarah. Today was bad enough but I just have this feeling that there's a lot more to come. That Krantz is just playing with us."

"Let's hope you're wrong," she said.

"We can always hope."

CHAPTER 22

Morning brought fresh shocks. The news was full of Paul Krantz. In the days when print dominated there had been deadlines for changing the copy. In the days of internet and digital media, deadlines could be ignored; breaking news could make it onto the screen within moments of it having broken. The rush to be first to present the public with that news was no longer timed in hours or even minutes. Each second counted and Krantz had taken advantage of that.

By 6 a.m. his face was on every channel, his claims being pored over by crime reporters, early morning presenters and the general public. *I did these things,* Paul Krantz proclaimed. *I killed and I cheated and I maimed and I'm going to do all of that again because prison couldn't hold me and the police can't find me. So watch out world.*

Ray was woken by the insistent ringing on his phone. "Turn on the television," Beckett told him.

"What channel?"

"It doesn't matter."

Ray did as he was told. Disbelieving, he flipped from channel to channel. "What the hell?" Krantz had itemized his crimes. The killing of his girlfriend, the attack on Dan Summers, the murder of DI Nightingale . . . instead of denying these acts he seemed now to be celebrating them all. On top of that it seemed that Krantz had a list of people he claimed had wronged him and had declared it was time for them and their families to suffer.

"Pretty much what I said. I'm sending an unmarked car for you. Bring all your stuff, once the press get wind of where you're staying you'll be inundated. Let Sarah and the rest know what's happening, anyone else you think might need a heads-up. I'm acting SIO, as of now, until someone comes up with a better option and there's a press conference been scheduled for noon, so you'd better think of something positive I can say."

Ray packed his bag and waited in his room until the officers in the unmarked car had let him know they had arrived. Dave Beckett had given him the registration number and the names of the officers. He checked both number plate and ID before getting into the vehicle. Once at police headquarters he made his way to the incident room and found Beckett.

"What's happening with the Summers family?"

"Dan's still in the ITU, in that same side room. He's apparently fit enough to be moved onto a surgical ward but they're keeping him where he is for the moment as it's more difficult to access than the main wards. They're trying to sort out transport for a nursing home the consultant suggested. It's got the facilities he needs in a private wing and accommodation for the family. We'll worry about who picks up the tab later. I'm assigning armed officers. Krantz may well still have him on his list."

"It's a pity he didn't send a copy of that out to the media. Then at least we'd know who he was after."

"Well, I think we should assume you're at the top of it."

"Thanks for that."

"Welcome. You've spoken to Sarah?"

"Yes, I woke her up. I suspect she's now woken the whole house. George has additional security on the house and we have to hope that Krantz will just be satisfied by making threats."

"I've arranged for extra patrols but I'd sooner they were all in a safe house."

"And you can't assume that anywhere is beyond reach. Nightingale changed his name and moved halfway across the country. That didn't stop Krantz."

Beckett sighed but didn't argue. "We're checking in with everyone he had a grudge against," he said. Someone called him away and Ray was left alone, watching as others manned their stations, took calls, added detail to charts and evidence logs. The television in the corner of the room was muted and the subtitles relayed the ongoing discussion. The reprise of events so far ran across the bottom of the screen. He saw pictures of Woods End Farm and the CSI moving slowly and methodically about the scene. Stock footage of the prison Krantz had escaped from. Old news reports of Ruth Edmonson and Polly Brown and of Ray and DCI Nightingale preparing to give evidence. Of Ashley Summers, of reporters now camped outside the George and Dragon pub, at the end of the lane that led to Woods End, outside the offices of Flowers-Mahoney, interviewing neighbours of DI Nightingale, who had known him by quite a different name. Krantz had been thorough in his media briefing, Ray thought.

He caught sight of Eloise going into the office they had been assigned, a wheelie suitcase in tow and guessed she too must have been told to leave her hotel.

"A fine mess this is," she said tartly as he followed her into the office.

"Can't argue with that. So, what next?"

"I carry on going through the old Paul Krantz interview tapes and you get back in the other room and keep looking at that wall till inspiration strikes," she said. "What else can we do?"

"What set him off last night? Robert Holt, I mean."

"I know who you mean."

"I was watching the interview. Nothing, well, not much, and then that."

"You say not much but you did notice something," she said. "What was it?"

"A tightening around the mouth, a . . . tension. Like he suddenly heard something unexpected and unwelcome. You've spoken to him since?"

He knew she had followed Krantz to the hospital and explained to her colleagues there what had happened.

"No, he's unresponsive, almost catatonic. They'll call me if anything changes but I think we're unlikely to get help from that direction. But I did review the tape." She grimaced. "Went straight for the eyes," she said. "It looked as though he intended to stop only when he reached the brain. It was horrible, Ray. Horrific. I've seen some dreadful things but not like that and not happening to someone I'd got to know. It felt far too close and far too personal."

Beckett appeared in the doorway. "More bad news," he said. "Tom Pollard is dead. Local officers went to do a welfare check when he didn't answer his phone this morning."

"How?"

"Stab wounds. Or rather, deep slashes across the abdomen with a very sharp knife. Dan Summers was lucky; Krantz only had time to strike once. He seems to have got Pollard multiple times. The officers that found him spotted him through the patio doors and called for backup. They didn't go inside. It was pretty evident he was well and truly dead."

"You're going over there?"

"Not just yet. The constables got to the house just ahead of the local press. It seems Krantz had contacted a producer at the local radio station and told them there would be something worth seeing at Pollard's address. He told them he was giving the station an exclusive. He'd told two local papers the same thing."

"Fuck," Ray said softly.

"Nothing to be gained by me going over there when there's a very competent inspector in charge. Crime scene photos will be sent within the hour and we've got a dedicated liaison on the team." He grimaced, "I've no doubt the investigation will be handed off to this team soon enough though."

Ray nodded. It would make sense for the Major Crimes team to have the overview. "And do we get more manpower along with the extra body?" *Do you*, he corrected himself, but Beckett hadn't seemed to notice.

CHAPTER 23

Mrs Caldwell had not been told that she was a potential target for Paul Krantz, but she had been watching the morning news and had drawn her own conclusions.

She'd not liked the man, not from her first sight of him, though she'd have been hard pressed to explain exactly what it was that made the hairs on her neck rise. She had always been able to recognize a predator, even those that dressed themselves as saints and lessons learned in childhood had stood her in good stead through adulthood.

"Too clever by half," Elsie Caldwell muttered to herself as she watched the news unfold. "Too eager to boast." She studied Paul Krantz's face as he spoke about the girlfriend he had killed, listened to the recitation of his deeds and misdeeds he claimed his followers had carried out on his behalf and then, as he looked directly into the camera she heard him say:

"And those who have wronged me they will suffer. They will wish themselves in hell because in comparison with what I can do to them, hell will seem like a picnic in the park."

"Bollocks," Elsie Caldwell said, enjoying the explosiveness of the word, but she could not help but recognize the frisson of fear that crept up the length of her spine.

* * *

Ray studied the crime scene images from Tom Pollard's flat. He lay slumped in a corner, as though he'd been backed up there and could retreat no further. His abdomen had been slashed so broadly and so deeply that his intestines lay exposed, fallen into the man's lap. Ray could imagine the stink. He did not have to imagine the blood; it pooled around the body, saturated the clothes, castoff decorated the walls.

Ray studied the castoff blood more closely. This kind of spatter was one he associated more closely with blunt force trauma, the blood thrown from the weapon when the assailant raised it for another blow and he wondered for a moment if the blood was in fact the result or arterial spray. But the pattern wasn't quite right for that either.

Experimentally, Ray stepped back from the table and imagined holding a sharp knife in his hand and then slashing that knife in a wide arc across the body, left to right, right to left, his arm continuing the extravagant arc before falling, to strike again.

He remembered Ashley's description of the incident with the rabbit corpses, of how the two boys and girl had honed their skills — though there was something artificial, almost staged and overdramatic about this method, about this . . . what would you call it? Training process? While he could understand the logic of the additional reach a slashing movement could give as opposed to a straight stabbing, surely even that called for more economy of motion than was evidenced here?

He thought back to the murder of Ruth Edmonson, the young woman bound and displayed in such barbaric fashion, as though Krantz had been presenting a piece of performance art. In Krantz's view impact was everything, Ray thought. How others viewed what he had done. Not just how much pain it caused to his victims but also how much pain and anguish it caused those called on to witness the aftermath.

* * *

The ring on Elsie Caldwell's doorbell took her by surprise. She had been expecting no visitors today and certainly no deliveries. It occurred to her that the police might be back in the building and seen fit to call on her again, but her natural caution, coupled with that heightened sense of self-preservation that had kept her out of a lifetime of trouble, caused her to pause.

On silent feet Elsie Caldwell crept down the hall and prepared to peep through her spyhole before opening the door. She halted a few feet from the door, suddenly aware that something looked wrong, that the narrowed glimpse of light that usually permeated the spyhole was absent. Someone was out there, Elsie thought, and was either blocking the spyhole or was trying to peer through.

That's not going to work, Elsie thought.

Silently she turned around and padded back into the kitchen. She picked up her bag and quietly opened the kitchen window, blessing the fact that she lived on the ground floor but less pleased with the fact that it was still a fair old drop to the ground. She sat on the sill, took a deep breath, and slid.

"Bollocks," she said for the second time that morning as she landed awkwardly, her ankle twisting beneath her and she tipped sideways with all the elegance of a brick wall.

Raw instinct told her that she couldn't just lie there, that she had to get away. Elsie's kitchen looked out onto a side road and across the road was a tiny park where children played on their way home from school. At this time of the morning there was little passing traffic and even the pedestrian school run was long over.

Struggling to her feet, Elsie crossed the road, wincing at every step and swearing softly to herself every time she took weight on the injured ankle. In through the park gate, swinging it closed behind her. Into the bushes beside the gate. She took her phone from her bag and then looked back through the railings at the kitchen window. As she dialled the nines and asked for the police she watched the window, careful to keep from view and conscious that she was going to feel really stupid if the person at her door had just been selling double glazing.

Then, as she spoke to the police officer Elsie caught her breath. "Oh my God. Oh my goodness."

"Madam? Are you all right?"

So shocked was she that it took her a moment to reply. Someone was standing in her kitchen, by the open window, and as Elsie Caldwell suppressed the urge to scream, a woman's head poked out and a woman's head turned to look this way and that up the narrow street.

"I think she's seen me," Elsie whispered.

"Stay where you are. Help is on the way."

But can it get here faster than she can cross the street, Elsie Caldwell wondered. Her ankle hurt abominably, but if it was life or death she could probably manage a little distance. But not fast enough, and besides, where was there to go?

And then she heard it. The loveliest sound Elsie could ever remember hearing. Voices, women's voices and those of young children, shrieking with excitement. Of pushchair wheels and little bicycles. Of the park gate being pushed open and three young women with their assorted offspring crowding through. They spotted her at once. She could see the shock on their faces at the sight of this old lady huddled on the ground.

"Oh my goodness, are you all right?"

"My ankle," Elsie managed to say. "I've hurt my ankle."

By the time the police arrived, Elsie was ensconced on a park bench, her leg raised and one of the young women — Janice, call me Jan —sitting at the other end of the bench and administering fizzy water, biscuits and quiet conversation, while her friends took care of children and swings and turns on the seesaw.

She thinks I'm dotty, Elsie thought. *She thinks I've wandered away from home and had a fall.*

The young woman looked very bemused when the police officer came into the park and made his way over to them.

"Mrs Caldwell?" He smiled, the relief on his face communicating to both Elsie and the young woman.

"Is there something wrong?" Jan asked, her expression now more anxious than concerned.

"I've hurt my ankle," Elsie said, that being the simplest thing to explain.

"Do you think if I help you, you could make it to the car?"

Jan was outraged. "She needs a paramedic, can't you see how swollen it is? The only reason I didn't call an ambulance was because Elsie said she'd already called for help. Oh," she added as it suddenly dawned on her that the help this elderly lady had summoned had not been medical. "Just what is going on here?"

Painfully, Elsie Caldwell slid off the bench. "You've been really kind," she said. "I'm so grateful."

She took the police officer's proffered arm and half limped, half hopped to the park gate. "There was someone in my flat," she said, her voice shaking a little as she remembered the shock and horror of it all. "She meant me harm."

If she had hoped for soothing contradiction, none was forthcoming. A second officer joined them as the first helped her into the car. "Door's been forced," he said. "I've called for backup. Are you all right, Mrs Caldwell?"

"You're saying it was a woman?" the first police officer asked.

"It most certainly was. A woman with short dark hair."

"Do you think you'll be able to give us a description of her?"

Elsie Caldwell smiled, clutched her mobile phone close to her chest. "Oh I can do better than that," she said.

CHAPTER 24

Nadine Carrington lived just a few doors away from a short run of shops; a newsagent, a small grocer's and a launderette. It had become a habit that she'd call into the newsagent and buy a paper and maybe some chocolate before she went out. She had bought the tiny house she now lived in partly because it had a good-sized back garden, but also for the off-road parking at the front and because she quite fancied being able to nip to the shops whenever she wanted.

She had just come out of the shop, having exchanged a short conversation with the owner and collected her morning paper, chocolate biscuits, bread and milk, and was in the act of fumbling for her house keys, intending to drop her shopping off before getting in the car when something made her look up, someone speaking her name. The voice was familiar and it was not a voice you expected to hear outside this small shop, on her quiet street on a Saturday morning.

She looked up in surprise, opened her mouth to speak and then gasped in shock and fell heavily to the ground, shopping and house keys falling with her.

* * *

The instruction had been to bring Elsie Caldwell straight to the police station and a first-aider had been summoned to look at her foot and ankle to see if she needed to go to the hospital. Her ankle was now bandaged and raised on a chair and the first-aider was pretty sure it was just a sprain. Elsie Caldwell was of the opinion that she had more important things to do than go for an x-ray and when Beckett arrived was busy explaining to both Ray and Eloise, and the constable who had "rescued her" just what had happened at her flat.

She had good, clear photographs of the woman who had stuck her head out of the window.

"So how did she get into my flat, did she break the door down? I thought I'd put enough locks on the thing."

"You had," Beckett told her. "We're not sure what she used, but she broke the panel. We're guessing that she had something like the hand-held battering ram that our tactical support units use to break doors down."

"Not exactly something you can buy from your local hardware store," Elsie commented a little sourly. "Would it not have made a lot of noise?"

"It would, but probably just one brief bang. It's likely anybody in the other flats that heard it would have thought it came from outside."

"Most of them are at work anyway." Elsie sighed. "Did she do any damage to my flat?"

"Apart from the door, no. She must've realized you had gone out of the window, but then she must have seen the women and children coming down the street and decided that retreat was the best option."

"And this is because he knows I identified him, that you were able to identify him because of what I said?"

"Either that or just because he knew you were Ashley's friend," Ray told her. "It seems he doesn't need much of an excuse."

A quiet tap on the door took Beckett away for a moment.
"I'm cold," Elsie said.

"You need checking over properly," Ray told her. "It's going to start to hit you now, what happened, the full shock of it. You're going to feel absolutely terrible for a while."

She laughed weakly. "Well thank you for that assessment," and then Elsie Caldwell burst into tears.

* * *

A few minutes later Elsie had departed for the hospital in the care of two constables and Ray and Eloise had gone in search of Beckett. He was on the telephone in the main enquiry room and Ray waited impatiently until he put the phone down.

"So what happened now?"

"Earlier this morning Nadine Carrington was stabbed to death outside a shop just close to her home. No theatrics this time, just a straight stab wound. Witnesses say that she was in conversation with a man and the next minute she was on the floor and the man got in a car and drove away. They say she definitely seemed to know him. She was dead before the paramedics reached her."

"Christ," Ray said. "Who's next?"

"There's more. She had her door keys in her hand, they fell on the floor when she did, so it seemed she intended to go back home and drop off her shopping. Police officers on scene went into the house and it very soon became obvious she'd had someone staying with her. A man."

"Paul Krantz," Ray said.

Beckett nodded. "It seems likely."

Eloise had gone across to the board to look at the photographs of Krantz's closest associates, the four that had disappeared when he had broken out of jail. One was Rob Holt, there were two other men and one woman. "Suzette Preece," Eloise said. "That's the woman who broke into Elsie's flat. I recognize her from the phone photo, she changed her hair colour, she's naturally quite grey and now she's dyed it a much darker brown but it's certainly her."

"Do we have the printouts from the phone yet?" Beckett asked, and a minute later they appeared. The image from Elsie's phone was placed beside that of Suzette Preece. It was definitely the same woman.

"So what do we know about this Preece woman?" Ray asked. Then, "Hold on a minute."

He picked up a copy of the phone photograph and went back down the hall to where the collage on the walls of Woods End house had been recreated.

The others followed him.

"Yes, she's here." Ray pointed to a news clipping on the first wall. It was a group photo of a social event, everyone dressed up in long frocks and bowties and gathered around some kind of trophy.

Eloise read the caption beneath the photo. "The garden committee celebrates best kept village, floral display," she said. "Not exactly what you'd expect."

"Paul Krantz was perfectly capable of leading an ordinary life," Ray pointed out. "We don't, I think, know much about Robert Holt yet; he seems to have been really under the radar."

Beckett nodded agreement. "He's something of a ghost. But it's no great surprise to find Suzette Preece turn up in a press clipping like this. She was a doctor's receptionist, member of the local WI, regular church goer, involved in organizing the local pony club events. In short, a pillar of her local community. The village she lives in is only a half-dozen miles from Woods End. She is somewhat older than Krantz."

"So how did they meet?"

"That we're not sure about, in fact it's possible they didn't meet face to face. According to other members of Krantz's little support group, she followed the trial avidly and contacted them after he'd gone to prison because she couldn't believe he was guilty. We know she did a lot of the admin for the early appeal, nothing technical, just organizing mailouts and then email campaigns and writing the odd press release. Then about three years in, she seems to have started writing to Krantz in person though it's not clear if he instigated that contact or she did. She was thoroughly embedded in his support team by then, even more avidly insistent that the man was innocent."

"So how does that square with the fact that he has just announced to the world that he was guilty of everything as charged and more beside. How come she's still cheerleading." Ray wanted to know.

"Some form of cognitive dissonance, I suppose," Eloise commented. "It's not uncommon for people to be able to hold opposite views or to be able to apply contradictory information to their lives and not see the contradiction. Or even if they see it they find a way to balance it in their own heads. How many meat eaters do you know that are devoted to their pets?"

"She's the oldest of the four," Ray commented. "We know that Robert Holt is the same age as Paul Krantz. Then there's Philip Carstairs, who we now know worked with him and alibied him on at least a couple of occasions."

"And the most high-profile member of the entire crew, Tom Beresford, who was on his original defensive team. He was involved in the early appeals for the last few rounds seems to have backed off from the whole thing. As often happens with these groups, large groups of people get enthused and aggravated by something to start with and eventually this dwindles to a few core members and the mix changes. Beresford is on record as saying that he had come round to the idea of Krantz's guilt over time, hence his distancing from the whole thing."

"And we are assuming that Tom Beresford has just taken himself off, and isn't lying in a ditch somewhere?" Ray asked.

"Both possibilities have to be explored," Dave Beckett agreed. "We know that these three, plus presumably Rob Holt, left home, disappeared from view, had no communication with friends or family from around the day Ashley Summers was abducted. All were eventually reported missing, but as all lived alone, and all had an excuse to disappear at least for the initial few days, it wasn't immediately noted that they had gone. Suzette Preece had gone on holiday and no one expected to see or hear from her for a couple of weeks. It was only when she didn't go back to work that alarm bells began to ring. She was always described as ultra-reliable.

"Tom Beresford had gone off on one of his fishing trips and it wasn't unusual for him to be out of touch for several days when he did that. Again, he lived alone, was divorced, no kids, no notice he was gone until he didn't turn up for a court appearance. His client was miffed to say the least, they'd already complained that Beresford hadn't been in touch to make final arrangements. The firm had covered for that, but it didn't initially seem to have raised any major concern. It turns out that his bills have been paid for the next few months, his house had been locked up and his milk delivery cancelled. So on balance I would say left of his own accord rather than being removed by Krantz, but we can't be certain that."

"And Philip Carstairs. From what I remember, he walked out of work on the Friday afternoon that Ashley Summers' flat was cleared out, didn't turn up on a Monday morning and hasn't been seen since," Ray said. "He still worked at the same company that Krantz had been working for when we arrested him."

"So where have they all been, and where has Robert Holt been living all of these years?" Eloise wanted to know.

Dave Beckett shrugged. "At least we now have some sense of where Paul Krantz was hiding out for at least some of the time," he said. "That's a little further on than we were this morning."

"That hardly balances the books." Ray's response was a little sour. "Two more dead and one surviving by pure luck. If she'd been followed into that park, Elsie would have had no chance."

"We need to talk to Nora Blaine," he continued. "It's likely she is next on the list and it's also likely she was telling the truth from the start, that she was not involved in assisting Krantz."

"She's been moved into protective custody, and I've arranged an interview for this afternoon." Beckett glanced at his watch, and reflexively Ray did the same. He was shocked to find that it was still only 1 p.m. So much had happened in so short a time he felt he'd already endured a long enough day.

CHAPTER 25

It had been agreed that Beckett should be the one to ask the questions but that Ray could sit in, as a courtesy, and also because Beckett recognized his observations would be useful. Nora Blaine looked exhausted, Ray thought, and it was evident that she was furious about the situation she found herself in. That they were suddenly doubting her guilt seemed to be something she found almost funny. He suspected that she was at breaking point and doubted that she'd ever go back to working as a prison officer, even should circumstances now allow it.

"I'm sorry she's dead, I'm horrified about it, but I kept bloody warning her that she was getting too close, that she was being taken in by him. She was all 'oh he's changed, he's a nice man really,' and she should have known better. She's been involved with people like him before, she had this boyfriend that was totally controlling, she couldn't even leave the house without his saying so. She got over that, she seemed to be doing fine, and then Krantz came along. Suddenly it was like she couldn't get enough of him."

"And yet she was telling everybody that it was you that was getting involved."

Nora Blaine nodded sadly. "It got to a point where whatever I said nobody listened. She was a senior officer, everybody assumed that she knew what she was talking about. I'd not been there that long, at the Grange, so of course everybody listened to her. I was the outsider."

"You claim that Krantz sought you out and that he made a big thing of being seen in conversation with you?" Beckett said.

"All the bloody time. I mean you do get that, and when it happens you report it, and generally you get shifted or they get shifted so that it doesn't happen anymore. Or when staffing is tight you grit your teeth and get on with it and that's easier to do in a high-security jail. Everyone's at arm's length and you're not left alone but everything is so much more casual at the Grange. I mean that was why I wanted to go there, they were doing fantastic work and to be honest I was sick of working in a place where I was just focused on warehousing. And at first it was great, I was able to organize so much educational stuff, sort out so much social stuff. The idea is that people went out able to cope with being in the outside world. That they would be employable but also socialized."

"And when did Krantz start to target you?"

"I'd been there maybe five or six weeks. There'd been a drama group before, but the guy that ran it had left and nobody picked it up. We canvassed opinion to see if there be any interest and there were about half a dozen guys who thought it might be something they'd like to do. I know it's not many but you've got to start somewhere, and a lot of these things start with just half a dozen core members and then grow. Anyway, Krantz got involved and next thing I know there's thirty or forty people turned up, he's convinced a whole load of people to give it a go, to support the new initiative and initially I was grateful. He was clearly popular and clearly had a lot of influence, and once you get someone like that onside it really makes a difference. It didn't take long to realize he had ulterior motives of course, but then usually they do. Suck up to the management, you get an easier time of it, or so some people think. Actually it just makes most of us suspicious." She laughed uncomfortably.

"But it's hard to complain about somebody being too cooperative," Ray said.

"Well, yes, especially somewhere like the Grange where the *raison d'être* is about cooperation and empathy and learning to be a social being." She rolled her eyes. "Saying it out loud sounds like I'm spouting the party line, but actually I believe in it. If you lock people up without any hope of rehabilitation, education, or socialization, well, like I said before, all you're doing is warehousing. So I was sort of stuck in this position, if I complained about him, well, it would sound downright stupid. I did report my worries and my anxieties to Nadine, it turns out she was just the wrong person to tell them to."

"It looks as though he was staying at her house."

"He was what? What all the time he was missing?"

"That we don't know."

"But if she was sheltering him, why did he go and stab her? Did she threaten to give him up or something?"

"Again, we don't know, but it seems unlikely. Maybe she just outlived her usefulness."

Nora was staring at him, a look of utter disbelief on her face. "Look, Nadine was obviously being stupid, but she didn't deserve that. I can't imagine what would lead her to . . ."

"Tom Pollard, what did Krantz do that set his back up so much? He obviously didn't trust the change that everyone else was applauding."

Nora shook her head. "I don't think it was any one thing, but Tom, he'd been around the block more than a few times. Everyone said he was old school, even old-fashioned, but he was a good, honest man and if he believed somebody was genuinely trying to change he would do everything he could for them. But Krantz just rubbed him up the wrong way from the beginning. He didn't believe Krantz should be at the Grange. Apparently there was some psychologist who had recommended that Krantz should be kept in a high-security unit but they were ignored, and Tom got wind of that somewhere and was trying to get a reassessment done. It wasn't that Tom was vindictive, but he knew, same as we all did, that in a place like the Grange it only takes one person to skew the balance. It's a very fragile environment."

"Can I ask something?" Ray said. Beckett gestured for him to go ahead.

"Did Krantz ever mention a house that he used to stay in as a kid, and a brother and sister that were the same age as him?"

She looked blank. "He never really talked about his childhood, not even in group therapy. We didn't run those, a psychologist came into do that, but there'd always be an officer sitting in, just in case of trouble. I remember one time they were all asked to think about their earliest happy memory and when it got to his turn he just got up and walked out."

"And were there any consequences from that?"

"I wasn't in the following session, but, yeah, he was challenged on it. He apparently said something about if he had any happy memories then he would share them. Why?"

"It's a line of investigation," Beckett said.

It's the heart of the investigation, Ray thought.

CHAPTER 26

When Paul Krantz had absconded eight months before, those who had kept in contact with him through his prison term were of course examined and in some cases their houses were searched. There had been absolutely no indication that Krantz had either been in touch with them since he'd left the Grange or had given them a heads-up about his intentions.

It had really only become apparent during the second round of interviews that Krantz had his favourites within the organization. Someone had mentioned it, others had been asked for confirmation, and the intelligence had developed from there. It was, Ray thought, as though everybody assumed that it was common knowledge and so it wasn't worth talking about. Interestingly Rob Holt had not been mentioned by name, although there were a couple of people who had made reference to a childhood friend that they thought Krantz was still in touch with. That in itself was interesting, seeing as how reluctant Krantz was to talk about his childhood or his teenage years.

In the second round of interviews since Krantz had so dramatically resurfaced, the investigation team had probed specifically about those closest to him, referencing the names that had surfaced eight months before. Philip Carstairs, who had worked with Krantz, had made no secret of being in touch with him. His employer was aware of this, as were various of his work colleagues. It was well known that Phil Carstairs did not believe in Krantz's guilt and thought he'd had a raw deal.

Looking at the timeline it seemed that Carstairs had been in work as usual on the day Ashley Summers had allegedly moved out of her flat but had called in sick the following Monday. He had not been heard from since. Suzette Preece had left for her holiday a couple of days before that, and before Krantz's involvement in the Summers' abduction was known. According to the statement she had made when Krantz had absconded, she'd had no contact with his support group for at least a couple of years, and this had been borne out by most of the others they had spoken to. A handful had thought that she and Krantz were still in touch and that certainly she had been one of the most tireless organizers in the early years.

Tom Beresford had simply not returned from his fishing trip. When asked about his involvement with Krantz, the law firm he worked for simply told the enquiry that of course he'd been in contact. He'd organized the appeal. So far as they were concerned all contact had ceased when the second appeal failed. According to others involved in the Paul Krantz fan club he had at one time been very active and there was a consensus that he still held to his client's innocence, whatever he might say publicly.

In light of their names having come up previously, another round of search warrants had been applied for and the urgency of that request had been emphasized by the revelation that Krantz seemed to have been staying with Nadine Carrington. When they left Nora Blaine that afternoon, Beckett received a call from the team searching the address of the lawyer, Tom Beresford, and a half hour later he and Ray arrived at a rather odd-looking, red-brick Edwardian house, set back from the road and surrounded by a strangely imposing garden wall.

The house itself was tall rather than large overall. It gave the impression of being stretched upwards rather than settling into the garden, Ray thought.

Entering, they were met with a tiled hall and a central staircase. Rooms off to either side. A narrow corridor led to the back of the house and into a kitchen diner that ran the full width and backed onto a rather lovely conservatory that looked to be period with the house. A door beneath the stairs led down to a tiled basement with windows set high up in one wall. Ray guessed this had been the original kitchen, when the space was occupied by servants who, presumably, didn't need a view.

Some of these details Ray saw for himself, others were shown to him by the photographer who was busy documenting the scene and who Ray chatted to while Becket was being briefed by the sergeant heading up the search team.

Ray followed Beckett up the stairs and onto the top floor and into what had probably been servants' quarters. One room was set out as a home office and two officers were involved in boxing up paperwork and laptops. The second room on the top floor was larger and gave Ray the impression of two connecting rooms having been knocked into one. One part was set out like a living room, with two easy chairs, an old-fashioned bureau desk, an open fire that had clearly seen recent use. A tiny drop-leaf table had been set beside the window, with a dining chair set beside it. An equally tiny improvised kitchen area beyond that. Table top oven, single ring hob, electric kettle. It looked, Ray thought, rather like a student bedsit. The bedroom led off, separated by a heavy curtain rather than a door and housed a single bed, neatly made, another easy chair and a narrow bookcase. There were no books on the shelves, instead a stack of what looked like old school exercise books. Donning gloves, Beckett opened one on top of the stack. Ray leaned in and read the first few lines.

"Robert Holt's stories," he said. "The ones he read to Ashley Summers."

* * *

178

Beckett hated press conferences, and Ray could sympathize. He watched from the sidelines as Dave Beckett took his place in front of the hall crammed full of local, national and international media. Krantz had caught the imagination of the world, Ray thought. This man who was attacking in so many places at once that the police seemed unable to keep up with him.

The room fell silent as Beckett took his seat. "I'm not here to make much of a statement," he said. "I'm here to appeal for help. You all have up-to-date images of Paul Krantz but we have reason to believe that there are others who are helping him and that we have now identified. I would like these people to come forward and I would ask for help from the public in finding them."

Ray heard the buzz in the room. A hand was raised and the question asked that they were all wondering. "You say these people are definitely helping him, you're not putting out an appeal for them as possible witnesses?"

"I'm saying this has gone beyond that. Now it might still be they have been caught up in Krantz's activities and are as much victims as those he has already killed and threatened. And make no mistake, once he has finished with people, once they are no longer of use to him, they can expect absolutely no mercy. The young woman who was stabbed in the street this morning, undoubtedly believed that she was doing the right thing in helping him and when she was no longer of use that was how he dealt with her."

"She's being named locally as Nadine Carrington," someone said. "A prison officer at Willingham Grange. Could you comment on that, Chief Inspector?"

"For the moment, no. Now there are four names I want to give you, together with the most recent photographs we have been able to acquire. One of these, Robert Holt, is already in custody but we are trying to trace his movements over the last weeks and months. He is believed to have been a childhood friend of Paul Krantz and also believed to be the man who held Ashley Summers prisoner after her abduction by Paul Krantz."

His image flashed up on the screen behind Beckett's head. Ray glanced around the room; Beckett, in this very unorthodox press conference, had grabbed everybody's attention. The fact that the press conference was also going out live would undoubtedly mean that they'd be overwhelmed by calls in a very short time and Ray himself had been seconded to man phones. This was now a question of all hands on deck. But Beckett had decided that this was worth the risk and had with some difficulty persuaded the higher-ups to sanction it.

"The second person of interest is Suzette Preece." Briefly Beckett gave some background information and appealed for the woman to come forward if she had found herself caught up in something which she could no longer control. Ray could just imagine the consternation that would be felt by friends and neighbours of this very respectable older woman.

"Philip Carstairs worked with Paul Krantz some years ago, before he was imprisoned for the murder of his girlfriend. According to friends and colleagues he genuinely believed that Krantz was innocent and it may be that he is trying to help a friend because he believed that is what was right. Mr Carstairs, if you can hear me, you now know that Paul Krantz was not innocent, he has declared as much to the world's media and you are aiding and abetting a murderer.

"The fourth person of interest is the lawyer who worked on the appeal for Krantz and it may well be again he has been drawn into this with the best of intentions and is perhaps now looking for a way to get out. Mr Thomas Beresford, if you are hearing this then please contact the investigating team. We can assure you that you will be given a fair hearing."

There was a restlessness in the room now, everybody knew that this was going out live, but even so they wanted to report back, to find out what background information they could lay hands on, to decide what particular spin could be put on this latest intelligence. They had come expecting platitudes, to be told that there were various lines of enquiry ongoing. They had not expected this.

Beckett was aware of all of these reactions, Ray could see that. He held his hands for quiet and then said, "I do also want to make a witness appeal. There is a woman known to Krantz when they were both teenagers and who may know more about his actions than she realizes. We have no reason to suspect that she is involved but we do ask that if she is hearing this that she does contact us. Kit, please get in touch."

The questions were immediate. Who was Kit, how was she involved, but Beckett had finished. He'd given them enough to be going on with, more than enough, Ray felt. This was a career-defining moment for him, good or ill. It would only be a matter of time — a very short time — before the media identified Kit as Kit Holt, sister to Robert, and he hoped fervently that she was somewhere neither they nor Krantz could get to her. It was one hell of a risk putting all of this out there.

As he and Beckett got in the car, he said, "If you need a job after all of this, I'm sure we can fit you in at Flowers-Mahoney."

Beckett laughed grimly. "If this goes tits up," he said, "I might well be taking you up on that."

* * *

Strange as it would later seem, she had gone through the entire day in total ignorance of what Paul Krantz had done. She had got in from her shift at 7 a.m., made tea and toast and fed the cat and then gone straight to bed. It was therefore late afternoon before she heard anything about the events of the day.

She had no shifts booked for the next few days so planned a quiet evening of TV, a good — normal — night's sleep and the next day of shopping, doing chores and then an hour or so with friends.

That was all about to change.

Kit turned on the TV for the evening news. She had cooked dinner and sat with it on a tray, the cat curled up beside her on the sofa. "So who is killing who today?" she asked him. It was her usual question. In Kit's opinion only the names and places seemed to change, the violence and unrest stayed the same day after day. She listened at first with casual interest to the press conference and then in increasing horror. Hearing Rob's name and then Paul's was like a punch in the gut and then at the end, when the detective spoke hers it was like a great, cold wave, knocking her sideways and leaving her gasping for breath.

She stood up, the tray crashing to the floor and the immediate urge to run as far and as fast as possible almost overwhelming. The cat meowed at her and then, because he was a cat, he jumped off the sofa to see if there was anything worth scavenging among the mess on the floor. Kit stared down at him and then her legs gave way and she slumped back on the sofa. What the fuck just happened?

For the next while she watched the television obsessively, surfing channel to channel and wondering what to do. Inevitably they reprised the original case and she remembered the horror she had felt back then when she had heard his name on the television and what he'd been accused of. She recognized the detective, Ray Flowers, she had followed that original case and read everything she could about the trial that followed. A more recent photograph of Flowers showed that he had scars on his face that had not been there before and she wondered what on earth had happened to him. For one terrible moment she wondered if Paul Krantz had been responsible for that as well and then remembered that Krantz would have been in prison.

What to do, Kit wondered, what to do? She had spent twenty years being someone else, Kit becoming Katherine and Holt becoming Cheney, for no particular reason than she had happened to hear the name on the day she'd had to come up with something. But she had grown into it, become Katherine — Kat — Cheney, an agency nurse with a little house, and a rather large cat, and a group of friends that might as well have not known she existed twenty years ago.

She had made up a false childhood, created a previous life that she could talk about with as much conviction as if it had really happened. She occasionally even went off to visit distant relatives, in other parts of the country. Relatives that had never existed but who nevertheless sent her birthday cards and presents at Christmas. She was someone else now.

So what to do, should she do anything at all?

By late evening she was calm enough to clear up the mess, make herself some tea and sit down to consider. By now she had learned about Ashley Summers, about the death of Inspector Nightingale, about the more recent deaths of the prison officers Tom Pollard and Nadine Carrington and she, like probably half the population, was madly Googling everyone else whose name was even mentioned in passing.

And she still had not decided what to do.

* * *

Paul Krantz had also watched the press conference, in his case with growing anger. He knew that Rob had failed the task he had been set, but had not known he had been identified. That was not in the script.

Krantz himself had taken care of Nadine Carrington and Phil had done a good job in dealing with Tom Pollard, but the others had let him down big time. Suzette, what the hell was she thinking? All she had to do was deal with one stupid old lady. An old lady who had brought this down on herself because she couldn't keep her nose out.

And Beresford, where the hell was he? Thinking about it, he should have realized that a bloody lawyer was no use to anyone. He'd managed to run Tom Pollard off the road that day, but then he had buggered off somewhere and neither hide nor hair been seen of him since. Krantz would catch up with him, and then he would be truly sorry.

Krantz picked up one of the mobile phones arrayed in front of him, there was only one number programmed into it. Suzette sounded truly nervous when she answered, apologizing yet again. He silenced her quickly. "That's done. Forget it. I've another job for you. Don't fuck up again."

* * *

It was the early hours of the morning when Ray finally got to bed. Calls were coming thick and fast and most of them he knew would be utterly useless. He felt sorry for the collators, sifting and cross-referencing and separating the wheat from the chaff. He called Sarah.

"Did I wake you?"

"Not really, I was just dozing. Well, that was dramatic."

"The press conference? It was not the usual, that's for sure. We have to hope it gets results. How is everyone doing?"

"Well, my boss called me this evening, having noticed you on the television and assumed my sudden illness must have something do with this case. So that's my cover blown, but I'm taking next week off so you better have it sorted by next weekend."

"Do my best."

"Maggie has decided to carry on as usual, so tomorrow we have the mothers' union in the morning, and I forget what in the afternoon. I'm just making tea for them all. I think she's right though, having people she knows in and out of the house will make her feel better if nothing else. John is of course just forging ahead, but I got to meet the Bishop."

"The Bishop, should I be impressed?"

"Bishop Charlie, he's nice. Doesn't quite know what to make of all of this, but came to give his moral support, which I suppose is good. The kids are taking it all in their stride, the only thing they're complaining about is that they were supposed to go across to Evie's place to play with all her grandkids, great grandkids or whatever they are and of course that's now been put off."

"So we'd definitely better get this sorted by next weekend, then."

"Absolutely. Nathan is restless, he's gone back to the cottage a couple of times to check on things and make sure his neighbour's okay. His neighbour was there when Robert Holt got arrested of course so Nathan's worried in case that comes to Krantz's attention. And he keeps going out to patrol the perimeter."

Ray laughed. "Is that what he said?"

"No, that would be very un-Nathan wouldn't it. All I know is he leaves and then suddenly reappears having checked that everything is all right. I tried watching him from the bedroom window but once he is out in the garden or the field you can't see a thing. Somehow he manages it without tripping the security lights."

If he can do it, Ray thought, *perhaps someone else might*. He had seen Nathan in action, he moved like a shadow but — "I might get George set something up, just in case."

"Ray, we have cameras everywhere, we have security lights everywhere, Nathan is just Nathan."

Ray yawned, he supposed she was probably right. "We'd better both get some sleep," he said. "I miss you."

"I miss you too and I want to go home. So—"

"So we'd better get this sorted by next weekend," Ray finished for her.

CHAPTER 27

The morning news was still full of Krantz and the press conference, Ray reckoned, had been played in part or in full
every half hour since the night before. He realized that was a
slight exaggeration, but not by much.

He met Beckett for breakfast in the police station can-
teen and was struck by how haggard he looked. "Anything
useful coming overnight?"

"Too early to tell. Sightings of all or any from Aberystwyth
to Aberdeen. The media have of course made the link between
Kit Holt and the Kit that we appealed for last night, they've
been chatting to the Beales and the people at the riding stables.
And there's a lot of speculation about the bodies we found, the
assumption being that this is the parents who lived at Woods
End with two kids all those years ago. We knew that would
happen. We also got the expected mix of people who went
missing in the area in the past three decades or so. People concerned that the bodies might be their missing relatives."

Ray nodded. All very much what was expected.
"Anything from Beresford's neighbours? Did they know he
had someone staying with him?"

"They spotted a young man coming and going, but only
occasionally. They didn't see Beresford all that often, he'd

come home, go to work, say hello in passing and have the occasional conversation about the weather. At weekends they often saw him going off with his rods. They knew about his involvement with Paul Krantz of course, or at least those who had lived in the street long enough. But nothing very useful. A couple of people called in about Suzette Preece, saying they thought she'd been behaving oddly lately, very absent-minded and distant, but it's easy to be wise after the fact and again no actual useful information from that."

Ray nodded. "Eloise and I will be looking over the notebooks this morning, that seems the best use of our time unless you want me back on the phones?"

"We've got enough bodies answering phones. No, I agree; it's possible, given your previous involvement with Krantz, that you might recognize something in the notebooks that is relevant. And Eloise might uncover something that helps us with the psychology of all this. Rob Holt is still refusing to speak though apparently he did eat and drink yesterday evening, so I suppose that's progress."

"If he spent all his life in Krantz's shadow it's going to be very difficult for him to break out from that and talk about it," Ray said. "We don't know what influence Krantz had when he was younger. We don't know who was responsible for those two skeletons in the garden. Do we have cause of death yet."

"The woman had a broken neck, and there are indications of stab wounds on the male skeleton, marks on the ribs suggest a long thin blade of some sort. As far as an absolute identification is concerned, no, we don't have that, but it seems most likely that it's Celeste and Robert Holt senior."

"So someone who could get up close and personal, not have to keep arm's length and slashy," Ray commented, remembering the passage that Ashley recalled having been read to her about the practicing of knife skills. "That would fit with one of the kids committing the murder. Rob or Krantz, perhaps even the mysterious Kit."

"As yet we have absolutely nothing tying Kit Holt to this. But I wish she'd come forward. Anything we can find out about Krantz's childhood, or what happened at that farm might prove very useful."

Ray drained his tea. "Hopefully there'll be something in the notebooks," he said.

* * *

It was hard to get any sense of continuity. It was almost as though Rob had picked up one book, written a few passages, then moved on to another before returning to the first. After a while Ray got up and taped a long strip of A4 sheets of printer paper together and started to draw up a kind of timeline. Eloise added to it but after a couple of hours there were so many crossings out and so much reordering was required that she began to transcribe what they had onto another timeline, leaving the reading to Ray.

It was a strange set of notebooks, Ray thought. Some seemed to have been written by Rob, some was written in third person and might have been put together by Paul. Or it was written by Rob but from an external perspective, as though he was distancing himself or dictating. The effect was oddly vertiginous.

Ray reread the last passage and then went back and read it again. This he was certain was the last entry Rob made. "Listen to this," he said.

"It was dark when we left in Paul's car. I sat in the front seat and Kit sat in the back. Kit was crying and she didn't want to leave, she thought we should have gone to the police. Paul was angry with her, he'd been angry with her for days and he had locked her in the cellar when she wouldn't stop crying. He said he'd come to help us and that he'd helped us and that she was just being ungrateful. He said she was being disloyal.

"We'd been driving for about an hour when he stopped the car and he told us both to get out. Kit was scared and she was shivering and I wasn't sure what was going on. I'd not seen him look like this before and we were in the middle of nowhere and it was very dark with no moon. He told us to stand in front of the car, in the light from the headlamps. The lights were bright and it was hard to see. Kit held a hand up to

*shield her eyes and Paul slapped it down. He had a knife in his hand
and he gave it to me and then he told Kit to take off her coat and her
shirt. And at first she wouldn't do it but he was so angry and I was so
scared that in the end she did. And then he told me to cut her, he said
he didn't care where, and he didn't care if I killed her not, but this was
to prove that I was loyal because she obviously wasn't.*

"And in the end I did. And now she's gone."

"Did he kill her?" Eloise wondered.

"Hard to know. It sounds final, whatever happened.
They would have been kids when this happened, late teens
if we are to assume that it was taking place at that point that
Paul Krantz left home and broke all contact with his family.
Their parents are now dead, and I think it's safe to assume
that one of them if not both were responsible for that. There
seems to be no clue in the notebooks as to the circumstances.
If there'd been abuse, would Rob not have mentioned it?"

"I don't know," Eloise said. "What he chooses to record
is often contradictory, totally out of order. There is no linear
narrative here at all and what he records seems to have been
selected because . . . Well, actually, I don't know why. It obviously has significance for him. I wonder if it would be worth
reading these passages to him to see if we can elicit a response?"

"Only if you can do it from another room, last time
we elicited a response you saw what happened then. He
half blinded the man he was responding to, I doubt DCI
Blatchford is ever going to get over that."

"Believe me, I've no intention of taking any risks. But if
there's a chance it might stimulate some other kind of response
then it's worth a try. From what I've heard he's eating and
drinking again so he's taking notice of his surroundings and
he might be approachable."

"Well, we'll talk to Beckett, see what can be arranged,"
Ray said.

CHAPTER 28

At Woods End Farm, the briar patch had been fully excavated but no more bodies found. The search of the house was now coming to an end and by the evening it was expected the CSI team would have packed up their gear and left.

Where the farm track joined the narrow road, the media had initially assembled and the local police who were managing the traffic had ushered them down the hill to the George and Dragon. The landlord was now making the most of the unexpected crowd. When the local constable told the media that there was nothing to see he was speaking quite literally; nothing at all could be seen from the road, not even the roof of the house.

However the media weren't doing so badly; curiosity brought villagers to drink in the pub, some of whom remembered when the house had been inhabited, some of whom even remembered the Holt family. Gossip and speculation made up for the lack of anything to actually look at.

It had become apparent to the team at the farm that members of the media that couldn't view the scene from one direction were trying another and on the ridge two men appeared, late morning, and it turned out they had a drone. The drone was an impressive size, larger than the crime scene manager, Eric, had normally seen, but he assumed it must be carrying a miniature video camera. He wasn't too bothered by this; the area where the bodies had been found was still tented and all they were going to see, even with decent drone footage, would be bunny-suited CSIs walking backwards and forwards between the house and one of the two vans, carrying samples in large plastic boxes.

A little later one of the CSIs spotted someone else on the ridge but assumed it was just another journalist. After a moment or two the woman she had seen disappeared from view and she radioed to one of the local constables on watch closer to the road, that it was possible a woman was on her way down to the farm. Could they intervene.

The drone had gone up again and it occurred to the CSI that they too had noticed the woman and were just as curious about her.

The CSI watched as the drone hovered above a clump of trees and then a moment later the woman emerged. She wasn't dressed for country walking, she appeared to be wearing a neat blue skirt and a crisp white blouse and, as she drew closer, the CSI noted court shoes. She called out to the crime scene manager, "Eric, something's off here," and a moment later she realized what it was. The woman had a shotgun and had raised it to her shoulder and was about to fire.

She and Eric both shouted to their colleagues at the same moment and by the time the first cartridge had been fired, everyone had either hit the ground or was taking cover behind one of the vans. The sound of the shot had brought police officers running. They too hit the deck when the second was fired. Eric, and one of the constables, both country lads, knew that she'd have to reload before she could fire again and a moment later they were both on their feet running at her, taking an oblique angle just in case she was the world's quickest loader.

It was only seconds later that they had the woman on the ground, had wrestled the shotgun from her and no doubt given some fantastic footage to the guy flying the drone, Eric thought.

"It's that woman from the telly," someone said. "That woman whose pictures they showed, Suzette something."

Everyone's attention had been so focused on the assailant with the shotgun they were utterly unprepared for what happened next. There was a crash, a bang like a small explosion and suddenly there was a fire in the house. Flames leaping at the ragged, moth-eaten curtains and immediately after, chasing across the floor.

A glance at the ridge showed the two men running away and Eric realized that they had crashed the drone into the house and that the drone had been carrying something that had exploded and started the fire.

"Is everybody out, is there anyone left in there?" This was all he was concerned about. He breathed a massive sigh of relief when it turned out that all his crew were safe and his next thought was to get the vans out of the area, just in case the fire spread. They filled buckets and anything else they could carry from the pump but the effort was pretty futile and by the time the fire brigade arrived, the fire tender clunking and churning its way across the field, the roof was ablaze and there was nothing anyone could do.

The woman they had identified as Suzette Preece was taken away. She hadn't spoken a word, neither had she resisted when they had handcuffed her and put her in the car. It seemed as though all the fight had gone out of her. She had completed her task and that was that.

Thankfully no one had been hurt.

"Was there much left to do in the house," Beckett asked once he had established that important fact.

"No, we would have been packed up by the end of the day." The crime scenes manager's voice kept breaking up. He was apparently walking across the field, and the signal was intermittent. "Sally spotted the woman coming down the hill and she thought she looked off, but she didn't realize how off until she opened fire. Frankly it didn't look as though she knew how to handle the gun properly, it was like she had just been taught to point-and-shoot and hope for the best but she could still have done some damage."

"Time to be thankful for small mercies I suppose," Beckett said. "But why set fire to the house, if you've gathered all the evidence? Krantz must know how long your team has been there, what the hell were they hoping to hide."

"Could be that he just wanted to cause maximum inconvenience. It could be just a show of strength."

"Very possible," Beckett agreed.

"Okay, I'm standing upon the ridge close to where we saw them. I'll comb the area but from the first glance it doesn't look as if they've left anything behind apart from some flattened grass. No tyre tracks, nothing on the road that I can see, but I'll work the scene just in case. And I'm sending everybody else back to base, they're all shaken up and who can blame them."

"You shouldn't be there alone," Becket warned.

"I won't be. I've got a couple of officers up here with me and a car at the end of the lane. But I'm not putting my people in the line of fire, that's not what they signed up for."

"Apparently the fire brigade are still monitoring the scene," Dave Beckett told Ray and Eloise. "They're letting the house burn itself out. They're currently just ensuring it doesn't catch anywhere else so are focusing their efforts on damping down the surrounding area. It's not easy getting sufficient resources across that field and there is nothing more they can do for the building."

"Did the CSI team mention a cellar or a basement?" Ray asked.

"I don't think so. DCI Blatchford didn't say anything about the cellar either. Why?"

"Because we came across the mention of one in Rob Holt's notebooks. About Kit Holt being locked up in the cellar by Paul Krantz."

Beckett got back onto the phone and it was confirmed that no cellar had been found. No sign that there had ever been an entrance into a cellar at least not from inside the house.

"They ripped up the floorboards in the downstairs rooms, so you would have imagined any kind of basement would be spotted if it was there," he said. "Could Rob Holt have been referring to somewhere else? Or could he have been making it up?"

"I have no idea," Ray said resignedly. "But we think we've established a timeline for the events he's written down. And we think it's possible that Kit Holt could be dead."

CHAPTER 29

If they had hoped to get any useful information out of Suzette Preece they were to be disappointed. She had remained totally silent in the police car and maintained that silence when they had booked her in. She was taken to an interview room and offered tea or water but she did not even look at the officers and did not respond in any way to their offers of refreshment or legal counsel. Instead she stared at the wall as much as Rob Holt had done, with her hands folded neatly in her lap, her back straight, and her feet placed precisely on the floor.

"Is she fit to be questioned?" Beckett asked Eloise.

"This looks like a conscious decision, I'm guessing it's something she's been told to do, pretty much the way Rob Holt was. But that doesn't mean she's fit to be questioned. Her behaviour so far has not exactly been rational. You need to get a second opinion, I'm too involved with this, but I think that second opinion will say that she needs treatment or at least observation."

Dave Beckett nodded, he had expected as much. "Do you think she's afraid of him? Afraid that he might somehow come and get her, come and harm her?"

"That wouldn't surprise me. I mean look at her, she's the epitome of a late middle-aged, respectable, middle-class woman. From what I've read of her background, she is well-regarded, she holds down a decent job, she doesn't step out of line. Only in this one regard, that she believed Paul Krantz had been sentenced unjustly."

"But she can't possibly believe that now. He confessed to his crimes about as publicly as it's possible to do."

"And he might well have told his followers this is part of some broader strategy. That they just have to keep the faith and . . . Whatever. He's playing a long game and we don't know what it is. It's possible he just gets a kick out of manipulating people but he might have something bigger in mind."

"He's behaving like a cult leader," Ray said. "He's created a narrative, and all of his adherents have to stick to that. To go against him is betrayal and people are punished for betrayal, we've seen that. The only difference is he's allowed his adherents to remain in wider society, encouraged them to be outwardly respectable and conformist. His personal communications have been a secret they keep, something that makes them feel special or that fulfils an emotional need. Or possibly if he can't make it work that way, he blackmails them, threatens them. Power is the thing; exactly what he has to do to get it is probably secondary."

"Ray and I were talking earlier, about the possibility of me reading some of Rob Holt's notes to him. See if we can get some kind of response out of him," Eloise said.

Beckett frowned. "I don't like the idea."

"You can see it has value."

Beckett sighed. "See if you can set something up with the unit but you are not to be in the same room as him and you are not to be alone."

"That goes without saying. He's in a secure unit; no one gets to be alone with him. But I think it might be useful."

"Agreed, see what you can do."

There was a knock on the door and the constable opened it. "A body's been found, the ID points to it being Tom Beresford. But it looks like suicide."

Beckett slid off the table on which he had been perching. "Mind if I tag along?" Ray asked.

"Be my guest," Beckett said heavily.

* * *

Tom Beresford sat in the driver's seat of his car. It was parked up on the top deck of a multistorey car park, in the far corner away from CCTV and, Ray thought, furthest away from anyone else that might want to use the car park. It was human nature that the top deck filled up last and that the spaces furthest from the exits, the stairs and lifts, were last to be utilized.

It would not have been immediately obvious to a casual glance from a neighbouring car that Tom Beresford was dead, unless you bent down to look through the window or, as the unfortunate young woman who had found him had done, you looked directly through your own windows and into his, while unbuckling your baby from its child seat.

"I thought he might have fallen asleep," she told the constable who was first on scene. "His head had kind of dropped forward onto his chest but he was a funny colour, and so then I thought he might be ill. So I tapped on the window and then I saw . . . And then I saw that he wasn't ill, that he was dead."

Ray had attended a fair few suicides in his time and he always found them desperately sad, but there was no doubt that Tom Beresford had meant to die. An empty bottle that had contained sleeping pills lay on the passenger seat alongside the knife that he had used to carve up his wrists and, Ray thought, there was no other way to describe what he had done.

"Poor bugger," Ray said. "He must have been in a desperate place."

A Manila envelope lay on the dashboard addressed to the SIO in the Paul Krantz case. With gloved hands Beckett eased the tab open and peered inside. "Photographs," he said. "They look . . . sexual."

He slipped them into an evidence bag and sealed it.

"Blackmail?" Ray speculated. "Whatever it was, it pushed him right over the edge."

* * *

Ashley Summers stared out of the window into the twilit garden. Dan was improving; she could hear him chatting to Libby in the background and the doctor's approving tone. They had been well looked after, though oddly Ashley had never felt so isolated. She could not have told Libby and Dan but she felt more alone now than she had when she had been imprisoned in that house, with the crazy man talking to her, telling the stories that she'd only half comprehended. At that point she'd only been half conscious so some of the fear had diminished but now, watching on the telly all the things that this man had done, this Paul Krantz, she felt isolated and fearful and guilty. She was safe, she was with people who loved her and that she loved. But she was having trouble getting to grips with the way she felt. Dan had been injured because of her, no matter who told her that was stupid thinking, it still impinged. If she hadn't been so stupid in the first place, if she had seen through this man's lies none of this would have happened. Well, maybe it would have happened but it wouldn't have involved her and Dan and Libby. She had thought when Aiden died that she had learned all about grief and guilt but it seemed life still had some lessons to pile her way. And the worst was there was absolutely nothing she could do.

So when the phone rang at four thirty that afternoon and the request was made, Ashley had no intention of refusing it.

"They had put it to him, asked if he'd agree to speak to me, or at least listen to me," Eloise told her. "I took his notebooks over there, yes, we found them, and we read them through and, well, they are a bit weird. I'd hoped maybe if I read them to Robert Holt, that I might get something useful out of him."

"And he's not cooperating?"

"Not at all. Or at least he wasn't until suddenly he came out with it. That he wanted to talk to you. That he wanted you to read to him."

Ashley felt the cold icy hand grip her stomach and squeeze. She had to sit down. But she also had to say yes. "Will you be with me?"

"Of course I will."

She could hear the surprise in Eloise's voice. The woman had put the question because she had to fulfil an obligation, but she'd assumed that Ashley would refuse. Ashley, terrified though she was, was also determined. "Then I'll do it, if you think it would help."

"Honestly? Look, please don't feel pressured. You've been through so much. As to if it might help or not, I don't know what to think. I don't know what might help or might not. I only agreed to put the question to you because frankly we're all a bit desperate and it feels like we've got to try anything. But I have to say, Ashley, I'm not happy about this."

"You've asked me now. So it's my decision, isn't it?"

Eloise sighed. "I'll be with you and you'll be in a separate room, he'll only be able to see you if you choose to let him. You'll be able to see him on screen but that's it, you'll be in a different part of the building. You'll be OK?"

"It's better than sitting here doing nothing," Ashley told her frankly. "Come and fetch me."

Predictably Libby was against the whole idea, but Ashley was determined now. At least it was doing something.

"I'll come with you," Libby said.

"No, you stay with Dan. Eloise will be with me and there will be police officers and I'll be in a different room, I'll be nowhere near him. I'll text you, and I'll keep letting you know what's going on. I'll be OK."

An hour later they were driving through the gates of the secure unit. An armed police officer accompanied the driver and another car followed on behind. Ashley and Eloise sat in the back of the car. Eloise held Ashley's hand, and Ashley had the feeling this was as much for her own comfort as Ashley's.

They were signed in through an airlock system, and then through another and then the armed police officer took up a position in reception and they were taken into a side room. Eloise sat off-camera while Ashley took her place in the chair facing the screen. A stack of notebooks had been placed on a table beside the chair and Ashley realized with a little jolt that these were the ones that Rob had read from.

"Aren't these evidence?" she asked.

"They've been processed; he wanted to know that you were reading from the actual books, not from photocopies. You ready to go?"

Ashley nodded, the screen in front of her flickered and suddenly Rob's face was there and Ashley wanted to scream.

* * *

Nathan stood in the garden, at the point furthest from the house where a gap in the hedge, filled by a rail-and-post fence, allowed him the view over the fields. In the spring there were hares in that particular field and Nathan had seen them boxing and chasing one another, disturbing the crows and the ponies. The ponies were still there, and the crows were always there, but the hares had gone off to wherever hares go in the summer. Maggie reckoned they congregated in the field on the other side of the little wood, where the summer grazing was better and they were less likely to be disturbed by people on the public footpath that crossed behind the house.

"What are we looking for?" Beth asked. Gavin had been allowed an extra hour of screen time, and was up on his computer playing games online with one of his friends. Beth had followed Nathan into the garden.

"What makes you think we're looking for anything?"

"Well, because we are standing here looking across a field. I just wondered what we're meant to be looking for."

It was a fair point, Nathan thought. He leaned on the fence and Beth came and stood beside him, hands on the top rail, chin on her hands.

"I'm not sure I'm looking," he said. "I think it's more feeling."

Beth considered this for a moment. "Last summer the farmer got a dowser to look for water. I had a go, the sticks really do move. It was amazing. The dowser said I'd found a water pipe and not a spring, but it was still amazing."

Nathan looked at her with interest. "Did the dowser find a water source?"

"Yes. And they brought this drill thing in, and they drilled down, and then they put pipes in so they could bring water into the field over there, the next one along, for the cows in the summer. Me and Gav watched, it was really interesting. Are you doing something like that?"

"Is there a disturbance in the force, you mean." He smiled at her. The kids had introduced him to the *Star Wars* films and film and pizza evenings had suddenly become part of Nathan's life. He had discovered, much to Maggie's amusement, that he actually liked pineapple on his pizza.

"Something like that," Beth confirmed. "It's like you know when you knock on the door, and you know that the house is empty. Or you go into a room and you know that someone's moved something. You know the kind of things you notice without understanding how you notice it?"

"Yeah, I suppose that's what I'm looking for. I suppose I'm also looking for weak points. If someone wanted to come to the house without anybody seeing, where would they come through?"

"They'd come from above, wouldn't they?" Beth said. "Like they did with the drone on that farmhouse. That's why you moved the cameras earlier."

"I think it's possible, but I don't think they will." He pointed. "You see those pylons and electricity wires. I think they might get in their way and anybody that wanted to fly a drone would either have to come into this field or go round onto the road and our cameras would pick them up."

"But even if we could see them, could we stop them?" Beth asked. "You can't exactly shoot a drone out of the sky, can you? I mean you can, but we can't. We don't have a gun."

That was true, Nathan thought. Should he even be discussing this with Beth, the possibility that their home might be attacked? Nathan wasn't sure what was appropriate here, but as Beth had raised the issue he didn't feel that he could dismiss her and he had never been very good at platitudes.

"When we were younger and I wanted to stop Gav going into my room I used to booby-trap the door," she said. "I'd hang things up so that if he tried to go in it would make noise. Then I'd hear and be able to go and drag him out of my room before he messed with anything." She shrugged, "I didn't like him very much then. When he was little he was really annoying. It got better as he grew up, and Mum says I got more tolerant as well. I like him now."

Nathan nodded. "I imagine younger brothers could be annoying," he said and then he wondered if that was really the point of what she was saying, or if it was something else. "Would you feel happier if we did something like that?" he said. "If we set up tripwires and things that made a noise if anyone tried to come through the garden?"

He saw from her face that he had hit the nail right on the head. She nodded. "Gavin and I talked about this last night," she said. "Mum and Dad, and Sarah, they might think that we were taking all of this too seriously and that we were getting too scared and then they might talk about sending us to stay with Grandma. I mean she's all right, but she's ever so serious and she'd freak out if she knew what was really happening here. So we thought we'd ask you, because if you think something is a good idea, the others will go along with it."

Nathan looked at her in some puzzlement. "I don't think I have that much influence," he said.

Beth just smiled and patted him on the arm. "Right, I'll go and tell Gavin what we're going to do, and we can start after dinner," she said.

* * *

"I'm sorry, I'm so sorry," Ashley gasped out. Her heart was racing, pounding against her ribs and she could hardly get her breath.

Eloise was holding her hands, kneeling in front of her, the screen was off now and Rob's face gone. Only the notebooks remained and Ashley was staring at them as though they were about to come alive and smother her.

Her screams had brought others to the doorway, a doctor and the armed officer now stood there, bemused and concerned and Eloise waved them away.

"Count slowly, breathe in for the count of four, out for six, that's right, you're doing fine. You had a panic attack, which is not surprising. I should never have brought you here."

"I . . . wanted to." Ashley struggled with the words.

"Don't try to talk, just breathe. Take it slow and as soon as you're ready we'll get out of here."

Ashley gripped her hands, feeling that if she let go the whole world would disappear. She was trying hard not to faint, her vision fading to red, glimpsing black, pulling herself back. Slowly her breathing eased, though her heart still pounded and she was trembling, head to foot. "I want to go now."

"Can you stand? Can you walk?"

"I'll manage, just get me out of here."

Slowly Eloise guided her towards the door. In the corridor they met with the doctor and she asked if he would go back and collect the notebooks for her. Ashley flinched, she wanted to be nowhere near those things, though she knew that they were just books and that her reaction was irrational, they symbolized those weeks of imprisonment, the voice, the stories, the feeling that she might not survive. She realized now that she had been working so hard to appear strong, untouched, able to get on with life, that she had fooled herself and others too. That the investigating team had wanted to believe that she was strong enough to do this. *That's how desperate they are,* she realized with a sudden shock. *My God, that's how desperate they are.*

They were in the lobby now, the armed officer standing back, his expression concerned and she had a sudden feeling that he'd be much happier shooting at something right now then dealing with a hysterical woman. Is that what she was, hysterical?

Eloise had an arm around her shoulders and kept her moving, through the airlock, into the corridor, through the second airlock, out into the fresh air. It had begun to rain, a half-hearted drizzly affair that seemed to heighten the scent of dust and summer heat rather than cleaning the air. But Ashley breathed deeply, grateful to be out in the open.

She knew it would be a long time before she wiped that memory from her mind. Rob's face suddenly appearing on the screen, looking at her, it seemed, even though she had been told that he could not actually see her, that he would not be able to see her unless she chose to switch on the video. But even so he knew that she was there and he was looking straight in her direction and he was laughing at her.

CHAPTER 30

"There's a call coming on the hotline but they're pretty insistent on speaking to you," Ray was told. "Asked for you by name, and referenced the old enquiry you were involved in."

"And does this person have a name?" Ray asked.

"Presumably, but they'll only give it to you."

Ray picked up the receiver of the phone he had been directed to. "Ray Flowers speaking, how can I help you?"

"You were the detective who arrested Paul, weren't you?"

"I was," Ray agreed. Paul, he thought, not Paul Krantz, not just Krantz. He waved a hand at Eloise and directed her to pick up the extension phone. "Can I know who I'm speaking to?"

The woman on the phone took a deep breath and he thought for a moment she was going to hang up. Then she said, "My name used to be Kit Holt. Robert was my brother. Paul was some kind of distant cousin, he used to stay with us in the summer. We grew up together, and then, then everything changed."

It was Ray's turn to take a deep breath. "We really need to talk to you," he said quietly.

"I know, but you'll have to come to me. I want to meet in a public place, I'm not coming to the police station."

"All right, we can do that. When and where?" He glanced across at Eloise, who was pointing urgently at herself. "And I'd like to bring someone with me, she's not a police officer but she has been trying to talk to your brother."

"And let me guess, he's not cooperating. So she's a psychiatrist or something?"

"Something like that. Her name is Eloise. Look, you tell me when and where, like you say somewhere public. A café maybe? We'll take a table close to the window so you can get a good look at us first and if you feel uneasy, walk away." He held his breath, wondering if he'd played this right and for a moment she didn't respond and he thought he had lost her. He said, "We have all of Rob's notebooks, we read them, we thought you were dead."

"I suppose the old me is," she said. "All right, but if I don't like the look of things I'm going to walk right on by."

Forty minutes later they were sitting at a table by the window of a coffee shop in the high street of a nearby market town. The street was busy, pedestrians walking by, kids on bikes, cars, buses, the usual to and fro of any town centre. Ray sipped his coffee and stared out of the window.

"Do you think she'll come?" Eloise wondered.

"I think she's made the first step, and we've opened the door." He paused. "I think that's her. Across the street. She looks like a slightly older version of Ashley Summers."

"Oh my God, she does."

The woman in dark blue linen trousers and a bright orange top studied them and then, glancing both ways to check out the traffic, she crossed the road and stood outside the café. Her skin tone was quite dark, her hair unexpectedly fair in contrast. Tight curls formed a halo around a very pretty face. She could have been Ashley Summers' older sister, Ray thought. It occurred to him suddenly that Paul Krantz had spent years punishing women who bore some passing resemblance to Kit Holt, just because Kit herself had escaped him.

Despite all he knew about Paul Krantz, he still found the thought profoundly shocking.

For a moment more, she looked through the window, moving restlessly, bouncing on the toes of her canvas shoes as though she wasn't certain whether to run or to come inside. Ray prayed that the police officers who were keeping watch on them would not make any move to spook her. Then abruptly she seemed to make up her mind and she came inside.

Ray started to get up but Eloise waved him back into his seat.

"Just wait," she said.

They watched as Kit went to the counter and ordered her coffee and then came over to the table. She examined them both carefully before deciding to sit next to Eloise. "Well, I'm here," she said. "But I'm still not sure it's a good idea."

"I think I can understand why you feel that way," Ray said.

"Can you? Can you really? I doubt that. What happened to your face and hands? I followed the trial, I remember you from that. I was really shocked but not surprised, if you know what I mean. I knew he had it in him, but the thing is he was probably right, you know, he probably didn't kill his girlfriend."

Ray felt things slowly coming adrift. "What do you mean?"

"I think she means that Rob probably did the actual deed," Eloise said.

Kit nodded. "I don't know for certain, but I think it's likely. Not because Paul isn't capable, you understand that, because it was his way of keeping people under his control. He'd make them do things. It was like a test. He liked to set things in motion and then he liked to watch."

"Did he make you do things?"

"He tried. By the time I left them everything was starting to get really weird. If I hadn't gone, I don't think I'd have survived. I began to doubt him, his friendship, his . . . sanity, I suppose. When we were all kids, we were like the Three Musketeers, all for one and all that. We were so close and then as time went on, I suppose we grew apart, or at least I did. I wanted other things. I wanted boyfriends, I wanted to go out with my girlfriends, I wanted to be myself."

She sipped her coffee and then said, "You read Rob's notebooks."

"Yes," Eloise said. "They were confusing, but revealing too. The last entry is about Paul ordering Rob to hurt you."

Kit's hand flew to her shoulder and then down to her collarbone. "He cut me. From here, across the top of my breast, down onto my sternum. Then we got back in the car and we drove away as if nothing had happened. A bit later on we stopped for petrol and I said I needed to use the toilet. He just shrugged, let me go. I don't think it occurred to him that I wouldn't come back. I think he believed he'd proved a point. He watched me as I went into the ladies but then when I came out he was paying for the petrol and Rob was already back in the car. I was hurting, and I was bleeding and I knew if I didn't get away then I never would. There was a door that said staff only and I went in there and there was this young woman and she told me that I shouldn't be there because it was for staff. And I told her I needed help. My shirt and jeans and everything was soaked in blood. It was only because my coat was really dark that you couldn't see it just from looking at me. She saw the blood, she was really shocked and she called the police and an ambulance and she phoned the guy at the front desk and told him what was going on, but by that point Paul had left the shop and was walking back to the car. I honestly don't know what I'd have done if she hadn't helped me."

"If the police came, why didn't they arrest your brother and Paul?"

"Because by then they'd gone. I made a statement, but I told the police I'd been hitchhiking and they picked me up. That was the biggest mistake I ever made. If they'd been arrested at that point, maybe he wouldn't have gone on to do the things he did but at the time I was just scared and wanted to be away from them."

"The chances are he'd have carried on anyway," Eloise said. "The pattern had already been established."

"That doesn't make me feel any better."

"You were a kid," Ray said.

"I was eighteen, nearly nineteen. I was hardly a baby."

"How did your parents die?" Ray asked.

Kit stared at him, colour draining from her face. "What do you mean?"

"We found graves at Woods End. A man and a woman. The woman had a broken neck, the man had died of stab wounds. The assumption is that they are the bodies of your mother and Rob's father."

Kit sat back in her chair and it seemed to Ray that this had been a complete shock to her.

"If you didn't know they were dead, what did you think happened to them," Eloise asked.

"I thought they'd just left us again," she said.

"Again?"

"They'd go off, days, weeks, they always left a credit card or debit card, made sure the bills were paid. I mean we were all right, we knew how to look after ourselves we'd been doing it for a long time. They always left instructions. What we had to do, what we mustn't do . . . like having anyone over at the house. If we missed school or anything there'd be big trouble. They'd always find out. We weren't allowed to be feral."

She looked pale, Ray thought. Though she spoke lightly, these were not easy memories.

"Did no one notice they were gone? Your mother worked, she was a receptionist or something."

"She worked for an agency, temping, reception jobs, I'm not sure what he did. He was a handyman or something similar some of the time, but the rest of it, God knows. There was always money, that's all I know. Sometimes he'd look after stuff for people. A van would arrive at night, we were told to keep out of the way, something or other would be put down in the cellar and then sometime later someone would come and pick it up. He wasn't really my stepfather, not properly, but we all used his name. I suppose it was just easier for filing in forms and stuff."

"And when did they start leaving you?"

"I suppose when we were about twelve or thirteen, maybe a bit younger. When we were really young they'd get an au pair or someone in to look after us for a bit but they never stayed long, that house is really remote and evenings at the George and Dragon with a cold walk back in the dark, were not really what they signed up for. Look, it wasn't that they weren't okay as parents, I guess, they weren't generally violent, abusive, anything like that. They just went off and left us."

"And were you there when your parents left that last time?"

"No, I'd gone on an Easter skiing trip. It was wonderful, it had taken so much convincing for them to let me go, I was away for two whole weeks. When I came back Rob said they'd gone again and Paul was there, and that was weird because he didn't usually come at that time of year. And it was also strange because he'd changed, he was kind of bossy. Aggressive. But if they were dead I guess that makes sense of a lot of things."

"And after you left, did you not try and get in touch with your parents?"

"How? We never knew where they were and they never left a number, not even for emergencies. I tried phoning the house a couple of times, but eventually the phone was cut off. I realized then the bills hadn't been paid. We'd been drawing on the card that that they always left but then one day there was no money in the account and I did get scared then. I thought something must have happened. I didn't realize it had happened at the house."

"And then Paul insisted that it was time to go. That you had to leave."

"The last week or two, all we did was argue. I wanted to wait for them to come back, I was sure there was just something wrong but they would come back. They would sort everything out. I wanted to take my exams, I wanted to go to university, I wanted a life."

"You mentioned a cellar, and Rob mentioned one in the books. He says that Paul locked you down there. But we could find no evidence of a cellar at the house."

She shook her head. "It's not under the house. There's a big slab next to the pump in the garden, that can be lifted and there's a space underneath it, leading down into the well. It was there so they could test the water I think. You have to lower a ladder into the well itself and then about halfway down there's a space, like a little tunnel. That's where Rob's dad used to store whatever it was he was storing. That's where Paul shut me in."

Ray tried to imagine what that must have been like and then he stopped trying to imagine it. He had something of a horror of enclosed, underground spaces.

"And so you managed to leave them that night. Then what happened?" Eloise wanted to know.

"We really should get this all down formally," Ray said.

The two women ignored him. "I wasn't very cooperative with the police. I spent a few days in hospital, I wouldn't say who I was or where I'd come from so they handed me over to social services. I got put in a hostel, it was tough but I've had worse. Eventually I went back to school, eventually I went to university. I had no criminal record so they couldn't find out who I was through fingerprints, so they used the name I gave them even though they suspected it wasn't my real one. I got registered with the doctor that looked after the hostel, I got registered at the school. I kind of built my identity from the ground up. It's difficult though but once you've got one piece of ID you can slowly but surely get others and they opened a bank account for me at the hostel, so I could have benefits paid into it, so that was kind of key."

It wasn't as simple as that, Ray thought, but he didn't press the point. The girl had survived to womanhood and made a life for herself and now she was willingly undoing that. Ray wasn't sure he'd have had the courage.

"We do need to get this down as a formal statement," he said quietly. "And then we'll probably need to get you into protective custody for a while."

"I've broken cover now, haven't I?" she said ruefully. "All right, but I just have to ring my neighbour so she can feed the cat."

She was, Ray realized, no longer the semi-mythical sister from Rob's notebooks. Twenty years had passed. This was a fully grown, middle-aged woman with a life and career and a cat and probably friends. He listened as she made a phone call and said that something had come up with a relative and she might be away for a couple of days. She dropped the phone back in her bag. She looked resigned, he thought. Unhappy.

"You want me to help you catch him, I suppose," she said. "But it's been years, I wouldn't know where to start."

"No, but Rob might," Eloise said. "Would you be willing to talk to him?"

She stared at Eloise, her expression as shocked as if the other woman had struck her. Finally she said, "This has to end, doesn't it. But you'll keep me out of this as much as you can?"

"If we can. As much as we can," Ray agreed.

CHAPTER 31

Slowly Kit examined the wall, the collage of images and events seeming to make sense to her, though Ray thought she seemed uncertain how to explain the thinking. Rob's notebooks lay on the table and from time to time she had glanced at them but she seemed to give them a wide berth as though reluctant even to be in their presence.

Dave Beckett had called the crime scene manager and they had looked for the so-called cellar, finding it exactly where Kit said it would be. Ray had now seen photographs of the place and it made him feel claustrophobic just looking at it. It might just about have been possible for a teenage girl to sit up but not to stretch out. She would have been cramped and confined and scared to death, he thought.

Kit paused and looked at the children's drawings, she seemed disturbed by them.

"Any idea what those signify?" Ray asked.

She shook her head. "They're the kind of thing all kids draw, I suppose, a house, big people that I suppose are parents and little people that I suppose are kids. And that big spidery sun. This one seems to have a dog and a cat in it and a rainbow. They look kind of new, though, not the sort of thing that Rob or I would have drawn when we were kids.

I mean I'm sure we did, but they would have been a lot older, faded, and the paper would be tatty by now. I didn't know Rob when he was that age anyway, we met when we were both about eight years old and our parents got together. These are little kid drawings, but what they doing here?"

"What was Rob like when he was a kid?" Dave Beckett asked.

"When he was a little kid I suppose he seemed quite normal, at least when I first knew him. But the teachers at school said that he was always in the world of his own and I think that got worse when he was older. He seemed to be kind of separate somehow; he could still function in the real world but it was like he was in two places one time, the real world and Rob's world."

"Did your parents try to help him?"

"I suppose they did in their own way. I mean they went to parents' evening and all that sort of stuff, and made a point of being visible when they needed to be. We weren't supposed to let people know when they were away and I don't suppose we did. And no one really came to the house. We used to walk down to the George in the morning to catch the bus, go to school, get dropped off at the George on the way home. If we needed groceries, we'd get them at the village shop or pick things up when we came out of school. We were really self-sufficient. I suppose for us it was normal."

"And the school never suspected that anything was wrong?"

"Why would they? We were clean and well fed and we got on with our lessons and we had a good attendance record. I'm not sure it ever occurred to us that we should truant or whatever. Nobody wanted to make our parents mad, it wasn't that they really did anything to us, it was just that . . . We knew it wasn't a good idea."

Ray wondered if he should pursue that. She was clearly not telling the whole truth, but he decided there were more important things to explore. "So your parents did talk to the school about Rob?"

"I think so, but the school would have said he was doing fine and he was. Rob was so good at acting normal and he never made any trouble. He was quiet and polite and he got his work done. He wasn't top in anything, not like Paul, but he was doing okay. No one saw Rob as a problem. At home it was different. I mean a lot of kids come home and shut themselves in their room, refuse to have a proper conversation with their parents, especially when they're going through teenage years, but it was more than that. Looking back, I think I ended up trying to shield him from them and them from Rob because if he was pushed too hard he'd explode. Or his dad would and then me and Mum would both be caught in the crossfire. To be honest, I liked it when they went away. Rob was calmer then. Maybe if I hadn't gone on the skiing trip and left him alone with them, things would have turned out differently."

"Was his father violent?"

"Only with Rob. Rob just seemed to push all his buttons without meaning to. Rob had been this sunny, cheerful, open kid and no one could really understand what had gone wrong when he got to about twelve or thirteen. I mean, a lot of kids change then but this was more than just ordinary teenage rebellion or angst."

"When did Paul start to come and stay with you in the summer?"

She hesitated for a moment and then she said, "I suppose around the same time. Maybe a bit earlier, I think the first time was when we were all eleven. He came for the summer and we all seemed to hit it off straight away.

"He was just so full of energy, we all went riding, he learned to ride that year and if you follow the footpath that started in the field next to the house, it leads down to a river. We spent a lot of time down there, just messing about. It was actually a great place to grow up, and Paul looked forward to staying with us."

"What was he like? Looking back can you see any indicators of the person he would become?" Eloise asked.

"How can you tell? He liked to get his own way, and so did Rob sometimes. I ended up acting like the peacemaker. He was always . . . No, *they* were . . . they were always egging each other on. Urging each other to climb higher, swim in deeper water, jump the bigger fence when we went riding and where one led the other followed. Sometimes it was Paul did the leading, sometimes it was Rob."

"And you?"

"I thought about it a lot, and looking back I think I just went along. It was easier just to go along with whatever they wanted to do. Sometimes they'd do what I wanted, but it was just things like going to the cinema, going swimming at the local leisure centre, just ordinary stuff. It was stuff they enjoyed too."

"And were you in touch much during the rest of the year?"

"As we got older, yes, we got computers and mobile phones and we could keep in touch with one another without having to ask permission to use the phone. We had limits, our parents paid a certain amount a month for the phone calls and we couldn't go over those, but email was good, and yeah, we communicated most days, I guess. Rob and Paul in particular."

"You mentioned that you wanted an ordinary life, boy-friends, trips out with your girlfriends and that this caused friction," Ray recalled.

"As we got older Paul had this attitude towards me, like I was his girlfriend. Or like I was going to be. He hated it if I went out with other people, even when he wasn't staying with us. He got very possessive. He would say things like you know we'll be together in the end, that nothing can tear us apart. That it will always be the three of us and after a while it got kind of creepy. I didn't look forward to the summer any more. The year we were all eighteen, that summer we all had our birthdays in the winter and that summer we were due to take exams and I was looking at university applications. Paul found it hilarious that I planned to go away to university. He said I'd never survive on my own."

"Did he plan to go to university?"

She nodded. "Yes, he was going to study mathematics and physics. Paul was really clever. Rob had no intention of doing anything of the kind, he'd got a job lined up at the riding stables and that would really have suited him. He used to help out at weekends and holidays and he was always really good with the little kids. It was strange, he could be so volatile and yet with little kids had so much patience. Paul couldn't stand kids. He just thought they were messy and sticky and unpleasant. We used to tease him about it but then he seemed to lose his sense of humour."

"In the notebooks, Rob records an incident with a fox," Ray said. He sorted through to find the relevant book. "He writes it as though it's a story about other people. At other times he writes in first person, like he's admitting he was there."

"I never read his notebooks. He was always writing, but he was kind of secretive about it."

Again, he noted, she eyed the notebooks cautiously, as though concerned about what they contained. Ray began to read.

"*He remembered how she had taken a brick from the pile next to the house, and how she had been so calm about it. The fox had flopped into the longer grass close beside the hedge and he had watched her as she approached slowly and so calmly the animal had barely raised its head. She had brought brick down so swiftly and so hard that it had no time to react. He remembered how he had wandered over, curious and disturbed. She had crossed back to the pump, washed the brick and replaced it on the stack while he and the brother had stared down at the now very dead fox.*"

"Did that happen?" Eloise asked. "Did it happen as he said?"

Kit turned away from them and once more looked at the wall, examining things carefully. "There are layers here," she said. "It's not linear, it's like he's gone over the same space several times, adding meanings or adding strata, I suppose is the easiest way of putting it. If you look at the stuff underneath, a lot of it is from when we were growing up."

They came over and stood beside her as she pointed to a news clipping. "The village fete was held on the green in front of the George and Dragon, and also in the pub garden. It was a pretty big thing every year and there was a fancy dress competition for the kids. When we were eight or nine, not long after we came to Woods End, we dressed up for the competition. Rob was a garden gnome and I was a flower fairy, I was into all that sort of thing back then. Mum made me a costume out of a ballet tutu by adding petals on the skirt and flowers and ribbons to the leotard and I think I had some kind of headdress. I remember it being a really happy day and Mum clipped the article out of the newspaper."

Ray looked closely at the newspaper clipping and then at what had been placed on top and beside. "So the next layer up, that would be the bonfire night?"

"I think so. There was a bonfire every year in the field at the back of the George and Dragon and there would be a kind of Guy Fawkes competition for the kids, so we'd stuff old clothes with straw to make a guy and make masks and that sort of thing and there'd be a bigger effigy burning on the bonfire. This particular year, things went wrong. The bonfire had been lit and all of a sudden there was this yowling and screaming coming from inside it. A cat must have burrowed down inside and not been able to get out again. I wasn't there, not that year, I think if I remember right. I was doing something at school, some kind of school play, and Rob was really mad with me for not being there because he said it wouldn't be as much fun on his own. Anyway, the cat got out but it was on fire and of course it died."

"That must have been horrifying, especially considering there would have been children there," Eloise said.

"I'm sure it was, in fact I don't know if they do the bonfire now. I know they took a couple of years break from it".

"You think Rob was responsible, don't you?"

Kit took a deep breath and then nodded. "It was my cat," she said.

They followed her as she walked round the wall, identifying early incidents in their childhood, places they had known or played or visited. Sometimes there were several layers where Rob or Paul or she had revisited the place, or another incident had happened. Some of these were major and significant, like the cat, others were simple day trips to a museum or a big house or a school visit when they had stayed in a youth hostel. In all cases a later incident had been added, a robbery, and assault, an act of violence or criminality.

Ray went and got a map, the same scale and area as the one on which they had plotted the most recent acts of violence; murders, stabbings, attacks, since Paul Krantz had broken out of jail. Together they plotted these early incidents and compared the two.

He was oddly disappointed to find that there were few correlations. He explained this to Kit who shook her head. "Why would there be, this is Rob's map, Paul would have had his own. Rob was a creature of habit, he liked to revisit the same places, he liked to do the same things, he liked to eat the same meals. Paul wasn't tied like that. He thrived on different. Rob had this thing about places, going back to the same place. Paul would pick on a person and either become very attached to them, or very against them. The attachment never lasted for long, he left a trail of broken hearts when he was a teenager, from being about fourteen girls would fall for him and he'd string them along for a little while, and then he lose interest and he'd just ghost them, not that we called it that back then, but you know what I mean."

"Okay, so looking at Paul's, can you tell me anything about the places?"

"No, like I say, it would be about people. He wouldn't care where they were, he would go after them anyway whereas Rob likes to be in a familiar place. Unfamiliar geography would throw him into a bit of quandary. He always got lost easily."

Ray nodded and Beckett who had been silent for quite some time then asked, "So what happened with the fox?"

"I killed it," she said, turning back to face him. "It was hurt, it looked like a dog had got hold of it, that much is true. But the first I knew about it was when I came out into the garden and the pair of them were pelting it with stones. Poor thing was too weak to run away and it was yelping in pain. So yes, I picked up a brick and I finished it off."

She held his gaze, daring him to challenge her on the truth of that.

"Would you be willing to talk to Rob?" Beckett asked.

She sighed, the tension and anger seeming to leech from her body. Ray watched as she thought about it for a moment and then nodded. "I've come this far," she said. "May as well go the distance."

CHAPTER 32

It was Ray who accompanied Kit to the secure unit. Rob Holt had been told that someone wished to speak to him and he had assumed it was Ashley. He had apparently told his doctors that he knew she would come back, that she would be unable to resist. No one had disillusioned him.

They passed through the airlock and into the first reception and then down the corridor and through the second airlock into the second lobby. They were led into the same room that Ashley had occupied earlier.

"Are you sure you're okay with this?"

"Of course I'm not okay with this. But it has to be done. I spent twenty years avoiding this, twenty years trying to be someone else. I'm not sure how I'm going to cope when all of this is over, but we'll cross that bridge."

Ray sat where he would be out of sight of Rob but was still able to see the screen and watched as Kit tried to control her breathing. It was ragged and too fast, and her hands were clasped tightly together. He wanted to give her a hug.

Rob's face appeared on the screen. He was smiling, smug-looking, Ray thought. Kit leaned forward and pressed the button on the keyboard that would allow him to see her.

Ray saw the confusion on his face, and then the sudden realization as she said, "Hello, Rob. Remember me."

His expression changed from one of smug expectation to one of real anger. Ray recalled the rage that had suddenly exploded in the interview room at the police station, and that had led to Rob's attack on DCI Blatchford, and was very relieved that they were separated from him by several rooms and a secure corridor.

"You left us." The rage exploded. "You left us. I should have killed you."

He lunged forward and a moment later his image was gone and Kit's screen went blank. His shouts and ravings could be heard even from this distance. An alarm began to sound.

An orderly appeared in the doorway and said, "We think you should leave."

Ray and Kit obeyed with alacrity. They were led out through a different exit and taken round the front of the building, the alarm still sounding in their ears.

"That was not a major success," Kit said quietly as they drove away. "Perhaps it's Paul we need to be talking to. If he's as angry with me as Rob is then perhaps if I reach out to him it might bring him out into the open?"

"Or he'll come after you."

"Pretty much the same thing I'd have thought."

"Kit, you asked me yesterday if I could keep you out of this as much as possible. You risk totally exposing yourself, you'll never be able to go back to the life you had."

"Perhaps it was never mine in the first place. If I had managed to get them arrested when Rob attacked me, then maybe . . ."

"Eloise already told you, they would have continued anyway. They were on a path that would lead to violence, that had already led to violence. One of them or both of them killed your parents. And before you say it, even if you had been there, there is no guarantee that would not have happened. Separately perhaps they might have been reasoned with, perhaps they might have been diverted, but the two of them together. Well, you told us they egged each other on when they were kids, it's likely they just carried on doing that, only at more than climbing trees and swimming in deep water."

She stared out of the window and he could feel the weight of guilt she carried and he knew that whatever he said she would feel responsible and, in a way, he supposed she was. If she had betrayed the identity of her brother and Paul then perhaps they would have been taken into custody, perhaps their direction would have been changed, perhaps a lot of things. Did he believe that? Ray asked himself. Probably not.

A phone call from Dave Beckett as they were travelling back did nothing to improve the mood or diminish Kit's resolve.

"One of the CSIs noticed a loose brick in the back of the little cellar place," he said. "They removed it and then realized that it had originally gone back further, that this was a false wall."

Ray eyed Kit anxiously, realizing that in the close confines of the car she could hear both sides of the conversation.

"And what was in there," Kit asked.

Ray was conscious of Dave Beckett hesitating but it was a bit late for reticence. "Two bodies wrapped in sacking," he said. "The guesstimate is they've likely been there about five years."

Kit was staring at Ray. "That space is small," she said. "They aren't adult bodies, are they?"

"No," Beckett said. "They are children, perhaps five or six years old. From the remnants of clothing, probably a boy and a girl."

* * *

"How is she doing," Ray asked Eloise as she came back into the central incident room and poured herself a coffee.

"We got her bedded down on a very uncomfortable sofa and the doctor's given her something to help her nap, I would say sleep, but I don't think that's going to happen. She is absolutely exhausted and she needs to take a break for a while."

"I imagine she does."

"Do we know more about the children?" Eloise asked.

"Well, I'm guessing we now know who did the drawings, but as Kit pointed out, these are the kinds of pictures that could be drawn by any kid. So if we are assuming that Rob killed them, he must have been close enough to the family to get hold of the drawings, perhaps, or at least had access to the house."

"It's a logical assumption, I guess. So what about the other things that are next to and behind them in the layers, can that tell us anything?"

"Dave and I have already talked about this, but it's a bit tenuous."

The two of them stood gazing at the children's drawings; these formed the top layer of three. The lowest of the strata was another press cutting. It was about the village of Ellsbury, which the map told them was somewhere around five or six miles from Woods End and which reported on a local gymkhana. "Any idea how old is this clipping is?" Eloise asked.

"There's no date on it, but it's likely to be from a local paper. With time I expect we could track down exactly when this was written but if we take on board Kit's idea that the lower layer is in some kind of linear order and then he backtracks two or three times over the top it wouldn't be so far out to guess that this was when they were eleven or twelve. Perhaps they competed? We know they rode." He frowned at the cuttings. "We have the drawings on the top, so what's between?"

Reports of an armed robbery at the post office in the same village. A shot had been fired, though no one was hurt and two men had been involved. "Apparently they didn't get away with very much," Ray commented. "A couple of thousand pounds but that hardly seems worth the effort."

"If one man was Rob Holt then who was the second?" Eloise said. "And then the third thing is the children. So did he take them from the same village?"

"My guess would be yes. There's already someone going through missing persons reports but they'll be dealing with a mass of data, this might be a way of narrowing things down. No harm in checking; if we draw a blank we've wasted no one's time but our own." They went through into the next room where their computers were set up and Ray logged on to the police national computer and input keywords for the village, missing children, and then as an afterthought, gymkhana. Eloise was carrying out a similar search on the internet, looking for media reports.

"Becky and James Deacon," Ray said.

"I've just picked those up too. Aged five and seven. James was competing in the gymkhana, his little sister was with their parents watching. She went with him after the competition to go and buy candy floss and that was the last anyone saw of them."

Ray swore softly and then went to find Dave Beckett.

"It makes sense he'd return to where he felt comfortable," Beckett said grimly. "Kit told us he liked familiar places. The fact that he had hidden the bodies in a place he knew well suggested he might also have taken the children from somewhere he knew well."

Ray nodded. "So what else has he been doing, what else are we missing?" He wanted to know.

CHAPTER 33

Kit was dressed in a simple white shirt and the blue linen trousers she had been wearing when she first met Ray. The shirt belonged to Eloise and they'd done their best with the trousers and a rather inefficient travel iron. She wore just a touch of make-up but nothing that could hide the exhaustion and distress.

At the press conference she came to the table with Dave Beckett and sat nervously as a roomful of people speculated on who she might be.

"You are all aware of the developments in this case," Beckett said. "Of the two further bodies found at Woods End. We are still waiting to confirm the identity of these two, and a further statement will be made when the relatives have been informed. You will also be aware that we found the body of Tom Beresford and that the cause of death is believed to be suicide. But I am looking for your help again. A statement is about to be read and I would ask that it is transmitted in full."

Kit cleared her throat and shuffled the papers on the table in front of her. She and Eloise had put this together in far too much of a hurry and all she could do was hope that they had said the right things.

"Paul, I'm sure you remember me. We were both eighteen when we last met face to face and when I left you it was not under the best of circumstances. You and my brother Rob and I, we were once good friends and it seems to me that, as Rob is in custody, if anybody can reach out to you now, then it has to be me. Paul, I don't know what went wrong for you and I don't know why you're doing this now but I do understand that you're angry and that you're hurting and that maybe we should sit down and talk. Paul, this can't go on, you must know that. You are hurting so many people and they don't deserve it. I can't help but think that . . . that some of this is because of me and because of Rob and if that's the case then I am so, so sorry. You don't have to carry on with this, you can be helped, you can stop this now."

She paused and glanced anxiously around the room and then swallowed nervously, she was clearly so far out of her depth that Ray stepped forward instinctively, wanting to help her. He moved back almost immediately; he'd agreed to come and give moral support but this was not about him and he had no wish to distract the media or draw attention to himself.

"Paul, I knew you when you were very young and you were an amazing person. I don't know what changed, or what happened to you but please know that you can talk to me and a number is going to be given out at the end of this for you to call or for anybody that cares about you to call so that we can get you the help you need."

He is going to hate this, Ray thought suddenly. He had been against Kit making this presentation, from the very beginning. He knew that neither Dave nor Eloise were convinced that it was going to be helpful but Beckett's bosses, having got wind of the fact that someone who was once close to Paul Krantz had come out of the woodwork and might be able to reach him, had been pretty much insistent that it be tried. Kit had her reservations . . . but desperate to help and, Ray thought, to assuage her own guilt, she had agreed.

"Paul, Rob is in hospital now, he is being treated and looked after. Contact me, Paul. Please. You and Rob have both done some terrible things and the police *will* find you so it's better that you come forward now, come and talk to me, let's get you the help you need."

* * *

Paul Krantz watched the television screen and fizzed with indignation. His ire grew as he caught just the swiftest glimpse of the one-time DI Ray Flowers step out of the shadows at the side of the room.

"Who's that then?" Philip Carstairs asked him. "She says she knows you from when you were young. Who is she?"

"Never you mind."

"No, but she's got a point, hasn't she."

His voice was shaking; Paul glanced contemptuously in his direction.

"Look, Paul, when I signed up to help you, it was because I thought you were innocent. Now, well, what you made me do to that man. He's dead now and I killed him and you made me do it."

"I didn't make you do anything," Paul told him coldly. "The choice was yours. You could have walked away."

"I did it for you! I did it because you—"

He fell silent, daunted by Paul's look of contempt. "You're weak," Paul told him. He gestured towards the television. "Weak, just like she was."

He watched as Philip Carstairs seemed to gather himself, bundle up his last bit of courage. Phil said, "We can't keep running like this, and you can't keep on doing what you're doing. What do you think, we contact them, we phone the number, we get to talk to someone. They're gonna catch up with us, Paul, and when they do they're going to lock you up, and me too and throw away the key. She says you can get help, we can tell them you're . . . you know, not quite right in the head."

"You think that, do you?" Paul Krantz's voice was flat and cold and he regarded his one-time friend with eyes that were dead and empty. Too late, Phil realized his mistake. He backed away, palms raised in supplication.

"I didn't mean anything by it, I'm just scared that's all. I've just bitten off more than I can chew here, you understand that."

"I understand that all too well," Paul Krantz said.

A half hour later, Paul Krantz left the empty house they had been holed up in. It was on the edge of a half-built estate, as far from the show home and reception as it was possible to get. An unfinished road led almost to the B road beyond, with only a short stretch of mud to cross and the 4x4 he was driving was well up to that task. He'd left Phil dead on the kitchen floor. Over the past days they'd kept moving, cheap hotels, empty houses, sometimes sleeping in the car — and this was the fifth car in as many days.

Paul Krantz was incandescent. That bitch was telling him that he was mad, that he had a problem, that he could be fixed. He should have made sure Rob killed her when they'd had the chance. But he'd been young then, he'd learned sense after that. Well, if they thought he'd caused chaos so far, just let them watch him now. No mercy, no holding back, he'd show her, he'd show the bloody lot of them.

* * *

Nathan was helping John to cook dinner and they had a small TV on in the kitchen. Nathan paused in his chopping, staring at the screen and John turned up the volume.

"Who's she?" John asked.

Nathan did not answer immediately, he listened to the rest of Kit's statement and then he said, "Someone who has just been allowed to make a very big mistake. This will just enrage him."

"You think we can expect trouble," John said. "I mean imminent trouble."

Nathan nodded. "This is just going to make him angry, it diminishes him, in his own terms. He doesn't want to be seen as mad; he wants to be seen as some kind of genius, able to strike fear into the hearts of those he is targeting." he said.

"Well, score one for that." John turned off the heat under the pan that he was stirring and went out into the hall. "Maggie, Sarah, kids, sweethearts, get a bag packed, just what you need for a couple of days."

Maggie and Sarah came out of the living room and stared at him and then Sarah looked at Nathan. "That bad?" she asked.

"I would think so."

"Kids, you heard your dad, go and pack," Maggie said.

Beth was staring down at them from over the banister rail and she too looked at Nathan for confirmation. He nodded at her and she grabbed her brother's hand. "I'll help Gavin," she said.

"I'll do that," Maggie said. "You go and sort yourself out."

"Beth's had a bag packed for the last three days," Nathan said. He could see the horror in Maggie's eyes as she took this in.

"Bloody hell," Maggie said.

Fifteen minutes later the dogs had been deposited with neighbours, John and Maggie and the family had gone and Nathan sat on the stairs wondering whether he should finish making sauce for the pasta. He could eat and then freeze the rest for when they returned. Sarah came out of the living room.

"You should go," he said.

"As should you. You're going to stay, aren't you?"

"He will come here eventually," Nathan said. "If there is someone here to raise the alarm, then there's a chance he can be caught."

"And that's not your responsibility. No one wants you to take risks, Nathan."

"Sarah, I think I am more capable of taking risks than anyone else I know," he said quietly. He got up and went through to the kitchen. "That's George's car, I recognize the sound of the engine. You should go. Be careful Sarah."

* * *

"That was Sarah on the phone," Ray said. "John and Maggie have taken the kids and left. They were spooked by the press conference. They all think it was a bad move, that it will just provoke him."

"I'm afraid of that too," Kit said. "He's not going to like the inference that there's something wrong with him." Ray knew she had worried at this idea when she and Eloise had written the script, that she had been certain this was a bad move, but those higher up the chain of command had been so keen on an appeal . . .

"So the house is now empty?" Dave Beckett asked.

Ray hesitated. Beckett did not share their wholehearted enthusiasm for Nathan. He had once suspected him of murder and that vague suspicion had never fully subsided. "Nathan's there," he said at last.

"Nathan," Becket said heavily.

"Look, I think he's just sorting things out for the Riverses. They left in a big rush."

"Who's Nathan?" Eloise asked.

"Good question," Becket countered. Then he sighed. "Not the concern at the moment." He turned to Kit. "We've had a dozen or so calls but nothing useful. So far as most people are concerned it's just another number to call with sightings."

"So what now?" Ray asked. "Apart from waiting for a call that might not come. We have to assume that he might not like the inference, but also that he's still got people on his list. He might decide to talk to Kit and then we've got some chance of talking him down. He might decide to go out with a bang."

Dave Beckett looked uncomfortable but he nodded. "We need to assume that you are still top of his wish list," he said. "You're certain that Sarah is in a safe place?"

"She's at George's. The Rivers family have booked into a hotel. John was certain there was no one following when they left."

"So, we're left with your home; there's a good chance he might go there. The Summers family are probably safe enough and we've already got an armed unit out there and the same with the secure unit where Rob Holt is being housed. Just in case he decides he wants to break him out. Then there's Nora Blaine, but she's in a safe house way up north."

Ray studied the map on which Krantz's offences had been mapped. It was a big area, if you included the killing of DI Nightingale, but the majority of the pins were in a more restricted area. Even so it was still around a hundred miles in radius. "Woods End is here, the attack on Dan Summers here. Tom Pollard was found dead at home, here . . . He sent Rob to my aunt's cottage where Nathan was staying and that's here." So spaced out, no sense of any pattern apart from people he wanted to target. As Kit had observed earlier, Rob was held to a centre by geography, by places he felt comfortable in. Paul Krantz had no such qualms. He had targets; he went where they went; he tracked them down.

"He could be anywhere," Kit said quietly. "But I think your friends were right to leave. What we should have done is let him know where I'd be. He'd come for me, you know he would."

"And probably with the worst of intentions."

"Probably, but at least you'd know where he was heading."

* * *

As he had done on so many occasions when staying at the vicarage, Nathan walked the boundaries and studied the access points, from the road, across the field. He and Beth had set the traps she had wanted to make, threading old saucepan lids, Christmas sleigh bells and even a pair of maracas onto a length of washing line and slinging this across the more open sections of hedge. The cameras covered most of the garden and, as Beth had observed, one looked up at the clear blue summer sky, should the attack come from the air.

Nathan thought this was unlikely now. Drones were pricey things and Krantz has already demolished one. Besides, the mix of power lines and trees close by the vicarage would make such an incursion much harder than it had been at Woods End. Reasonably satisfied there was nothing more to be done, Nathan went back inside and locked the doors, then set about finishing the ragout he and John had been preparing before they had left.

CHAPTER 34

As it happened, Krantz had decided to keep everyone waiting. For a good chunk of the night he just drove, taking little notice of where he was or where he was going, but just allowing the anger and the sense of injustice to build, feeding the flame with a slow inventory of all who had betrayed him, let him down, proved inadequate to his needs.

By morning Paul Krantz had built a bonfire from his rage and it blazed higher than it had done even on the night that Kit deserted him. He had been angry enough to kill her that night and now, here she was, back like a bad smell and inviting him to contact her, so that he could get help. Help! She'd be the one needing help when he got hold of her. Her and all the rest of them.

It was not lost on Krantz that in killing Phil he had perhaps done himself a disservice. While Phil travelled with him he had an errand boy; someone to get food, to interact with people on the odd occasion they were forced to do so. To fill up with petrol . . . That was Krantz's most immediate concern. When they had taken this car, it had had about half a tank of fuel and now it was way down in the red.

Krantz pulled up on the forecourt and filled the tank, wishing he could have pressed the button that allowed him to pay by card. Last time they had risked using Phil's card, the card had been rejected, the screen bringing up the cheerful suggestion that they try another method of payment.

The realization that the bank must have blocked Phil's account, that the police realized he must be with Krantz had shocked his one-time partner in crime. Unsettled him and, Krantz felt, led in part to their unfortunate confrontation that had in turn led to Phil's death. Krantz had viewed this as inevitable; in fact it was only that their cash needed to be preserved until it could be topped up that he had even permitted Phil to try.

Rob was supposed to bring more cash. Rob who had also failed him. Rob who couldn't keep two ideas straight in his head these days.

Briefly he considered getting in the car and driving off, but that was certain to raise the alarm. There were cameras every bloody where these days.

He took the right money out of his pocket and crossed the forecourt, entered the little convenience store and crossed to the counter. His picture had been everywhere — of course, that was exactly what he'd intended — but he'd not intended having to go and pay for his own fuel.

Sunglasses on, hair dyed to take out the grey, he knew he looked different but was he different enough?

Paranoia wriggled inside him, fuelled by anger, fired by the sense that everyone had let him down.

A woman taking milk from the fridge glanced his way, seemed to be holding his gaze for a little too long. A man passed him on the way out and Paul Krantz was sure he'd done a double take. He approached the counter; the assistant looked up, smiled and then reached beneath the counter for something. Paul convinced himself that he'd pressed an alarm.

The anger, fuelled by paranoia, boiled over. He hurled himself at the plastic screen on the counter. It gave under his weight and a moment later he was on the floor, struggling with the assistant. The female customer screamed, he could hear someone else calling the police. His fury, as he rose to his feet and dived back towards them, cleared the way, but not before he had caught the woman's arm with the knife he now held.

Then he was out on the forecourt and running for his car. Seconds later, he was gone, leaving in his wake a woman with blood pouring from her arm and a shop assistant dead on the floor. It was not yet nine in the morning.

* * *

"Well, we now know how he's going to play this," Ray said grimly. "But what the hell set him off?" One moment Krantz was walking sedately across the forecourt and into the shop and the next he was in full attack mode. The CCTV showed him pull the knife from his pocket and throw himself into the plastic screen. He was holding an ordinary kitchen knife with a slim blade. It looked to Ray like a paring knife or possibly for filleting fish. Not long or flashy, but big enough to leave a man dead.

"Did he think he'd been recognized?" Kit was unable to take her eyes from the split screen that played the scene from several angles. She was, Ray could see, shaken and pale, no doubt remembering that other time, that other petrol station where she had escaped from a younger and less experienced and perhaps, Ray thought, a less crazed version of Krantz than they witnessed here. He had then been at the beginning of his journey when some restraint and caution remained. There was nothing of that evident now.

"Well, he's heading back in the direction of his first murders," Ray observed. "Or rather, the ones we arrested him for."

"So he wants to get to you," Kit said.

"Or those I care about," Ray added, hoping fervently that everyone was indeed in a safe place.

CHAPTER 35

They managed to pick up the car on CCTV, but then lost it when he headed out of town. Krantz surfaced again when the car was spotted at the end of the road where Nora Blaine had been living. By now the media had caught wind of what was going on, film of Krantz, taken at the petrol station, had been uploaded onto social media. The witness with the phone had thought he was filming someone driving off after failing to pay. It was moments later when he realized what else was going on and a few minutes after that when he realized just who he had caught on camera.

Something must have alerted Krantz at Nora's house because he turned in the middle of the road and drove at full speed back to the junction, once more heading out of town. He was picked up next close to Ashley's flat and must have spotted the police car parked in the little side road, across which Elsie had escaped. This time he stopped the car.

One officer left his own car and began to approach.

Wrong move.

On the dashcam footage from the police car, Krantz was seen to throw something and a second later that something exploded into flames at the officer's feet. The next images showed his colleague running from the car and beating out the flames. Then Krantz was gone.

"He's not badly hurt," Beckett said. "He jumped back as the bottle hit the ground but it could have been a hell of a lot worse."

"He's playing with us," Ray said. "Tying us up in knots." Quite literally, he added to himself, thinking of the numbers of officers currently manning phones, following tip-offs, fielding demands from the media, covering those locations that Krantz might target next.

* * *

Ray and Beckett kept their eyes riveted to the screen.

The footage playing was of Krantz's car, parked at a set of lights. A police car pulled up beside him. Krantz sat, waiting for the lights to change. As the lights turned green Ray saw the police car start to turn across the junction and only then did Krantz react. Whatever impulse seized him in that moment, it was too much to resist. Accelerating hard, Krantz drove straight at the patrol car, centre-punching it and sending it skidding back across the junction and into oncoming traffic. Then he was out of the car, flinging open the door of a vehicle waiting in the queue, ordering the startled driver out before driving away.

"What the hell was he doing?" Ray demanded. "He could easily have been injured. Does he want to get caught?"

"So long as he gets caught doing something spectacular, I don't think he cares," Beckett said.

Then, just as they had put out details of this new car, it seemed he had changed vehicles again. This time at a junction with no cameras, he had blocked in a vehicle, climbed into the passenger seat and held a knife at the driver's throat, ordering her to drive. She'd had to mount the pavement to get past the car he had now abandoned but then they had gone.

The man who had reported this had tried to intervene and pull Krantz from the car. Krantz had stabbed him in the

238

thigh for his trouble. The only reason he'd not bled to death was that a passenger in a following vehicle was an ex-army medic.

"Someone's guardian angel was working overtime today," Ray said.

So now where would Krantz go?

For the next two hours there was nothing. It was, Ray thought, as though everyone held their collective breaths. Where was he? Was the woman still alive?

They had a name for her now, the car having been picked up on CCTV further along the road. The driver was Jennifer Samms and she was just nineteen. Ray watched the rolling news on the television, the ticker tape of breaking news repeating what details were known, along the bottom of the screen. The knowledge that there was nothing he could do gnawing in his gut.

Kit brought him another cup of tea. He took it from her but set it aside. If he drank another one he'd be drowning from the inside. "You think he's killed her?" Kit asked.

"I'm hoping he just wants a hostage," Ray said.

An hour later they got the call they had been anticipating. The car had been spotted, heading along the main road that would eventually take Krantz to the vicarage. He was now in the back of the car, sitting directly behind the driver and as the car pulled up to a halt it was clear he had a knife at her throat.

"Can you get a clear shot?" Beckett wanted to know.

Negative, he was told. There was no clear line of sight.

Krantz had hold of her now. Was walking backwards towards the large front door. "I know you can see me," Krantz shouted, his glance taking in the camera set above the door. "So you'd better let me inside. I can kill her slowly, bit by bit. You want that?"

The door opened and Krantz began to back inside.

"No, I don't want you to do that," Nathan said.

It was probably the calmness in his voice that took Krantz by surprise, that made him turn his head, that lessened his attention just for that split second. But for Nathan it was enough.

* * *

Krantz felt a sudden blow against the side of his head. The girl he held was grabbed tightly and, confused and in pain, Krantz felt her slipping from his grasp. He felt the shove in the middle of his back and he fell heavily, back through the door and onto his knees on the gravel path. Then he heard the front door slam.

* * *

Jennifer Samms had lost her balance, collapsing onto the hall floor, unable to process what was happening to her. Instinctively, she rolled aside and then curled up tight, her brain unable to grasp the idea that she was actually free. A young man knelt beside her, told her that she was safe and that she need not be afraid. Jennifer curled tighter, sobs convulsing her now and she felt the young man gently taking her hand.

And then came the chaos of running feet, outside, of shouts and orders. And then someone banging on the door and the door opening again and sunlight streaming into the hall.

Someone helping her to her feet and sitting her on the stairs and Jennifer seeing the man who had threatened her. He was lying on the ground, his hands cuffed behind his back, surrounded by armed police.

* * *

"We've got him," Beckett was told.

"And Jennifer Samms?" Would have nightmares for the rest of her life, Ray thought. But at least she would have a life. "And Nathan?"

"Your crazy friend is making tea," Ray was told. "What the hell did he think he was doing. He could have been killed."

Wouldn't be the first time he risked that, Ray thought.

240

CHAPTER 36

Kit had agreed to speak to Paul Krantz. He was refusing to say a word to anyone until she was brought to him. Ray had agreed to be with her.

Krantz was handcuffed and the cuffs attached to a metal D ring on a table that was in turn bolted to the concrete floor. Kit took her place at the other end of the table, Ray standing beside her. There were armed police standing by the door.

"And a visit from the great detective," Paul Krantz's voice was mocking. "I suppose you're satisfied now?"

Ray remained silent. He really had nothing more to say to this man.

"You wanted me here," Kit said. "So what did you want to say?"

He smiled at her and Ray, to his surprise, caught something of the genuine pleasure in the expression as though Paul was momentarily glad to be seeing an old friend. "I want you to confess," Paul Krantz said.

"Confess to what?"

"To what started all of this. Way back then. To what set events in motion, if you like. That made me the way I am, that opened up the possibilities."

"I don't know what you mean."

"Oh, I think you do," he said. "I think back to how much you hated them and I really, really think you do."

"Who am I supposed to have hated? My mum and Rob's dad?"

"You did, we all knew it. Not that I blame you, of course. Useless pair of bastards, weren't they. Not to mention the violence and the unpleasantness. All show, weren't they, all, look how happy we are, look how much we do for our children. Ballet lessons and riding lessons and after-school clubs and trips and . . . well. But once no one was watching, you and I both know what they were. So no one could blame you for what you'd done, not if they knew the truth of it."

"Your truth, Paul, not mine," Kit said heavily. "I wasn't even there when you and Rob did what you did. I wasn't even there."

She stood then and said, "If that's all you have to say, then I'm done. I walked away twenty years ago and I kept on walking and that's what I'll be doing now. Goodbye, Paul."

His laughter followed them down the hall.

"Were you there, Kit?" Ray asked gently as they got into the car.

She shook her head. "I was on a skiing trip," she said quietly. "I wasn't even there."

But as they drove away, she closed her eyes, leaning her head against the window and she remembered. Another row with her mother. Celeste, eyes blazing, arms waving, blows falling on Kit's head. She wasn't even sure what had set her mother off this time. Lashing out, trying to make her mother back off, making contact with a woman whose temper had already thrown her off balance, who stood so dangerously close to the stairs. Kit could still remember the scream as she fell, the crack as she hit the floor, the shout of rage from Rob's father as he raced into the hall. The cry of pain as he slumped to the floor. Rob standing over him, hands bloody as he pulled the knife free. A slim-bladed kitchen knife now clutched in his fist.

"He would have hurt you like before," Rob had said. "He would have hurt you again and worse this time" And then he'd taken a deep breath and looked at his hands and the mess on the floor and he had said, "Best phone Paul. He'll know what to do."

And Kit remembered how her heart had sunk. He would know and he would help and then he would control them forever. They'd just be trading one set of bullies for another.

She sat up, rubbed her eyes with the heels of her palms. "What happens now?" she said. "I'll have to leave and start again. Just as well I'm renting, I suppose."

"You'll get help to settle somewhere else," he told her.

"Yeah, I suppose." She was silent for a moment and then asked, "Ray, do you know anyone who could look after my cat? It might be a while before I'm settled. It doesn't seem fair to him."

Ray looked curiously at her and he wondered.

EPILOGUE

There were too many funerals to attend, Ray thought. Too many loose ends to tie up. Too many random events that obviously had meaning for the likes of Paul and Rob and even Kit, but which made no sense to him. He pulled up in front of what had been his aunt's cottage and took the pet carrier from the back seat. The cat meowed plaintively.

Nathan opened the door and they went through into the kitchen. "His name is Mr B," Ray said. "I don't know what the B stands for, but he's a lovely cat. Hopefully he'll settle in here."

Nathan opened the carrier and stood back, allowing the cat to make his own decision. Typical Nathan, Ray thought.

"I've never lived with a cat," Nathan said. "I think it will be interesting."

Later, with Nathan sitting in the old rocking chair and the cat sitting on his lap, Ray poured himself a second cup of tea. "We know why Rob killed those children," he said. "He finally decided he wanted to write it down. And the reason is so damned pathetic it makes me want to vomit."

He watched as Nathan stroked the cat and waited for him to go on. Nathan was good at waiting. "Their mother and Kit competed against one another in pony club type events and on this one occasion, she beat Kit by the tiniest of margins and Rob and Paul were both furious. Not just with her for winning but with Kit for not caring. A whole lot later Rob heard she'd got married, and later that she'd had kids and later still that they were learning to ride."

"Does it matter," Nathan said, "if someone who kills a child has a big reason for doing it or what you see as a small and unimaginable one. The outcome is just the same. It's still a great wrong."

"Is killing an adult a smaller wrong?" Ray mused.

He could see Nathan considering that and no doubt one day, when Ray had forgotten even asking the question, he would give Ray an answer.

THE END

THE JOFFE BOOKS STORY

We began in 2014 when Jasper agreed to publish his mum's much-rejected romance novel and it became a bestseller.

Since then we've grown into the largest independent publisher in the UK. We're extremely proud to publish some of the very best writers in the world, including Joy Ellis, Faith Martin, Caro Ramsay, Helen Forrester, Simon Brett and Robert Goddard. Everyone at Joffe Books loves reading and we never forget that it all begins with the magic of an author telling a story.

We are proud to publish talented first-time authors, as well as established writers whose books we love introducing to a new generation of readers.

We have been shortlisted for Independent Publisher of the Year at the British Book Awards three times, in 2020, 2021 and 2022, and for the Diversity and Inclusivity Award at the Independent Publishing Awards in 2022.

We built this company with your help, and we love to hear from you, so please email us about absolutely anything bookish at feedback@joffebooks.com

If you want to receive free books every Friday and hear about all our new releases, join our mailing list: www.joffebooks.com/contact

And when you tell your friends about us, just remember: it's pronounced Joffe as in coffee or toffee!

ALSO BY JANE ADAMS

RINA MARTIN MYSTERY SERIES
Book 1: MURDER ON SEA
Book 2: MURDER ON THE CLIFF
Book 3: MURDER ON THE BOAT
Book 4: MURDER ON THE BEACH
Book 5: MURDER AT THE COUNTRY HOUSE
Book 6: MURDER AT THE PUB
Book 7: MURDER ON THE FARM
Book 8: MURDER AT THE WILLOWS

MERROW & CLARKE
Book 1: SAFE
Book 2: KIDNAP

DETECTIVE MIKE CROFT SERIES
Book 1: THE GREENWAY
Book 2: THE SECRETS
Book 3: THEIR FINAL MOMENTS
Book 4: THE LIAR

DETECTIVE RAY FLOWERS SERIES
Book 1: THE APOTHECARY'S DAUGHTER
Book 2: THE UNWILLING SON
Book 3: THE DROWNING MEN
Book 4: THE SISTER'S TWIN
Book 5: THE LOST DAUGHTER

DETECTIVE ROZLYN PRIEST SERIES
Book 1: BURY ME DEEP

STANDALONE
THE OTHER WOMAN
THE WOMAN IN THE PAINTING
THEN SHE WAS DEAD

Milton Keynes UK
Ingram Content Group UK Ltd.
UKHW010009240823
427351UK00004B/203

9 781835 260975